YOU ONLY DIE TWICE

**Center Point
Large Print**

**This Large Print Book carries the
Seal of Approval of N.A.V.H.**

YOU ONLY DIE TWICE

EDNA BUCHANAN

CENTER POINT PUBLISHING
THORNDIKE, MAINE

This Center Point Large Print edition
is published in the year 2001 by arrangement with
Morrow and Company, a division of
HarperCollins *Publishers*.

The text of this Large Print edition is unabridged.
In other aspects, this book may vary from the original edition.
Printed in Thailand. Set in 16-point Times New Roman type
by Bill Coskrey.

ISBN 1-58547-124-0

Library of Congress Cataloging-in-Publication Data

Buchanan, Edna.
    You only die twice / Edna Buchanan.
        p. cm.
    ISBN 1-58547-124-0 (lib. bdg. : alk. paper)
    1. Montero, Britt (Fictitious character)--Fiction. 2. Women journalists--Fiction. 3.
Miami (Fla.)--Fiction. 4. Large type books. I. Title.

PS3552.U324 Y68 2001b
813'.54--dc21

                                                          2001017320

FOR MICHAEL CONGDON

IT WAS DÉJÀ VU ALL OVER AGAIN.

YOGI BERRA

THAT WHICH HATH BEEN IS NOW; AND
THAT WHICH IS TO BE HATH ALREADY BEEN.

ECCLESIASTES 3:15

1

Hot sand sizzled beneath my feet. An endless turquoise sea stretched into infinity. Bright sailboats darted beyond the breakers, their colors etched against a flawless blue sky. Playful ocean breezes kissed my face, lifted my hair off my shoulders, and ruffled my skirt around my knees. The day was perfect, a day to die for. Too bad about the corpse bobbing gently in the surf.

She appeared serene, a drifting, dreaming mermaid, narrow-waisted and full-breasted, with long slim legs: an enchanting gift from the deep. She wore seaweed in her hair, which was long and honey-colored, streaked by brilliant light as it swirled like something alive just beneath the water's glinting surface.

Had she been caught by the rip current, that fast-moving jet of water that races back to the sea, or did she plunge from a cruise ship or a party boat? Perhaps she was a tourist who went wading, unaware of the sharp drop-off only a few feet from shore. But if so, why was she naked?

Clearly she was no rafter drowned in a quest for freedom and a new life, or gold chains and designer jeans. Her fingertips and toenails gleamed with a pearly luster, as though polished to perfection by the tides. This woman appeared to have lived the good life. None of the grotesqueries that the sea and its creatures inflict on the dead had overtaken her yet. Obviously she had not been in the water long.

I had overheard the initial radio transmission on the "floater" while working on a story at Miami Beach police headquarters. My ears had perked up. My name is Britt Montero, and I cover the police beat in this city where everything is exaggerated, where colors are too vivid to be real, where ugly is uglier, beautiful is breathtaking, and passions run high. Every day on this job, I see new faces. Many are dead. My mission is to chronicle their stories and preserve them permanently—on the pages of the newspaper of record, in our files, and on our consciousness, forever.

My editors at the *Miami News* share a somewhat different view of my job description. As a result, I had been dutifully poring through tall gray stacks of computer printouts in the police public information unit. The art department planned a locator map for Sunday's paper, to accompany my piece on the crime rate. My task was to compile the crime statistics zone by zone and identify the scene of every rape, murder, armed robbery, and aggravated assault.

I hate projects based on numbers. If words are my strength, decimal points are my weakness. Calculating the number of violent crimes per hundred thousand population has always been problematic for me. Is it 32 crimes per 100,000, 320 or 3.2? A live story on a dead woman is infinitely more intriguing.

Studying the body more closely, I could see that we shared characteristics in common. We were close in age and appearance. My plans, to bodysurf and sunbathe today along this same sandy stretch, had been ruined by the DBI (Dull But Important) project I had agreed to complete on my day off. Her plans had also been ruined. All of them. Permanently. Some quirk of fate had delivered us both to the coastal strip I had yearned for, sun on my shoulders, sea breeze in my hair—but it wasn't the day at the beach either one of us had in mind.

Along with a lifeguard, two uniformed cops, and a growing crowd, I watched a detective trudge toward us across the sand. Emery Rychek was an old-timer, one of the few holdouts who had not opted for guayaberas when Miami Beach police dress codes were relaxed. Unlit cigar clenched between his teeth, his white shirt open at the throat, his shapeless gabardine jacket flapping in the breeze, Rychek handled more than his share of deaths, most of them routine. Young cops want sexier calls, not grim reminders of their own mortality. Rychek never seemed to mind the unpleasant tasks that come with a corpse.

"So, you beat me here, Britt," he acknowledged, his voice a gravelly rumble.

"I was at the station, working on a story about the crime rate. I heard it go out."

Rychek chewed his cigar. His smelly stogies often came in handy, to mask the stench of corpses gone undiscovered too long, though colleagues routinely debated which odor was more nauseating. No need for him to light up here. This corpse was as fresh as the sea air.

"Well, lookit what washed up." He appraised her for a moment, fierce eyebrows raised in mock surprise, then turned to the cops. "Whattaya waiting for, the tide to go out and take her with it?"

"Thought maybe we should leave her like she was till you guys took a look," one said.

Rychek shook his head in disgust as the two cops stripped off their shoes and socks, rolled up their pant legs, pulled on rubber gloves, and waded gingerly into the sun-dappled shallows. Green water streamed from her hair as they dragged her ashore. Her pale half-open eyes stared hopefully at the sky, her expression reverent. Her only adornment was a gold earring, the delicate outline of a tiny open heart.

Excellent, I thought. Distinctive jewelry is a good start for those of us trying to identify the dead. But this woman's youth and beauty guaranteed she'd be no lost soul. I dreaded the cries of her loved ones, sure to appear momentarily, frantic with grief, hearts breaking.

"A great body is a terrible thing to waste," one of the cops muttered.

Rychek ignored him, as he straddled the naked woman, cigar still clenched between his teeth. He grunted as he tugged her pale form one way, then the other, seeking wounds or identifying marks. I watched, painfully aware that there is no modesty, no privacy in death.

"Hey, Red." Rychek glanced over my shoulder.

Lottie Dane was elbowing her way through the growing throng of gawkers. She is the best news shooter in town and my best friend. Her red hair whipped wildly in the wind as she strode across the sand in blue jeans and hand-tooled cowboy boots, her twin Canon EOS cameras, a wide-angle lens on one and a telephoto on the other, slung from leather straps around her neck.

"Hell-all-Friday, who is she?" Lottie murmured, shutter clicking. "Sure don't look like the usual coffin fodder that washes up on this beach. Where's her clothes? How'd she git here?"

"Gimme a chance," Rychek protested. "I just got here myself."

The big eyes of a small boy were fixed on the dead woman's breasts. Runty and pale, wearing baggy swim trunks a size too large, he gaped from the forward fringe of the crowd. Where is his mother? I wondered, as a beach patrolman brought the detective a yellow plastic sheet from his Jeep.

"What do you think?" I asked Rychek, as he peeled off his rubber gloves.

"No bullet holes or stab wounds," he said. "We'll know more when we get a name on her. Most likely it's an accidental drowning."

"Is the M.E. coming out?"

He shook his head. "The wagon's on the way." Medical examiners don't normally attend drownings these days, except in cases of mass casualties, obvious foul play, or refugee smugglers who routinely drop their human cargo offshore—sometimes way too far offshore.

"My Raymond saw her first!" The boy's proud mother had finally made an appearance. She wore big sunglasses, pink hair curlers under a floppy sun hat, and a bikini that exposed a ruddy hysterectomy scar on her glistening belly. She smelled strongly of coconut-scented suntan oil and spoke with a New York accent.

Raymond, pail and shovel forgotten, still stared, transfixed, at the sheet-covered corpse.

"Unbelievable," his mother told all who would listen. "Raymond kept trying to tell me, but I didn't pay attention. That kid is always into something." She shook her head smugly. "I shoulda known.

"He kept saying, 'Mommy, Mommy! There's a lady with no clothes on!'

"I was in a daze," she acknowledged, "working on my tan, half asleep. Thought it must be another one of them damn foreign models, you know, stripping topless on the beach. Most got nothing to show anyhow. The ones with the pierced nipples and belly buttons are the worst." She snorted in disgust.

I crouched down to Raymond's level. It was tough to compete with the naked lady. "Raymond? Raymond? My name is . . ." He tore his eyes off the corpse and stared at me, perplexed.

"Does she have wings now?" he asked, in a small high voice. "Can she fly? Like on TV?"

"I don't know," I told him. "I hope so."

His mother had used the cell phone in her beach bag to dial 911. But according to Rychek she had not been the first to notify police. The initial call had come from a regular, he said, in a sixteenth-floor apartment at the Casa Milagro, a high-rise condominium behind us. The resident had scanned the horizon with high-powered binoculars and spotted the body riding the incoming tide.

Rychek's handheld police radio crackled. The detective listened to the message, squinted toward the upper floors of the graceful tower with its turquoise-blue trim and wrap-around balconies, and turned back toward the water.

"Anybody see anything?"

Scores of eyes scanned the sea's sparkling surface.

"I do!" somebody shouted. Murmurs swept the crowd. A flurry of excitement: Something was floating beyond the breakers, a hundred yards down the beach. One man broke into a run, sprinting across the sand, pursued by several others who splashed into the waves in a race for the prize.

"Take it easy. Don't kill each other over it!" Rychek shouted after them.

A young Spanish-speaking man with a killer tan and drop-dead pecs waded out of the surf triumphantly waving the trophy above his head like a banner: a rose-red bikini bathing-suit top.

The detective dangled it by its thin strap, holding it up for me to scrutinize.

"Whattaya think, Britt. Her size?"

"Looks about right. Only one way to tell if a bathing suit fits."

"We'll try it on Cinderella at the M.E. office. No sign of the bottom half. Some pervert probably took it home as a souvenir," he said. "Musta thought it was his lucky day."

Lottie left for a feature assignment at the Garden Center. I knew I should leave too. Instead, I walked the sand as far north as 34th Street, looking for an unattended beach towel or lounge chair the dead woman might have left, along with her personal belongings. No luck. That didn't mean they hadn't been there. A thief may have found them first.

Rychek was talking to a buff jogger in his late seventies when I returned to the scene. A local who'd been around for years, the man did push-ups and headstands in the sand each day, then ran and swam miles along the beach, rain or shine. I occasionally encountered him in the supermarket, in the produce department. He was slightly hard of hearing and spoke loudly, with an eastern European accent.

"I saw her." He nodded, gesturing broadly. "This morning. She vas svimming, right there." He jabbed a gnarly index finger at a deep-blue spot in the water. "She looked like a good svimmer. It vas early, vhen it looked like rain, before the sky cleared up. There vas almost nobody on the beach."

"She was alone?" Rychek asked.

The man paused. "There vas another svimmer. A man. I thought he vas vid her, but"—he shrugged—"maybe not."

He had not seen her arrive or leave and could describe neither the other swimmer nor the color of her bathing suit.

"I vasn't paying attention," he said. "I vas exercising. I guess the guy vasn't vid her. . . ."

"Why do you say that?" Rychek asked.

"Vell, if he vas vid her"—he shrugged and opened his hairy, muscular arms—"vhere is he now?"

"Good question," Rychek said.

"You think they both got in trouble and there's another body out there?" I asked. Women have a higher fat–muscle ratio than men, whose leaner bodies are less buoyant. If both had drowned, she would probably surface first.

We stared at the sea, valleys and troughs, rising and falling like the ebb and flow of life, with all its pain and joy.

"Terrible." The old man shook his head. "A terrible thing. She vas young, so attractive."

He was right. Sun, sea, and sky usually lift my spirits. Instead, a wave of sadness washed over me. My feet sank in the coarse sand, irritating my toes as I trudged back to my car, illegally parked at a bus stop, my press card prominently displayed on the dash. The blinding sun made my head throb, and I suddenly felt thirsty and dehydrated.

I sat in my superheated T-Bird, wondering if her car was parked nearby. If so, the meter must have run out by now.

Expired. Like its driver.

The woman's image shimmered in the heat waves that rose from the street as I drove back to the *Miami News* building. Did she wake up this morning, I wondered, with a premonition, a bad dream, any clue that this day would be her last? How many hearts would break, how many lives change because hers had ended early?

Bobby Tubbs was in the slot at the city desk. His round face wore its perpetual scowl of annoyance. "Did you get the stax for the art department? They need them right away."

"Sure," I said. "I've also got a story for tomorrow. A drowning on the beach, an unidentified woman."

"Keep it short," he snapped.

I double-checked the figures, turned in the crime statistics, and reread my notes on the dead woman.

Rip currents might be to blame, I thought. Sometimes they seize scores of swimmers, setting off mass rescues, as TV news choppers swarm the skies. I'd experienced them myself. When the sand beneath your feet seems to be moving rapidly toward shore, it is actually you who are moving fast—out to sea. Swimmers panic, tire, and drown. By swimming parallel to the coastline, one can escape the narrow band of savage current. Or simply relax and let Mother Nature sweep you away. Enjoy her wild ride. Eventually, out beyond the breakers, she'll set you free to swim back to shore.

I made some calls. The beach patrol reported no rescues, no other casualties, no rip currents. So my lead depended on who she was. I was sure she would be identified by deadline. I was wrong. A medical examiner's investigator returned my call at 6 P.M. She was still Jane Doe, not scheduled for autopsy until morning. I called Rychek.

"Nuttin'," he reported grimly. "Do me a favor, wouldja, kid? Put her description in the newspaper."

"That's why I called."

"Good girl, a woman after my own heart." I could hear him flipping the pages of his notebook and imagined him adjusting the gold-rimmed reading glasses he kept in his shirt pocket.

"Lessee. You saw 'er yourself: probably early thirties. Nice figure, good-looking, five feet four-and-a-half, weight one twenty-one. Hair blondish, a little longer than shoulder length; you seen it. Eyes blue, bikini tan line. Nice manicure, good dental work. We'll know more after the post."

"And the earring," I reminded him.

"Yeah, we shot pictures," he said. "Can you put one in the paper if we don't have her ID'd by tomorrow?"

"Sure," I said. "But if you ID her tonight, before our final at one A.M., call me so we can change the lead."

"You'll be home?"

"If I'm not, leave word. I'll check my messages."

"So, how is your love life, kid? Hope you dumped the cop. You're too good for 'im."

"You don't even know him," I protested.

"He's a cop, so I know you're too good for 'im."

I smiled. Rychek was funny and smart, with a professionally acquired insight into human nature. I hoped he was wrong about my love life, but maybe not. I had begun to seriously question it myself.

I led the story with a police appeal to the public to help identify the victim.

Lottie stopped at my desk, her turned-up nose sun-burned, hair frizzy from the humidity. She is forty-one, a statuesque five-eight, eight years older, four inches taller, and twenty pounds heavier than I am. "So who'd your floater turn out to be?"

"No clue," I said.

She frowned. "Gawd, think she just swam out too far?"

"Could be, or maybe she was on drugs or had a seizure." One of my first stories at the *News* was about a teenager from Brooklyn who drowned in a hotel pool, in full sight of witnesses who thought he was playing. They didn't know, until too late, that he suffered from epileptic seizures. "She may live alone," I said, "and won't be missed until tomorrow, when she doesn't show up for work. Then somebody who reads the story will put two and two together."

"She don't look like somebody who'd be high as a lab rat or living solo," Lottie said. "A woman with her looks . . ."

"*We* live alone," I reminded her.

"God-dog it to hell, you just got to rub it in, don'tcha?" She laughed. Born in Gun Barrel, Texas, she has seen it all in the pursuit of breaking news all over the world, capturing heart-stopping moments in every major trouble spot. Long divorced, no children, she wants nothing more than to settle down.

"Don't knock it," I said wistfully. "Maybe we're lucky that our jobs and the hours we work keep us single and celibate."

"We need to get you a blood test, to see if any is getting to your brain. Like I keep telling you," she said, in her molasses-smooth Texas twang, "you ain't gonna catch any fish if you don't throw your bait in the water."

I passed on the invitation to join her for a night of line dancing at Desperado's. Leaving the newsroom, I noticed that some wag from the photo desk had posted one of Lottie's unused prints on the bulletin board: skinny little Raymond knock-kneed in the sand, clutching his pail, his tiny shovel in the other hand, the covered corpse in the foreground. A caption had been added: a tourist slogan— MIAMI, SEE IT LIKE A NATIVE. Not funny. I glared around the newsroom. The usual suspects were all hunched over their terminals. I yanked the photo off the board and locked it in my desk.

As I drove home though twilight's tawny glow I wondered what tomorrow's story would reveal about the mystery woman. That's the beauty of this job, I thought; it's as though I live at the heart of an intricate and endless novel, rich with characters, ripe with promise, and rife with mystery.

I fed Bitsy and Billy Boots, the cat, and then took Bitsy, the tiny mop of a poodle I inherited from a dead cop, over to the boardwalk. We sat on a wooden bench in the moonlight, watched the surf, and then walked home along shadowy streets.

No messages waited. The sense of melancholy acquired on the beach earlier was still with me. I didn't bother with dinner. Instead, I poured a stiff drink from the first-aid kit in my kitchen cabinet, drank it down hopefully—as though Jack Daniel's Black Label was a magic elixir concocted to erase the images better left unseen—and went to bed.

In the morning I called the Miami Beach detective bureau

but Rychek was out, they said, across the bay at the medical examiner's office. I took the MacArthur Causeway west, dodging tourists, their rental cars careening as they eyeballed and snapped photos of the *Ecstasy*, the *Celebration*, and the *Song of Norway*, all in port preparing to depart for such exotic destinations as Cozumel, Ocho Rios, Half Moon Cay, St. Lucia, and Guadeloupe, the ships and trips that dreams are made of.

The cheerful receptionist at number 1 Bob Hope Road said Rychek was "with the chief, down in the autopsy room." She called for permission, then waved me on.

I left the soothing pastel lobby, trotted past records, through the double doors, descended the stairs, and hurried through the breezeway into the lab building. My footsteps echoed along the brightly lit corridor, its walls lined with poster-size photos of the towering oak trees and resurrection ferns along the Withlacoochee River in Inverness. The chief medical examiner, a history buff, shot them himself in a wilderness as unspoiled today as when Chief Osceola and his warriors holed up there during the second Seminole War. U.S. Army Major Francis Langhorne Dade led his doomed troops into ambush at that now-historic battleground. On hot and bloody city nights I wonder if Miamians invited bad karma on themselves by naming their county after an inept leader whose sole claim to fame was being massacred.

I passed the photo-imaging bureau, the bone and tissue bank, and found the star attraction at an autopsy room station, attended by the chief, known both as "the titan of medical examiners" and the genius who designed this one-of-a-kind building, and a scowling Emery Rychek.

She lay supine on a tray, her body incandescent, bathed in the light of sixteen fluorescent bulbs. A rubber block beneath her shoulders had tilted her head back, exposing her throat. The tray she occupied, neutral gray for color-photo compatibility, was designed to facilitate X-ray transmission and mounted on wheels, so that bodies only need to be lifted twice, on arrival and on departure.

They had finished the autopsy. Her vital organs had been scrutinized beneath a high-powered surgical lamp on an adjacent stainless-steel dissection table. The Y-shaped incision in her torso and the intermastoid cut that opened her skull had already been sewn shut with loose running stitches of white linen cord. Every surface was scrupulously clean, not a single drop of blood. Instruments gleamed, their blades as immaculate as the chief's surgical scrubs and apron, a source of pride with this man. He acknowledged me with a cheerful nod.

"Hey, kid," Rychek growled. The detective stood at the woman's head, just outside the splash zone. He, too, wore an apron.

"Got an ID yet?" I slipped out my notebook.

"Not a single call. Not even the usual nutcases who love to flap their yaps. Zip, zilch, nada."

"Huh." That surprised me. "Maybe she was a tourist. . . ."

I stepped closer, then gasped in shock.

"What happened to her?" When I last saw her, the dead woman was as ethereal and haunting as Botticelli's Venus emerging from the sea. Today she looked like the loser in a bad bar fight. The autopsy incisions were routine. What shocked me was her nose, raw and skinned, as were her knuckles and ears, and the ugly red-brown bruising on her forearms, wrists, and legs.

"Nothing new." The chief spoke briskly. "Abrasions from the sand and other injuries are almost invisible on moist skin. They don't show up right away. They only become noticeable after the body's been dried off and refrigerated. Drying tends to darken wounds."

"But her eyes," I protested. Still slightly open, the whites were now black on either side of the irises.

"*Tache noir:* black spot," he said. "Though to be literal, it's actually dark brown. Part of the evaporation process. Common in seawater drownings. The water, being five percent salt, dehydrates the tissues and draws out the moisture, and when the tissue dries it's dark brown."

"But all those marks. Are they fish bites?"

The chief shook his head. "I'm afraid not."

"The news ain't good." Rychek nodded at the doctor.

"It appears our detective friend here has himself a homicide," the chief said pleasantly. "She was murdered."

"Why me?" Rychek sighed.

I was not sympathetic. She was the one murdered.

"So," I said. "You mean she was killed, then dumped in the ocean?"

"No," the chief said. "As I was just apprising Detective Rychek, she was deliberately drowned." The chief consulted his notes. "Those bruises on her wrists and upper arms were inflicted during a struggle, as she fought being submerged. See here?"

He turned her head to one side.

"Note the bruises on the back of her neck. Someone grabbed her from behind and slightly to her left and pushed

her head down. See the marks? His right hand was here"—
he placed his own gloved fingers over the bruises—"on the
back of her neck. Fingers on the right, thumb on the left.
Look close and you can see the little horizontal linear abrasions where his fingernails penetrated the skin on her neck
as she twisted, trying to escape his grasp."

Chills rippled across my skin, and the room, a constant
72 degrees, felt colder. I imagined her fighting to breathe,
coughing and choking as she inhaled water, her panic. I
have nearly drowned—twice. Once in a dark Everglades
canal, the second time at sea, in sight of Miami's bright
lights. Somehow I survived both, but nobody had been
deliberately holding my head under water.

The chief was pointing out injuries to the woman's left
arm, ". . . bruising beneath the skin, about a centimeter in
diameter, three or four fingernail abrasions where he apparently grasped her wrist with his left hand to stop her from
flailing and grabbing at him. See the visible bruises on the
flexor, here, on the underpart of her left wrist, and another
fingernail mark?"

"None-a them were visible at the scene," Rychek said
morosely.

"The guy swimming near her," I said. "It had to be him!"

"Could be," the detective said.

"How did he do it?" I asked. "She had to be difficult to
subdue, struggling for life. Why didn't anybody see it or
hear her screams?"

"The pattern of injuries looks as though he used a scissors grip," the chief said. "Wrapped his legs around hers
from behind, pinned her ankles together, and used his own
body weight to submerge her. Her body supported his

while he held her down."

"How long would it take to drown somebody like that?" Rychek asked.

"Two to three minutes. She'd be struggling, of course, ingesting seawater. Most likely unable to call out for help."

The thought of her terror, her helpless last moments, outraged and sickened me. Savagely attacked in the water, like a victim in *Jaws*, she had to be so scared. But this primitive predator was a man.

"All these bruises and abrasions make it difficult to ascertain what's post- and what's antemortem," the chief mused. "Some are obviously the result of wave action sweeping her body back and forth on the bottom."

"What else?" Rychek peered over his little half glasses, notebook in hand.

"See this?" The chief pulled down her lower lip to expose the pinpoint hemorrhages. "On the inside, a linear abrasion, the shape of a tooth. Apparently done when he grabbed her face to push it underwater or stop her from screaming.

"And here, on the earlobe, a one-millimeter tear where an earring was forcibly ripped off. She was still wearing the other one when found."

"What about the bathing suit?" I asked.

"That top could be hers. It fits," the chief said. "No way would a swimsuit simply fall off in the water. The killer either removed it deliberately or tore it off accidentally during the struggle."

"Was she raped?" I asked.

"There's no trauma to the genitalia," the chief said. "The rape workup was negative, but of course that doesn't rule out sexual battery."

"It starts out a simple drowning," the detective said, his tone aggrieved, "and now it's not only a whodunit, it's a who-is-it."

Our eyes met across the dead woman's body.

"You will catch the SOB who did this," I told Rychek. "Right?"

"No way," he said, "till we know who got killed. We need her name." He turned to the chief. "Whattaya say, Doc? Anything else here that could help me out?"

The chief frowned at her chart. "Dental work looks excellent. Porcelain veneers on numbers eight and nine. Good work. Expensive, sophisticated. We'll have Dr. Wyatt take a look and do an impression. And we'll have her prints for you shortly."

A slender olive-skinned morgue attendant had joined us. He uncurled and stretched out the fingers of the dead woman's right hand. One by one he inked, pressed, and rolled them into a spoonlike device lined with narrow strips of glossy fingerprint paper.

"She had a bikini wax," I murmured, thinking aloud, "and her hair . . . when you release her description, be sure to mention that she has frosted highlights, probably done in an expensive salon. See those lighter streaks? They cost big bucks and half a day at the beauty parlor. Somebody might recognize that."

"So that ain't natural, from the sun? Humph." The detective peered more closely at the dead woman's hair. "What else? She healthy, doc?"

"No signs of disease, prior injuries, surgeries, or chronic conditions," the chief answered. "But there is one other thing that might help. She was a mother."

"She has children?" I was startled. "How can you tell?"

"She had some stria—stretch marks—on her abdomen, and the cervix of her uterus showed an irregularity. The nipples tend to be a bit darker, as well."

"How many kids?" the detective asked. "More than one?"

"No way to know." The chief shrugged. "But she'd experienced at least one pregnancy. Possibly more."

Somewhere there was a child, or children, without a mother. Why does no one miss her? I wondered, as we left. As birds sang in the sunny parking lot outside and traffic thundered along the nearby expressway, Rychek filled me in on what little he knew. The condition of the body indicated a time of death four to five hours before she surfaced, placing the murder at between 5:30 and 6:30 A.M.

"More likely closer to six, when that elderly jogger saw her," I told him. "He's probably right on target about the time. He's a creature of habit, a good witness. I see him every morning that I run. I can set my watch by him."

Rychek gave me two black-and-white five-by-seven photos: a close-up of the earring next to a small ruler, to demonstrate scale, and a head shot of the corpse. "Think you can get these in the paper?"

"The earring, sure. On the other . . . I'll try," I said, frowning. My editors have an unreasonable prejudice against pictures of dead bodies in the morning paper, when readers are at breakfast. "They probably won't go for it," I warned.

The last time I talked Tubbs into using a morgue shot, it was an absolute success. Readers quickly identified the corpse, a college student dead of a drug overdose in a motel room. Instead of praise, we received reprimands. He still had not forgiven me.

The argument I had used to persuade him was that the overdose victim didn't look dead, he might have been sleeping. The woman in this photo was definitely dead.

It wouldn't matter, I thought, if the right message was waiting for me in the newsroom. Rychek had had no calls. That didn't mean I wouldn't. Some people will talk freely to cops but not reporters—and vice versa.

Unfortunately, none of my messages were in response to the morning story. The sole new clue came from an unlikely source: my mother.

I had comp time coming for working on my day off and had arranged to meet her at La Hacienda for lunch.

Her white convertible was parked jauntily outside, the top down. At age fifty-four, she looked stunning in cool ice blue. I basked in her bright and bubbly chatter about her burgeoning social life, her career in high fashion, and the new winter cruisewear, grateful that she was not criticizing my clothes, my job, or my love life.

I enjoyed a delectably seasoned crisp-crusted baked chicken with *moros* and green plantains. Lunch was relatively uneventful until I fished through my Day Timer for my credit card and the photos, tucked inside, fell out.

"Oh," my mother chirped cheerfully, as she picked one up to study before handing it back. "Those are my favorites."

"Excuse me?" I said. "You recognize this earring?"

"Of course, the Elsa Peretti open heart. Exclusively for

Tiffany's." She shrugged. "*Everybody* knows that."

"You're sure?"

She stared, as though I were not her only child but some alien creature from a third world planet.

"Of course. They're a signature design for Tiffany's." She snatched up the second photo.

"Good God!" She squinted at the image. "Is this woman . . . alive?"

"No," I murmured unhappily. "Not anymore."

She slapped it face down on the table like a playing card, shoulders quivering in an exaggerated shudder.

"What *happened* to her? No, no." She held up one hand like a frazzled traffic cop. "Please. Don't tell me. Spare me the details. I don't want to know."

She studied me in pained silence for a long moment, her expression one of suspicion. "What on *earth* would you be doing with a thing like this?"

I realized again what a disappointment I am to her. Most women my age happily share baby pictures, while my handbag reveals close-ups of corpses.

Appetite gone, I pushed away my caramel flan and fortified myself against the usual barrage with the dregs of my *café con leche*.

Instead, she turned up one edge of the photo with a beautifully manicured fingernail for another peek, her expression odd.

"Gruesome." She grimaced as she turned the photo face up. "I swear, something about this poor creature . . . who is she?" Her questioning eyes rose from the photo to me.

"You think you know her?" I leaned forward. "She's the unidentified woman who drowned at the beach yesterday."

"I saw your story," she said pointedly, as if the tragedy had somehow been all my fault. She stared at the photo, closed her eyes for a moment, studied it again, then pushed it toward me. "I guess not," she whispered. "Her own mother wouldn't recognize her now, I'm sure."

"You know," I said quickly, "it's entirely possible that you do recognize her. You meet so many people: the fashion shows, the models, the buyers, your clients. She may have moved in those circles. Here, take another look," I urged. How ironic, I thought, if my mother could help solve this mystery.

"No!" She shook her head emphatically, refusing to look at the picture again. "It was just a passing thought." She was strangely silent as we walked to her car. A quick hug and she was gone, flying out of the parking lot at an uncharacteristically high rate of speed, tires squealing as she floored it.

The Bal Harbour shops sit near the sea, a short drive across the Broad Causeway, light-years away from newsroom deadlines, inner-city woes, the county jail, and the morgue. Who would believe that during World War II this site was a swampy mosquito-infested German prisoner-of-war camp guarded by barbed wire and armed men? Today, beautiful people sip wine and cappuccino at outdoor tables, surrounded by the swank shops and boutiques of Chanel, Gucci, and Versace, as strolling models strike poses in designer fashions.

My eyes lingered on the silk scarf worn by the elegant woman who greeted me at Tiffany's. It was draped perfectly, tied just so, a coveted knack I have never mastered.

Her eyes lingered on my wristwatch, registering dismay. The little Morris the Cat number was a gift of sorts from Billy Boots, who obligingly consumed enough cat food to acquire the necessary labels.

The earrings, she said, could have come from any one of more than one hundred and fifty Tiffany stores in both the United States and such world capitals as London, Paris, Rome, and Zurich. Or they could have been ordered from the store's glossy catalog, which for some reason had never found its way to my mailbox.

I could not bring myself to flash the morgue photo in this posh emporium where everyone spoke in hushed and genteel tones. I would leave that to the cops. Feeling seriously underadorned, I thanked the sales associate, took a catalog, and drove back to the *News*. I called Rychek on the way and told him what I had learned at the store.

I showed Bobby Tubbs the earring photo, which he agreed to run with the story if we had the space. "I've also got a picture of the victim," I said cheerfully.

His head jerked up, eyes narrowing. "Is she dead in the picture?"

"It's not that bad," I said. "We can touch up the nose a little."

"I don't want to see it. Ged it the hell outa here!" He spun his swivel chair and turned away, fuming.

"Putting it in the newspaper may be the only way to reunite her with her loved ones. . . ." I was pleading with the back of Tubbs's head.

"Don't even think about it!" he barked. He did not look up from his editing screen.

Of course I thought about it. Missing people intrigue me.

Perhaps because my father, lost on a mission to liberate his Cuban homeland, was missing for most of my life, or because human beings lost and never found baffle me. "Everybody's got to be someplace." That punch line, from a long-dead comedian named Myron Cohen, says it all.

I turned in my story, dropped a handful of business cards in my pocket, told the desk I was taking comp time, and departed for the day. At the beach, I parked ten blocks south of where the dead woman was first spotted and began to canvass, trudging from one hotel lobby to the next, inquiring about any female guest or employee who might be missing.

I could have done the job faster by phone, but I like to look people in the eye when I ask a question. And I like being out of the office. Nothing excites me more than picking up the scent of a good story, and I had begun to believe this was one. I could feel it in my bones.

I pressed my cards into the hands of desk clerks, managers, and bartenders, asking them to call if they heard anything.

I stopped ten blocks north of where she was found. Which one? I wondered, my eyes roving the pastel skyline of hotels, condos, and conversions—aging hotels updated, renovated, and converted into high-priced apartments. If you were here, I whispered to the woman from the water, where?

I beeped Rychek at sunset. We met, shared drinks, ate a pizza, and compared notes.

Our victim matched no missing persons reports, county, state, or international. The detective had checked on cars towed or ticketed for overtime parking near the beach since her final swim. Two were stolen, one from Miami, the other in Chicago. The first had been used in an armed-robbery spree; two pounds of marijuana, a sawed-off shotgun, and a cemetery headstone were found in the other. Neither appeared linked to a missing woman.

The detective had visited Tiffany's too. I imagined him, with his smelly cigar and unpretentious swagger, bombarding the staff with blunt questions. No one recognized the dead woman's picture. Copies were faxed to other stores, but that was a long shot. She probably didn't buy the earrings herself.

"She looked like the kinda broad guys buy presents for." He sounded wistful.

I sipped red wine and wondered about his marital status. For as long as we had known each other, he had never mentioned his personal life.

"Want to bet that the call will come tomorrow?"

"From your lips to God's ears, kid." He raised his glass.

Tomorrow came and went. So did the next day and the day after.

"Every right turn I make is a dead end," Rychek complained at our next strategy session a week later. "It's like she dropped outa nowhere." Her fingerprints had come back NIF, Not In File. No criminal record. "It's like she came to Miami to die," he said. "Why she hadda do it on my watch, I dunno. What the hell did she have against me?"

"Maybe she's foreign, a tourist, and the folks back home haven't missed her yet. What did Wyatt say?"

Dr. Everett Wyatt, one of the nation's foremost forensic

odontologists, sent one of the nation's most savage serial killers to Florida's electric chair by identifying his teeth marks, left in a young victim's flesh.

Rychek shrugged. "He says her dental work looks like it was done in the States."

Like the jail, the streets, and the court dockets, the morgue was overcrowded. Rychek said the administrator at the medical examiner's office was talking burial.

"We don't come up with answers soon," the detective said, "they're gonna plant her in Potter's Field."

The prospect made me order another drink.

Backhoes dig trenches twice a month and prisoners provide free labor as Dade's destitute and unclaimed go to their graves in cheap wooden coffins. Stillborn babies sleep forever beside impoverished senior citizens, jail suicides, AIDS victims, and unknown corpses with no names and no one to mourn them. Their graves are marked only by numbers at the county cemetery, otherwise known as Potter's Field, in the hope that a John, Jane, or Juan Doe will one day be identified by a loved one eager to claim and rebury the body. That rarely happens.

"No way," I said.

"Right." The detective's jaw squared. "Somebody must miss her."

He took it personally. So did I.

Rychek left and I wandered back to the beach, contemplating endless horizon and big gray-and-green sky, over a wine-dark sea. Who are you? I asked her. Who wanted you dead?

She appeared in my dreams that night, trying to answer,

eyes alight with desperation, pale lips moving beneath sun-splashed whirls of blue water. I reached out to her, over and over. But the water, like something cunning and alive, kept her just out of my grasp.

How can somebody like you and me just get lost?" I groused to Lottie the next day. She straddled a chair she had pulled up to my desk after deadline for the first edition.

"Maybe she wasn't like you and me," she said, thumbing idly through my Tiffany catalog, with its sterling silver baby cups, jewelry, and crystal.

"Well, if she shopped there regularly," I said, "she wasn't. But rich people are missed quicker than the rest of us. And there's a child out there somewhere with no mother. Where the hell are her relatives, neighbors, co-workers, her boss, her best friend? Hell, you'd think her hairdresser would report her missing, if no one else. She looked like high maintenance."

"Dern tootin'. By now, she's due for a touch-up, a manicure, another bikini wax. The works."

A much-anticipated evening with the man in my life, Miami Police Major Kendall McDonald, began with promise but ended badly. He smelled good, looked *guapismo,* and greeted me with such an ardent embrace that I discerned that he was not wearing his beeper. Hormones slam-dancing with the neurochemicals in my brain, I deliberately left my pager behind, too. Tonight would be for us alone.

The first sign of trouble occurred en route, when he reached for me, I thought. What he actually reached for was his beeper, which he removed from the glove compartment.

Our destination, a barbecue at the home of a police colleague, was in Pembroke Pines, a suburban neighborhood densely populated by cops, who are always happiest with other cops as neighbors.

I mingled with friendly police wives, some of whom I'd met before.

"I thought Ken and Kathy—" a small dark-haired woman blurted, before being silenced by a sharp look from our hostess.

"I guess Kathy couldn't come," another commented, almost but not quite out of earshot.

My longtime suspicions were confirmed. McDonald and Rape Squad Lieutenant K. C. Riley had been, and apparently still continued to be, more than friends.

The men gathered around the grill on an outside patio, while us gals nibbled nuts, crackers, and pita chips and chatted. Childbirth was the topic: morning sickness, labor pains, pre- and postnatal depressions, and the horrifying details of actual blessed events.

Pictures were passed, baby pictures. Though cute, the infants all looked amazingly alike. How, I worried, would the mothers get the right pictures back? Did it matter? My life lacked interest. With no babies, meat-loaf recipes, or suburban small talk to share, what could I say?

I am haunted by a dead woman with seaweed in her hair.

McDonald's beeper sounded as we dined outdoors with the night soft around us, laughter and music in the air, and the pungent aroma of citronella candles to repel mosquitoes.

He returned from the phone, his expression odd, stopping to whisper in the ear of a homicide lieutenant, who reacted as though shot. They exchanged expressions of disbelief.

"What happened?" I asked expectantly, as McDonald reclaimed his seat beside me.

"Nothing," he said, eyes troubled.

That was his final answer. I hate secrets. On the way home, I coaxed. He lectured on ethics. I pried. He protested. One thing led to another.

I slammed out of his car at my place and marched to the front door without looking back. As my key turned in the lock, his Jeep Cherokee pulled away.

He doesn't trust me, I lamented, after all we've weathered together. He shares everything in common with the other woman in his life, the one he sees every day on the job. How do I compete with that? I asked myself. Do I even want to try?

Ignoring the blinking red eye on my message machine, I took Bitsy for a walk. Each time a car slowed beside us, I hoped it was his, but it never was. How did this happen to us? I wondered.

Dressed for bed, I was warming a glass of milk in the microwave when someone knocked softly.

I swiftly smoothed my hair and threw open the door, grinning in relief.

My visitor's balding dome shone in the moonlight. "You ain't gonna believe this, kid."

"Emery, what are you doing here?" I clutched my cotton robe around me and glanced at the wall clock. "It's one A.M."

"You tol' me to call you if I got a break. You didn't answer. I was passing by and saw your lights."

I swung the door open wider and Rychek stepped inside.

"I got me the name of the mermaid," he announced. "Been working the case all night. Thought you'd wanna know. It's a hell of a thing."

"How'd you find out who she was?" Eagerly, I led him into my small kitchen. He looked rumpled and needed a shave. "You want coffee?"

"No, but I could use a stiff drink. I'm headed home after this. You expecting somebody?"

"No." I took out the Jack Daniel's. "How's this?"

"Perfect. Nothing on the side." He looked puzzled. "What's with you, kid? Didn't you ever learn to check who it is before you open your door in the middle-a the night? You of all people."

"You're right. I wasn't thinking."

We sat across from each other at my kitchen table, him with his booze, me with my milk, our notebooks in front of us, the air electric. I love these moments.

"I knew you'd do it." I smiled as we raised our glasses in mutual salute. "Who is she?"

He took a swallow, then sighed. "A Miami native, born and raised."

"Wow. How come nobody identified her sooner?"

"Because the corpse we fished outa the drink that day was a dead woman." Fondly, he contemplated the amber liquid in his glass, prolonging the moment.

"So? We knew that." I frowned and put my pen down.

"She was a murder victim . . ."

"Emery," I implored impatiently.

"... more than ten *years* ago. She was *already* dead." His deliberate gaze met mine. "Ran her prints again, this time through local employment records. Came back a hit. Her prints positively identify her as Kaithlin Ann Jordan, murdered in 1991."

2

But that's impossible!" I gasped. "She'd only been dead a few hours. Did you notify her next of kin?"

"Not yet." His eyes glittered. "That would be the lady's husband, and he's sitting on death row as we speak. Been there ever since he was convicted of her murder."

My jaw must have dropped.

"In fact," he said, "he lost his final appeal, and the governor signed his death warrant last month. He's set for execution next week. Obviously that ain't gonna happen now. All of a sudden, the man's got himself a future."

I shook my head in disbelief. "Incredible! What a close call. Did you say Jordan?"

He nodded. "High-profile case. Big headlines. Big bucks. He's the Miami department-store heir—you know, Jordan's."

"Of course!" I nearly spit up my milk. "My mother worked at Jordan's! I was just out of J-school, not at the *News* yet, but I remember the stories and everybody talking about it. She was killed upstate somewhere, right? They never found the body."

"Now we know why," Rychek said. "At the time, they

figured he dumped her in the Gulf Stream or buried her up in the woods where he used to hunt. From what I hear, they had more than enough to convict."

"But he didn't do it," I whispered. "My God, what an injustice. He'll be a free man."

"Correctamundo. He didn't kill her, but he's damn lucky somebody did. Her murder saved his ass."

"You're sure it's the same woman?"

"You kidding? Think I was happy? I had 'em recheck the prints three times. They finally gave me the fingerprint cards and I checked 'em myself."

"What a story!"

"Helluva story," he agreed, and rolled his eyes. Mine flew to the clock. Too late. The final had gone to press.

"Who else knows?" I demanded, mind racing. "When is this gonna break? It's too late to get the story in the paper until Sunday. I'd hate to see TV beat us."

He shrugged. "It'll probably hit the fan sometime tomorrow. Couldn't catch hold of Jordan's lawyer right away. He's in trial over in Tampa. Gotta touch base with him first thing in the morning. Already broke the news to the prosecutor who convicted him. Poor bastard built his reputation on winning that case. Ain't easy to get the death penalty without a corpse, especially in a high-profile case with a big-bucks defense. He's state attorney up in Volusia County now, planning to run for the senate on a tough law-and-order campaign. Probably rethinking his game plan tonight."

"Damn," I said. "The lawyer is sure to call a press conference as soon as he talks to his client. Somebody should tell Jordan right away. Tonight. Imagine what the man has endured." I stared accusingly at the detective. "Think how he must have felt when nobody believed him."

"I had nuttin' to do wit' it. I'll leave it to the lawyers to break the good news. I never set eyes on the man. And I'm damn sure sorry I ever set eyes on his ol' lady." He leaned back heavily, an eyebrow arched. "Surprised you didn't have the scoop already, with your connections. The city knows. Somebody from Miami homicide was over there when I got the news. They had an interest. They were trying to make the guy for some kinda embezzlement when the homicide went down. The alleged homicide. Even if he didn't do her, Jordan was no choirboy. Had a history of domestic violence down here and the prosecution up in Daytona used it to prove a pattern."

That was it, I realized, the telephone call Kendall McDonald had stonewalled me about. Hell, my own mother might even have had a clue. Forget your enemies, it's your loved ones who double-cross you every time.

"My connections," I said flatly, "aren't worth crap. I wish I'd known sooner."

"Tried to call you at nine." Emery shook his head. "Even had your office beep you."

While I uneasily perused baby pictures, the biggest news story of the year had been slip-sliding through my fingers. I should have known better than to abandon my beeper in the pursuit of happiness. Mine and McDonald's probably would have chirped in concert. Why do my good intentions always turn around to bite me?

"Where the hell was this woman for the past ten years?" I asked Rychek. "Did she fake her own death? Was it amnesia? Was she kidnapped? Or traipsing around Miami all along, under everybody's nose?"

"Beats me," he said wearily. "All I know is, when she washed up on my turf, she didn't look like she'd been starved, abused, or chained up in an attic since 1991."

His mournful eyes drifted to the bottle on the table.

"This was 'sposed to be a routine drowning," he said regretfully, as I refilled his glass.

Energized, I paced my small kitchen, then, from force of habit, began to brew a pot of Cuban coffee. I set the grinder on extra fine and fed it the dark fresh-roasted beans, as their aroma permeated the room. "I wonder if her parents still live here? You think Jordan was the real victim?" I filled the lower chamber with water up to the steam valve, added the basket of coffee, screwed the top chamber on tight, and set the little pot on the stove.

"The case wasn't ours," he said. "But I gotta find out in a hurry. Gotta build me a file. Think you could slip me copies of all the stories that ran in the *News*?"

"Sure," I said. "No problem." Providing old news clips to cops is not newsroom policy, but it isn't police policy to personally deliver tips on murder cases to reporters in the dead of night. Life is a two-way street.

"I'll have them for you first thing in the morning," I promised, as he rose to leave. "Get some sleep and eat something." I smoothed the lapels of his wrinkled jacket as he stood in the doorway. "Wear a shirt that looks good on TV, just in case. But try not to talk to any other reporters until you have to. Jeez, I hope we don't get beat on this."

He looked perplexed. "What kinda shirt looks good on TV?"

"Blue. Light blue."

"Hell, I don't even know if I got me a clean shirt, much less a clean blue shirt."

"Sorry, I don't do laundry."

"See ya, kid," he said, his face close enough for me to smell the whiskey on his breath.

He was several steps away when I called after him.

"Emery?"

He turned.

"This is no practical joke, right? You didn't make this one up, did you?"

"Kid, I'm flattered you should think I'm that creative."

"Sorry. Shoulda known better."

Warm milk usually makes me drowsy but I was already wired as I dressed, even before I swallowed that first sip of lethally powerful black Cuban coffee. I took a mug full with me, knowing the *News* cafeteria was closed and the stuff spewed by the coffee machine undrinkable.

Moonlight glinted off dark water as I speeded west across the causeway. The glittering city skyline beckoned as my spirits soared on the high that comes when you know that you alone have the story everybody will want. She had a name now, but the woman in the water still hid her secrets. The mystery that had swirled and eddied around her from the start had become darker and more intriguing. I wondered what was it like for a man to lose ten years and nearly his life for a murder that never took place—until now.

I parked the T-Bird in the shadows beneath the *News* building and let myself in the heavy back door. Caught by the wind, it slammed like a gunshot behind me. The dark, deserted lobby was as cold and forbidding as my thoughts.

The only elevator operating overnight seemed slower and more sluggish than ever. My footsteps echoed down the hall. The newsroom was empty, the library locked. I could pull up the old stories on my computer terminal, but I wanted to see the hard copies, the headlines, the pictures and the faces in them.

I fumbled in the receptionist's desk, searching for the key. Suddenly I froze, aware I was being watched.

"Hold it right there!"

A figure stepped from the shadows behind me. A boyish security guard, fingering his mace canister, his lanky body tense. He was a stranger.

"Hi." I breathed again in relief. "I need a key to the library. You have a set, right?"

"Who might you be, ma'am?"

"Oh, for Pete's sake, I work here. That's my desk over there. The messy one, with all the papers on top. Who are you?"

"Rooney D. Thomas, ma'am. *News* security. May I see your photo ID?"

Impatiently, I dug it from my purse. He scrutinized the card, eyes moving to my face and back to the photo; then he focused on the small print.

"Britt Montero!" He looked elated. "Why didn't you say so? My fiancée is a friend of yours!"

"Who?" I asked, uncertainly.

"Angel. Angel Oliver."

Lord, no, I thought. I had met Angel, a welfare mother of seven, when she was charged with her baby daughter's death. Doctors later discovered that a rare congenital defect had killed her and Angel was cleared, but not before her ex-husband brokered a hit on her with a homicidal teenage gang. Life was a death-defying experience every time our paths crossed. Twice we narrowly escaped being shot. The woman nearly got me killed. No matter how well-meaning, she was a headache looking for a host. Last time we spoke, she had completed a work training program and had been thrilled to tell me she'd landed a job as a *News* advertising department secretary, once her new baby arrived. This must be the father.

"Oh," I said. "I thought you were in the navy," then bit my tongue. Was he the same man? Or some new fiancé?

"Discharged last month," Rooney said, beaming. "Security work is just to tide me over till I land something better, but once Angel starts, it'll be perfect. She'll work days, I'll work nights, and one of us will always be home with the kids."

She is really coming to the *News*, I thought dismally.

"Has she had the baby yet?" I asked.

"Any day now. I'm wearing a beeper." He grinned and patted the device clipped to his belt. "We're getting married right after the baby comes."

Traditionally, I thought, such events took place in reverse order, but who was I to be picky?

"And how's Harry?" I smiled in spite of myself. Angel's son Harry, age five, was my favorite.

"A great kid. Talks about you all the time," he said. "Claims you carry candy in your purse."

"Listen," I said urgently. "I'm working on a story and need to get into the library."

"Sure thing." He dug in his pocket. "I've got the master key." He dangled it enticingly in front of me, with a sort of crooked, goofy grin.

"Let's go," I said briskly, "and bring the key to the copy machine, too."

While he warmed up the copier, I pulled the clip files on Robert Jeffrey Jordan, better known as R. J., and his beautiful wife, Kaithlin.

Filed by date, the stories read like a novel. I would write the next chapter and hoped I'd get to write the ending, too. I sat at a librarian's desk and started at the beginning.

R. J. Jordan was the scion of a pioneer family that established South Florida's first trading post on the Miami River before the turn of the last century. The Jordans bought pelts from the Indians who paddled downstream in canoes and sold supplies to early settlers. One hundred years later, the trading post had grown into a hugely successful department store chain that sprawled across seven southern states.

R. J. was tall and handsome, a football hero and a party animal, according to the early clips: expelled from one prep school, suspended from another. A tragic teenage car crash had killed a passenger in his new Corvette and gravely injured four teens in a Camaro. Only R. J. walked away unscathed. He led a charmed life. Despite allegations of drinking and drag racing, he was never charged. He and several fraternity brothers also escaped accusations of a sexual nature against them after a wild party on the University of Miami campus.

Everything the bad-boy darling of Miami society did, from piloting his own plane to mountain climbing to escorting Miss USA to the annual Miss Universe ball, made the newspapers.

The most eligible of bachelors, he romanced beautiful and well-known women. His marriage broke countless hearts, although his young bride's story warmed the cockles of the women's-page writers. Kaithlin Warren first caught his eye when she worked part-time at Jordan's cosmetics counter during the Christmas season. She was only sixteen, the child of a hard-working widow who had raised her alone in a modest apartment. R. J. was twice her age.

Four years later their nuptials, the "wedding of the year," took place at the picturesque Plymouth Congregational Church. A reception for three hundred followed at the swank Surf Club. Jordan's prominent parents said they were thrilled and elated that he had settled down at last.

The bride was radiant at the center of a group photo on the society page. R. J. smiled, rugged in a tux. The bride's mother wore the only face without a smile. Severely dressed and clutching a crumpled handkerchief, Reva Warren looked older than R. J.'s parents, and her pained expression was that of somebody just kicked in the ankle. Tears, I thought. Only natural. My mother would weep in sheer relief if I ever married.

Rooney startled me again, his awkward silhouette filling the doorway.

"Machine's all warmed up," he said jauntily, and sat down across from me. "You should hear how excited the kids are 'bout the wedding. Harry wants to carry the rings. The twins are scattering rose petals, and Misty's gonna be a bridesmaid. Won't be a real big affair, but we want you to be there."

How can they keep it small? I wondered. Angel's kids are a crowd.

"Can you copy these clips for me, while I go through the rest? Two of each. Okay?"

He hesitated, gray eyes uncertain. "One of my responsibilities is to prevent unauthorized persons from coming in after hours to use the copy machines. Am I authorized?"

"Raise your right hand," I said. "I'm deputizing you to officially assist me on a story."

" 'Kay," he said, doubtfully. "I'll finish my rounds, just take five minutes, then I'll be right back to help you out."

I sorted the stories I wanted for my file and for Rychek's into a separate stack as I read. A business-page writer reported that the groom's father, Conrad Jordan, had put R. J. in charge of the chain's flagship downtown Miami store shortly after the wedding. He apparently hoped the responsibility would commit his son to the family enterprise.

Instead, subsequent stories indicated, it seemed to be Kaithlin who developed a dedication to the business. At age twenty-five, she became the store manager.

I remembered my mother's praise for the woman's business acumen, style, and panache. Kaithlin Jordan blossomed into a sleek and stunning executive with leadership qualities and a commitment to civic responsibility in subsequent stories and pictures. She founded a mentoring program to help inner-city single mothers get off welfare by teaching them skills, then sending them to job interviews attired in business suits donated by the store. She personally saw to it that they were provided with matching accessories and confidence-boosting cosmetic makeovers. Who knows what more she might have accomplished had her success not been cut short, along with her life.

A gossip column item reported the first hint of trouble

six years into the marriage, a trial separation while the couple "worked out their difficulties." A Jordan's spokesperson confirmed that Kaithlin would remain executive manager of the flagship store and continue to serve on the board of directors, along with both R. J. and his father.

The marriage careened downhill. Kaithlin and her mother obtained restraining orders, alleging threats of physical violence. Soon after, R. J. was stopped for drunk driving, fought the cops, and was arrested. A gossip columnist reported that Kaithlin met with a well-known local divorce lawyer.

A business-page writer broke the story about scandalous financial irregularities at the flagship Jordan's. If it was embezzlement, it was big: three million dollars unaccounted for. R. J. and Kaithlin had been questioned, as was the chief financial officer he had hired and other executives.

Then Kaithlin Jordan vanished. Her mother and her best friend reported her missing on a Sunday night, February 17, 1991. The circumstances were ominous.

R. J. and Kaithlin had flown off together for a romantic weekend getaway, an apparent attempt at reconciliation. He was at the controls of his twin-engine Beechcraft King Air, their destination the Daytona 500. NASCAR races seemed an unusual choice for a romantic reunion, particularly after the couple's storybook Parisian honeymoon, but there is no accounting for taste, and R. J. always felt the need for speed. Racing was a passion.

Kaithlin's mother and Amy Hastings, the missing woman's best friend since kindergarten, said Kaithlin had expressed doubts about the trip but still hoped to salvage their six-year marriage. Kaithlin called Amy that Sunday. She said R. J. was angry, violent, and out of control. The trip had been a terrible mistake. All she wanted was to go home to Miami "in one piece." Amy offered to drive the 250 miles to Daytona to rescue her friend, she said, but Kaithlin declined, saying she'd be all right.

But she was weeping an hour later in a call to her mother. She sounded frightened. "R. J. wants to kill me!" Her mother tried to calm her but they were abruptly cut off. Terrified, unable to recall the name of the motel, the desperate mother dialed 911. Told to contact the proper jurisdiction, she phoned Daytona police, who left her on hold. Eventually, after being transferred from number to number, she was advised to call again if she did not hear from her daughter by Monday.

The couple had planned to return to Miami that night. The mother called Opa-Locka Airport. R. J.'s mechanic said the Beechcraft had landed an hour earlier. R. J. had already gone. Kaithlin? He hadn't seen her.

Reva Warren finally reached R. J. at home that night. When she asked for her daughter, her son-in-law lashed out with a string of epithets, she said, and slammed down the telephone.

She called police again.

The next morning, the Daytona police checked the motel room occupied by Kaithlin and R. J. and made an ominous discovery. A shattered mirror. Signs of a struggle. The telephone ripped out of the wall. Bloodstained bedclothes and a missing shower curtain.

The prosecution later hypothesized that Kaithlin, dead or fatally injured, was wrapped in the shower curtain, con-

cealed in the trunk of R. J.'s rental car, and driven to the airport hangar where his plane waited.

If she was aboard, dead or alive, when he took off from
Daytona, she was not when he landed in Miami. Airport
witnesses, including his own mechanic, said R. J. arrived
solo. He was upset, they said, and had stalked off, carrying
only a single suitcase.

Police found traces of blood on the fuselage. Hounded by
police and reporters, R. J. insisted the weekend was
peaceful, the marriage patched up. He denied quarreling;
the scratches on his face and arms had been accidentally
inflicted by Kaithlin's fingernails as they'd wrestled playfully.

Kaithlin had left the plane to buy soft drinks from a
vending machine as they were about to take off for Miami,
he explained. She never came back. Impatient, he went to
find her. Even had her paged, he said. When she did not
respond, he flew home, alone and furious.

Kaithlin's luggage, name tags inside, was found the next
day, broken open alongside U.S. 9 west of Cape Canaveral.
Her scattered belongings, torn and bloodstained, were
identified by her mother and her friend Amy.

R. J. reluctantly conceded to police that he lied initially.
They had quarreled, but she was fine when she left for the
sodas. Police found no record that Kaithlin had been paged
at the airport. Under siege, R. J. admitted he lied about that
too. But he never hurt her, he insisted; she just walked off.
Detectives computed the time between takeoff in R. J.'s
Beechcraft, with a range of a thousand miles and a cruising
speed of 175 mph, and his Miami arrival, then plotted the
areas over which he could have flown. Unfortunately they

included Ocala National Forest, a thousand miles of ocean, the Loxahatchee National Wildlife Refuge, and the vast reaches of Lake Okeechobee. R. J. had filed no flight plan. Police aircraft equipped with heat sensors designed to detect decomposing human remains flew low over the forest. The Coast Guard was alerted that the body might have been dumped at sea. Authorities in more than a dozen counties between Daytona and Miami-Dade launched a major search for a body.

"Hell, it's like looking for a needle in a haystack," a detective said in one story. "He could have landed on any back road or at any ranch or farmland airstrip and put her in a shallow grave."

As the furor mounted, R. J.'s parents issued a statement. Their son's marriage had "hit a rough spot, which all couples experience at one point or another, but he would never harm Kaithlin, whom we all love dearly." They offered a $50,000 reward for her safe return. In public they proclaimed R. J.'s innocence, in private they hired South Florida's best criminal defense attorney.

"On advice of counsel" R. J. refused to speak to police any further. He'd made too many damning admissions already. But he did talk to the press. His attempt at damage control backfired when his temper surfaced. Swearing he had not harmed his missing wife, he departed from his lawyered script to send her a message. "Stop playing these childish games," he snarled, "and come the hell home!" He glared into the camera lights and refused to answer questions. He looked strained, scared, and guilty as hell in the accompanying photo.

Women's groups boycotted Jordan's and the women she

mentored demonstrated at the downtown store, chanting "Justice for Kaithlin Jordan!"

When hope of finding her body faded, police and prosecutors took their case to a Volusia County grand jury. Jurors promptly indicted R. J. on first-degree murder charges. Police watched his plane and caught R. J. attempting to take off at midnight. In his duffel bag was $75,000 in cash, his passport, and a handgun.

Held without bond, he sat in a Volusia County jail cell for five months before trial. Though prosecutors warned they would seek the death penalty, R. J. refused a deal, a guilty plea in exchange for a life sentence. Insisting he was being railroaded, he trusted a jury with his life.

Our daily trial coverage was reported by Howie Janowitz, who was still with the *News* today. He had captured all the drama, the color, the detail.

Jury selection experts hired by the defense apparently considered R. J.'s charm and dark good looks appealing to women. They accepted eight, along with four men and two alternates.

Eunice Jordan, R. J.'s elegant mother, wore high-fashion black to court every day. The victim's mother, red-eyed, fingernails chewed to the quick, had to be warned frequently by the judge to control her emotions.

A powerful witness, Reva Warren focused a malevolent stare on the defendant as she described R. J.'s abuse of her daughter and what happened when she tried to intervene.

"He threatened to kill us both," she wept on the stand.

Amy Hastings testified that Kaithlin knew R. J. was unfaithful and feared he was responsible for the missing money. But he had been the only man in her life since she was sixteen. When he refused marriage counseling, Kaithlin went alone. As he became more abusive, she had turned to the courts, even appealed to her in-laws—but the mentor who helped others found none for herself.

R. J.'s own mistress testified against him. Dallas Suarez strutted to the stand wearing a tight white blouse and a black skirt, a bombshell witness for the prosecution. Now contrite, she provided motive. She was the flight instructor who had trained R. J. on the Beechcraft. Their passionate affair began in the cockpit. They scuba-dived, went flying, and air-boated in the Everglades while Kaithlin worked. R. J. bought Suarez a Jaguar convertible and made the payments on her condo apartment.

The high point of her testimony came when she flashed a soulful look at the stony-faced defendant and burst into tears, blurting, "I never thought he'd kill her." R. J., she said, had vowed to dump his wife for her but never said it would be out of a plane.

Prosecutors theorized that R. J. embezzled the money to finance his womanizing lifestyle, then murdered Kaithlin to prevent her from exposing him to the police—or his parents. It was during the testimony of Dallas Suarez, Janowitz noted, that several of the female jurors began to glare unrelentingly at the defendant.

They continued to do so as Miami police officers testified about domestic battery calls to the big home R. J. and Kaithlin shared on Old Cutler Road. Other investigators testified that the embezzlement suspects had been narrowed down to three employees, Kaithlin, R. J., and Walt Peterson, the store's financial officer, an old college fraternity brother hired by R. J. himself.

Peterson took the Fifth, declining to testify about financial matters on grounds that he might incriminate himself.

The cash confiscated from R. J. at his arrest could not be traced to any legitimate source. The prosecution contended that it was part of the money he and Peterson conspired to steal.

An employee at the Silver Shore Motel in Daytona testified that he heard a man's voice, loud and angry, in the couple's room.

The bloodstains in that room, on the plane, and on the clothes in the shattered overnight case were all the same type—Kaithlin's. Her mother had given a blood sample for DNA testing, and results confirmed that chances were astronomical that the blood could have come from anyone other than her child.

The defense was in trouble. R. J. was all they had. Still cocky, he took the stand. Sure, he had lied at first. Who wouldn't? he asked. The police were clearly out to get him. The weekend had been stormy, he belatedly admitted. They had quarreled. He did slap her. But that was all, only a slap. She had scratched him, he conceded, but R. J. swore he never hurt Kaithlin. He loved her. Dallas Suarez, he said, was a mere diversion because his wife was busy working and he was bored. His interfering mother-in-law, he stated bitterly, was the cause of their problems. The cash he had when arrested, he swore, came from his own private funds, gambling winnings kept on hand for emergencies. He had intended to use the money to launch his own investigation to prove his innocence, he said. The prosecutor caustically pointed out that R. J. must have planned to do so from a distance, since he'd been carrying his passport as well.

He last saw his wife, R. J. insisted again and again under cross-examination, as she walked off across the Daytona Airport tarmac to fetch Cokes from a vending machine.

The defense used the usual blame-the-victim tactics, hammering on the theory that Kaithlin was alive, in hiding, to exact revenge on a cheating husband. If she was dead, they said, it was at her own hand, despondent over her marital woes.

The prosecutor scoffed. Did she commit suicide and hide her own body? He introduced Kaithlin's engagement calendar, crammed full of appointments and notes on future plans. If she was alive, why had none of her cash, checks, or credit cards been used? Nothing was missing from the Key Biscayne apartment she had occupied since their separation. Bank accounts, valuables, her driver's license and passport—all left behind. Her car, coated with dust, was still parked in her reserved space.

It was all proof she was dead, they said, and that R. J. had killed her.

Despite creativity and fancy footwork from a battery of high-priced defense attorneys, the jury returned a verdict in less than forty-five minutes: guilty of murder in the first degree. They took even less time to recommend death in a subsequent penalty phase. The judge agreed. R. J. stood sullen at sentencing and continued to proclaim his innocence.

Lead defense attorney Fuller G. Stockton later confided to reporters that the most he had hoped for was to save his client's life. The charge never should have been first degree, a death-penalty case, he said. It should have been second degree, unpremeditated and committed in the heat of passion.

Appellate courts upheld death, citing R. J.'s history of domestic violence, his prior run-ins with the law, the victim's restraining order, and his complete lack of remorse. On appeal, the state supreme court ruled that, though circumstantial, the evidence established both premeditation and corpus delicti and called the sentence consistent with other cases that warranted execution.

Another aggravating factor, Janowitz concluded in his final story on the case, was that R. J. was tried in upstate Volusia County, actually the deep South, a place where rich arrogant Miamians with slick big-city lawyers were unpopular, if not downright despised.

Questions flooded my mind. Was R. J.'s conviction a conspiracy of women? Did Kaithlin's mother know all along that her daughter was alive? I ran Reva Warren through the *News* library. Her name had appeared only once after the trial: May 11, 1996, dead at seventy. No story, only a brief agate obit.

Amy Hastings's name had not appeared in print at all since the trial. Had she left town, I wondered, or changed her name through marriage?

I punched more names into the search mode. Another casualty surfaced: Conrad B. Jordan, R. J.'s father, dead of complications after heart surgery in 1994 at age seventy-three. The 110-year family dynasty ended, the chain was sold to a Canadian conglomerate. The saga read like a Greek tragedy.

R. J.'s widowed mother, Eunice, still lived in Miami. Society columns noted her frequent attendance at charitable functions and benefit luncheons. Her most recent photo, at an Adopt-A-Pet fund-raiser, had appeared in the newspaper only a month ago. Still elegant, she still wore black. How would she react to the extraordinary news of her son's return from the valley of the shadow?

3

A figure loomed, silhouetted in the doorway, as I swallowed the last cold and bitter dregs of my coffee.

"How's it going?" Rooney asked.

"Great," I said. "Greed, sex, violence—the story's got it all."

"Didn't think you'd be here at this hour if it didn't." He sat in a chair across the desk from me and smiled. His uniform was crisply starched, and he smelled optimistically of shaving lotion.

"Brought you something." He placed a cellophane-wrapped packet of peanut butter and cheese crackers before me like an offering. "Thought you might be hungry. It was all that was left in the machine," he said shyly.

"My favorite," I said. "Thanks."

"I never thanked you for all you did for Angel and the kids while I was at sea," he said. "Times were tough. I coulda lost her."

"Angel is pretty feisty," I said. "She can take care of herself."

"Well, I'm taking over that job now. I'll be looking after her and the kids and they won't be having any more problems." He looked terribly young, his honest brown eyes solemn in the shadowy room's half-light. Did he have any idea, I wondered, what he was getting into? He must have read my mind.

"Some of my friends say I'm crazy to marry a woman with children."

"They're probably concerned about you," I said. "Step-parenting is no picnic."

"But I'm looking forward to it," he said enthusiastically. "Taking care of kids, raising 'em right, is the most important thing in the world. Every child needs a daddy."

"That's true." His sincerity touched me. "I never knew mine," I said. "He was killed in Cuba, by a Castro firing squad, when I was three. But I think I have some good memories, him lifting me up onto a pony, holding me up high to see the star on top of a Christmas tree. Maybe they're real, maybe I imagined them, but I think of him always."

"See how important dads are?" He rocked in anticipation, his face aglow. "I know it'll be a madhouse, but I love kids. My daddy always said, 'When you have a big family, you're never alone, and you're never bored.'"

"That's right, you're too busy."

He grinned and stood up. "Need to get back out on my rounds, but I'll keep an eye on you. Let me know if you need anything and give a holler when you leave so I can escort you to your car."

His jaunty footsteps retreated down the hall as I gazed again at the wedding photo of the rich and beautiful Jordans who had it all. What chance did Angel and this goofy kid have, I wondered, beginning with nothing but children in a world where love is so often fatal?

I put together the background for the main story, then researched for a sidebar about other death penalty cases in which no corpse was ever found.

In the movies and on TV cop shows the rule is always: "No corpse, no crime, no case." Not true. I found more than I expected, including the high-profile case of a politically connected Delaware lawyer who murdered his sweetheart, the governor's secretary, and disposed of her body in the Atlantic. He's probably the only rich white lawyer on death row in this country, though lots more surely belong there.

Another case, also in Daytona Beach, involved a teenage schoolgirl. Her name was Kathy. Her grandparents dropped her off at a convenience store, where she met two teenage girlfriends and a young man. Eventually Kathy left alone with him. She was never seen again.

Police questioned the young man. He said they had stopped at another store where he talked to two other girls while Kathy used a pay phone. Next time he glanced up, he said, she was gone. The officers saw scratches on his skin and a bruise on his side. Shaped like a footprint, the bruise was consistent with the shoes worn by the missing girl.

The suspect, who had a violent record, told acquaintances that a teenager had resisted sex with him, forcing him to slash her throat and hide her body. She was sixteen.

His lawyers, like R. J.'s, argued that there was no proof of a crime without a corpse. Appeals-court judges rejected the argument. Kathy had never run away. She had left her purse in her grandparents' car, saying she'd only be gone a short time. Her small bank account and personal possessions remained intact and, as a new member of the high school dance team, she had eagerly anticipated the fall semester. The combined circumstances convinced the judges that she was dead—murdered.

Young girl gone, without even a grave for loved ones to visit. As I sat there alone, in the dead of night, her piquant face smiled up at me from her photo, a typically curious teenager, too young to realize that a moment's bad judgment is often fatal.

So much sadness, so much evil loose in the world.

By 6 A.M., impatient for the sun and the rest of the city to rise, I called my mother.

"Britt, darling, is something wrong?"

I felt a moment's guilt, but hell, I was wide awake, shouldn't everybody else be?

"No, I'm working on a story."

"You're certainly off to an early start." She sounded more hoarse than sleepy.

"Mom, you don't sound like yourself. Are you coming down with something?"

"No, I'm fine. I just didn't sleep well."

"I didn't sleep at all. Why didn't you tell me the dead woman in that picture was Kaithlin Jordan?"

There was a long silence. "It did remind me a great deal of Kaithlin . . ."

Swell, I thought. She *did* recognize her.

". . . but the poor thing, bless her heart, has been dead and gone for years now." The words sounded oddly hollow.

"No. She was gone but not dead, at least not until now."

No response, another silence.

"Britt, darling," she finally said, voice wary, "what an

outlandish thing to say. Are you sure you're all right?"

I explained why I'd been up all night, told her what I had learned. "You could have said something, Mom. I mean, you knew them, didn't you?"

"Of course," she said softly. "I knew Kaithlin. Such a bright and quick-witted young woman, with the most wonderful laugh. I trained her; then, before I knew it, she was my boss. I didn't mind. She worked so hard that no one could begrudge her anything. She was special."

"What about R. J.?"

She gave a quick, impatient sigh of disapproval. "He was spoiled. Never really interested in the business, except to flirt and sweet-talk all the young sales associates, who, of course, loved the attention from the boss's son. On good days, R. J. could charm the sharks out of the sea; on others he was perfectly dreadful. Always volatile and short-tempered when everything didn't go his way. Once, while he was still in college, he and his dad had a fight, a brawl, right in the executive offices. No one who knew him ever doubted that he killed poor Kaithlin.

"It was so terribly sad." Her voice dropped to a near whisper. "Conrad and Eunice wanted to build a dynasty, but Eunice miscarried twice, and a premature daughter died at birth. All they had was R. J. They were so grateful that he was healthy and beautiful. . . ."

She paused and I could hear her light a cigarette. I thought she had quit.

"The Jordans never could say no to him, and he knew it." She exhaled deeply. "With all that followed . . . maybe some people are just not meant to have children."

"How did they get along with Kaithlin?"

"In their eyes, she came from the wrong side of the tracks. But once they saw R. J. was serious they were thrilled, at first. She was their great hope for the future of the bloodline—and the family business. I heard they promised to double R. J.'s inheritance if he and Kaithlin produced a male heir. I'm sure it was true."

"What was the courtship like?"

"Well, that Cinderella story was a tad exaggerated. Made it sound like the glass slipper fit and he instantly dropped to one knee to propose. Actually, it was turbulent. R. J. wasn't easy. They were on-again off-again for years before the ring and the fairy-tale wedding. She was so young, her mother was so upset, and he—well, he was just R. J. They ended it at one point. He saw other women. Everyone breathed a sigh of relief. But apparently they simply couldn't stay apart. Young as she was, nobody could hold a candle to Kaithlin. She had a certain . . . something."

"So what happened? Why wasn't it happily ever after?"

Silence. I heard her breathing; otherwise I would have thought the line was dead.

"I see from the clips," I offered, "that she became manager."

"That's right," she said quietly. "Kaithlin chose to work until they started a family. She was immensely talented. Her promotions and young ideas gave new style and energy to the Jordan image. Annual sales increased by more than thirty percent, she was so resourceful. R. J. was relieved that somebody—anybody—was taking care of the business, as long as it didn't have to be him. But I think he resented it when she became so successful."

"If she wanted to disappear," I said impatiently, "where

do you think she'd go? What would she do?"

"Britt, dear, I simply can't imagine Kaithlin doing such an implausible thing. I can't believe she's been alive all these years. You're sure?"

"Absolutely," I said.

"How awful. How cruel." Her voice faded, so distant that I strained to hear. "The stores never would have been sold . . . and Con would still be alive, I'm sure of it. He never got over seeing his son sentenced to death."

Con? "You were friendly with Jordan senior?"

She hesitated. "I worked for him—with him—for many years."

Slowly, as I grow older, I learn more about my mother, but the process is long, slow, and never easy. I decided this was not the time to try to draw her out.

"Did Kaithlin have affairs? Did she steal the money?"

"Of course not! R. J. was her first and only love, Jordan's her first and only job. She had ethics. She was loyal."

"Then who took the money?"

"What's the point of all this now?" she asked irritably. "It was so long ago."

"It matters, Mom. This is a major story."

"The Jordans dropped the investigation into the missing money after the murder—or whatever it was," she said reluctantly. "R. J. was in enough trouble. Everybody suspected him and Walt Peterson, that accountant he hired. They were long-time chums, involved in dubious escapades together ever since high school. Peterson was fired, of course. I think Con and Eunice covered for them both. They attributed the loss to poor accounting practices that had been corrected. Lucky for them it was a family-owned company."

I closed my tired eyes for a moment. "How do you remember her?" I said. "What was she like?"

"I don't like talking about this," she said. "But there was something about her eyes, even when she smiled. The months before her mur— whatever, you know what I mean—her eyes looked darker, as if she saw things others didn't. I remembered that later. She didn't laugh as often. She looked almost haunted, or hunted. . . . Listen to me rambling on like this. I sound ridiculous. Have to go now, sweetheart, I have an early meeting."

"But Mom—"

"Love you, dear."

The line went dead.

Conversations with my mother often left me uneasy, not so much about what was said as what was left unspoken. Why did those words always seem to be the most important?

I met Rychek at the employees' entrance at 6:45 a.m. Eager to stretch my legs, I trotted briskly down five flights from the newsroom. Despite my protests, Rooney trotted dutifully at my heels, hell-bent on protecting me whether I needed it or not.

The detective waited, clean-shaven, his sparse hair neatly combed, wearing a fresh light-blue shirt. The bad news was that up close the garment had the look of something from an end-of-season clearance sale at Kmart.

"Hey, kid."

"Here you go." I pressed the thick manila envelope into his hands. "It's everything we ran on the case, plus some background on the cast of characters. Get any sleep?"

"A coupla hours. You?"

"Not yet. I'll make up for it later. Kaithlin's mother died, by the way, in 'ninety-six."

"Humph," he growled. "That's what they all say."

"Whoa." The idea hadn't occurred to me. What if reports of the mother's death were also highly exaggerated? What if she had simply disappeared to join her daughter in hiding? "Jeez, I better check vital statistics and the funeral home. What's your game plan?"

"I'm gonna go over this stuff, brief the chief, then drop the bombshell on Jordan's lawyer. Hope he's wearing his hard hat. He's 'sposed to call me at eight-thirty." He squinted over my shoulder. "Who's your sidekick?"

Rooney stood sentinel at the door, hand on his mace.

"*News* security," I said softly. "Brand new. I'm trying to figure out how to get him out of here. Maybe the police academy?"

"Make sure I'm retired before you send 'im," he said quietly.

I flashed my warmest smile. "You look sharp," I told him. "Knock 'em dead. Solve this one, and the media will give you your fifteen minutes. Oh, yeah," I added, patting the envelope, "R. J.'s dad is dead too. The widow sold the stores and the big house in Cocoplum. She lives at Williams Island now and works the ladies-who-lunch circuit."

"Anybody see *his* body?"

"Sure. He died in the hospital after surgery. His heart. They say it broke when his son went to prison."

"Nice work, kid. I owe you."

Rooney escorted Rychek to his car as I escaped back into

the building and boarded the only working elevator. I may scamper down five flights to stretch my legs, but on the return trip, with no sleep, I want a ride. The increasingly sluggish elevator ascended in fits and starts, so slow that Rooney, who took the stairs, beat me there, beaming and barely winded.

"You know," he said enthusiastically, "Detective Rychek said a new academy class starts in April. I never thought of being a cop, but when he told me about all the benefits . . ."

Thank you, Jesus, I thought.

Back at my desk, I dialed a number.

"Get outa that bed!" I shouted repeatedly into the machine.

"Who the hell is this?" Janowitz finally mumbled, his voice groggy.

"It's Britt. I'm in the newsroom and I've been working all night. Why aren't you here?"

"What the fuck time is it? Shit, it's not even seven A.M. I'm not due in till ten. What the hell's going on? Somethin' I should know about?"

"Remember R. J. Jordan?"

"That murdering bastard. Hell, yes. I covered his trial."

"He didn't kill her. His wife was alive until two weeks ago. She was that unidentified murder victim who washed up on the beach."

"You're shittin' me." The groggy mumble gone, he sounded awake and alert.

I filled him in. "Think her mother was in on it?"

"Not a chance," he said, without hesitation. "If she was, she deserved an Oscar. No way that frail little old lady could work up so much emotion and anger day after day unless she really believed her daughter was murdered. All that pain was no act."

"But how could they convict him when she wasn't even dead?"

"I'da voted guilty myself, on general principles. You shoulda heard 'im. The son-of-a-bitch came across as an arrogant rich bastard from Miami and a bully to boot. Hell, that jury couldn't wait to fry 'im. And shit, no, he wasn't railroaded; the prosecution had a helluva strong case. Look at the clips."

"I did. Your trial coverage was great. Only problem, the crime didn't happen."

"Shit. Not only will that son-of-a-bitch walk, he'll be a martyr, patron saint of every anti–death-penalty group. They'll jump all over this one. Jesus Christ, if Kaithlin Jordan put the whole thing together, she oughta be charged with attempted murder. His. Hard to believe she'd do that to her own mother. You sure she wasn't on ice somewhere all this time?"

"The M.E. said the body was fresh. They could tell if her blood had been frozen."

"Damn. Need a hand on the story?"

"Nope, I've been working all night, got it all under control."

"Yeah." He sounded disappointed. I pitied him, but not enough to share. This story was mine.

A computer search of the Bureau of Vital Statistics data base showed a death certificate for Reva Warren but, of course, one had been issued for her undead daughter as well. I wondered how state bureaucrats would cope with the process of issuing a second death certificate for Kaithlin Jordan. Did they have an official policy to cover those who die twice? Or is it only one to a customer?

I reread Reva Warren's obit and called the funeral home. The woman on duty pulled up the file. Services were conducted at St. Patrick's Church, with burial at Woodlawn Park. "Says here she collapsed on the street. A stroke," the woman said cheerfully. "Had a history. Hypertension."

I asked for the name of her next of kin.

"Looks like she didn't have family. Predeceased by a daughter."

"By a husband too, right? She was a widow."

"No husband mentioned here. She had prearranged." The contact in the file was listed as Myrna Lewis, a family friend. I took down her address and the plot number at the cemetery.

A happy yodel echoed in the hall, and I waved. Lottie must have had an early assignment.

"How'd it go last night?" Wide awake, she was eager for details.

"Amazing! Lottie, you won't believe this!"

"Hell-all-Friday! The man proposed?"

She took in my blank stare, the files and notes strewn across my desk, the blocks of copy glowing on my computer screen, and rolled her eyes.

"Uh-oh. We ain't at the same address, are we? Not even the same zip code." Her expression changed to one of alarm. "Don't tell me you got stuck here on a story and didn't git to go?"

My ill-fated evening and the baby pictures came back to me.

"I went," I said. "Bummer. But wait till you hear the story I'm working on! Let's go for breakfast and I'll tell you about it."

She dropped off her film, art of an out-of-control brush fire on the fringe of the Everglades. I left the city desk a detailed memo on my story, and we went to a Cuban coffee shop a few blocks away.

I filled her in on the story between bites of flaky cheese-filled *pastelitos* and thick hot black coffee that resuscitated my brain cells and set my blood on fire,

"Now I need to go find a grave." I put down my cup and checked my watch. "It shouldn't take long."

"Is it in a cemetery?" she asked, daintily patting crumbs from her mouth with a paper napkin. "Or do we need a shovel?"

"Woodlawn," I said. "I have to see it, to make sure it's really there."

"You don't need me for that. But I want in on this one, Britt. Call me when there's something to shoot. Helluva story."

"Damn straight."

Pink and mauve streaks lit the sky as a fiery orange sun burned its way through banks of purple and a misty haze rose off the lush green grass at Woodlawn Park Cemetery.

Noisy traffic streamed in every direction. There was gridlock on the Palmetto Expressway after a tractor-trailer rollover. Motorists were trapped by construction on I-95, and wheezing Metro buses exhaled poisonous fumes at every stop, but here the grass smelled fresh and clean, insects buzzed, and flowers bloomed. In this place of death, I felt overwhelmed by life. Birds sang, water trickled merrily in a stone fountain, and time stood still. Nobody who slept here was in a hurry.

I found no one at the caretaker's cottage, so I studied the map posted outside, drove to the designated section, and set out on foot.

Mounds of fragrant fresh-dug earth piled high with damp and dewy floral arrangements marked a burial site less than twenty-four hours old. I stopped nearby to study the heart-breaking beauty of a stone angel that had been weeping over a child's grave since 1946.

If she's here at all, this must be the place, I thought, reading the lettering on stone markers and bronze plaques. Then I found it and saw why I had missed it at first. I was not expecting a freshly tended, recently visited gravesite. Somebody had neatly cleared away the weeds and tangled vines and placed a bouquet of long-stemmed white roses in the bronze flower holder. The double plaque bore two names.

MOTHER

Reva Rae Warren
April 25, 1926–May 11, 1996

BELOVED DAUGHTER

Kaithlin Ann Warren Jordan
January 27, 1965–February 17, 1991

The roses had withered and shriveled, crisped by the sun. Dried blossoms and buds had fallen away from the thorny stems. The weathered bouquet looked as though it had been there for about two weeks, since just before Kaithlin Jordan arrived unclaimed at the morgue.

What was it like, I wondered, to kneel at your own grave?

4

I found the groundskeeper back at the cottage, pointing out a section on the map for a middle-aged couple to whom he was giving directions. A stooped, slightly built man in his fifties, he nodded, eyes curious behind the tinted lenses of his eyeglasses when I told him the name and plot number.

"That one's had a lotta company all of a sudden," he said, his look quizzical.

"Oh?" I said.

"Never had any action, any visitors, far as I know," he said, self-consciously covering his mouth with his hand to mask ill-fitting dentures that clicked as he spoke. "Then, maybe six weeks or so ago, some fella came by looking for her."

"A man? What did he look like?"

He shrugged. "Shortish, Anglo, dark hair, late thirties, early forties. Had a sly way of looking atcha. In a big hurry, wanted help to find 'er. Didn't stay long. He came back right quick, wanting to know if anybody else had been asking 'bout 'er or visiting that plot lately."

"Did he leave his name or a card?"

"Nope." He readjusted his baseball cap over wispy hair.

"Did you see his car?"

"Looked like a rental."

"Who brought the flowers?"

"Must have been the woman. I seen her out there a coupla weeks ago. She'd been tidying it up. Didn't speak. When I rode the mower acrost that strip between the front row and the fountain, saw 'er just kneeling there, real quiet. Didn't really see her face, hidden by sunglasses and a scarf, but she looked young. It's funny," he said from behind his hand. "Nobody all these years till now. What's the sudden interest in that one?"

"I hoped you could tell me," I said. I gave him my card and asked that he call me if anyone else came looking for Reva Warren.

Across the street, within a block or two of the cemetery entrance, were three small florists' shops. White roses, I asked at each one, sold about two weeks ago? The first two shook their heads when I showed them a glossy *News* file photo of Kaithlin Jordan.

"*Tal vez,* maybe," said the third, a flower importer from Colombia. He set down the sharp cutting tool he'd been using to snip the thick stems of a bird of paradise, wiped his hands on his apron, and picked up the photo in an exaggerated, almost theatrical gesture. Lips pursed, he studied it thoughtfully, the air around us moist, cool, and fragrant.

"*Un poco mayor,* a little bit older." He raised huge, sad eyes from the photo. "When was this taken?"

"More than ten years ago." I held my breath. "*Más de diez años.*"

"Maybe, maybe not." He studied it again, shrugged dramatically, and stroked his sleek mustache. *La cliente,* if she

72

was the one, wore a scarf, he explained. He never saw her eyes. She never removed her large dark glasses. He suspected at first that she might be a celebrity but he couldn't place her face, and a celebrity would not be alone. *"¿Sí? There would be a bodyguard, an entourage. ¿No?"*

American and well dressed, she had come by taxi and paid in cash. His red roses were beautiful, a fresh shipment that morning, full, lush, and passionate. But she had insisted on white. *"Una dama muy bonita, pero triste. ¿Sabe?"* He gestured expansively. A pretty lady, but sad. She said little, but left the impression that she had come from a distance to pay her respects to a loved one. After she left, he watched from his front window and saw her cab swing through the cemetery's wide wrought-iron gates. He could not remember the name on the cab but thought it was yellow. Yes, yellow.

Something clandestine about her, he confided, made him suspect *el muerto* was an old lover, a former husband, perhaps someone else's husband. Of course, he confessed, he was dedicated to *amor*. He wished he had seen her eyes, he said. They always tell the story.

I left his tiny shop, full of fragrance and romantic fantasies, and called Rychek. "The mother is definitely dead," I told him. "I'm at the cemetery. Guess who was here?"

Rychek told me that Fuller G. Stockton, R. J.'s lawyer, was already en route to Florida State Prison to inform Jordan. Stunned by the revelation that his client was actually innocent, he had hastily regained enough presence of mind to schedule a 6 P.M. press conference. He'd be back by then from the prison, in Starke, a small north-Florida town surrounded by pinewoods. Motions were already being filed for R. J.'s immediate release. The timing was good for me. TV reporters would have scant time to report and fill in background. They might air the news flash first, but only we would have the complete story.

As I drove north, I called the city desk and Lottie to alert them to the press conference and asked that she photograph the flowers at the gravesite. Twenty minutes later I found the address I sought.

Miami's skyline changes constantly, as do the names of streets, banks, and businesses. It is not uncommon for locals to find themselves confused and disoriented on suddenly unfamiliar street corners, their intended destinations, stores, shops, or restaurants vanished like missing persons, without a trace.

My adrenaline spiked at my good fortune. What a surprise. The Southwind Apartments, an aging three-story structure, was still standing.

Among the names on a rusting bank of mailboxes in the crumbling foyer I found LEWIS.

I buzzed the apartment.

"Who's there?" A woman's voice rasped from the squawk box.

"Mrs. Lewis? Myrna Lewis?"

"Who is it?" Another voice, speaking nonstop in the background, sounded oddly familiar.

"Britt Montero, from the *Miami News*. I'm a reporter. I understand Reva Warren was a friend of yours."

"She passed away some years ago."

"I know. I need to talk to you about her daughter."

"Kaithlin's dead too."

"I didn't mean to interrupt. It's important. I won't take much of your time."

"Well," she said reluctantly, "only a few minutes."

In her late sixties, or even older, her face was worn and deeply lined. She had attitude and a certain dignity, despite her shapeless housedress and arthritic limp, as she showed me into her small and scrupulously clean kitchen. Neatly pressed curtains, the color nearly washed out of them, framed the single window, which overlooked a parking lot. Her companion, the other voice I'd heard, continued to speak from a radio on the kitchen counter, a woman talk-show host dispensing life-changing personal advice to callers.

"I know why you came," Myrna Lewis said, and gestured to a chair at the wooden table. An empty cup sat on the scarred tabletop. A used tea bag sat puddled in a saucer on the stove. She switched off the radio as the host admonished a caller: "Without a ring and a date, you don't have a commitment."

"You do?" I said.

She nodded solemnly. "Because they're going to execute the man who murdered Reva's daughter." She struck a match to light the gas burner beneath the kettle. "Would you like some tea?"

I'd already had too much coffee, I said.

"I wish Reva was alive to see it," she said wistfully. She extinguished the match at the water faucet and dropped it into the trash. "She planned to go, you know. She wanted to be there. I think that's what kept her alive in the last years, when she wasn't well. She hung on to see that man pay for what he did. But all those appeals." Shaking her head, she limped to the table and slowly lowered herself into the chair opposite me. "The system is so slow that the son-of-a-bitch outlived her. It wore her down and he won again. There'll be no real justice the day he dies because she didn't live to see it."

"It's even more unfair than you think." I opened my notebook.

Her pale, faded eyes widened as I explained. Her mouth opened. Her lips moved, but she made no sound.

"Impossible," she finally whispered. "You say she wasn't dead?"

"Mrs. Lewis, do you think there's any possibility that Mrs. Warren knew that? That she and her daughter might have been in contact through the years?"

"How could you even think such a thing?" She rose painfully to pace the length of her tiny kitchen, murmuring as though to herself. "Reva was religious, a good Catholic. That little girl was her life. She worked so hard, two jobs, to put that child in a good school, give her dance lessons and pretty things." She eased herself back into the chair, shoulders slumped, as though my questions were a heavy burden.

"You were good friends?"

Her stricken eyes focused on mine. "We worked together when we were young, years ago, piecework in a dress factory in Hialeah. New owners came in, Cubans, who only wanted to hire Cubans, so we got laid off. Reva found another job, on her feet all day in a bakery. She also helped out part-time at Discount Office Supply, where I worked, over on One Hundred Twenty-third Street. At night she sewed and did calligraphy—you know, that elegant old-fashioned penmanship? She was an artistic woman. People paid her to address their invitations—to weddings, parties, bar mitzvahs. She did birth announcements, even Christmas cards."

The teakettle's shrill whistle interrupted and she rose to silence it. Hands shaking, she poured boiling water over the used bag.

"Sure you won't have some?" she offered. "I would give you a fresh bag, of course. I only reuse them because it's less caffeine that way and they go further."

I shook my head as she stirred.

"Can you imagine," she went on, "that some people don't even write their own Christmas cards? Reva would work all night at her dining-room table, addressing envelopes to strangers, and then go to her day job. As she raised a daughter, took her to church and to music and ballet lessons. She made all Kaithlin's clothes herself, beautiful things, handmade and embroidered."

"It had to be difficult," I said, scribbling notes. "When did Reva's husband die?"

She averted her eyes and hesitated. "The bum didn't die. He left when she was six months pregnant. Saw the baby once, maybe twice, then left town with his latest girlfriend. Last Reva heard, maybe twenty-five, thirty years ago, somebody saw him in New Orleans. He's probably still alive. People like him, they lead charmed lives, do as they please. . . . Never paid a nickel in child support, all those years. These days they chase them down, call them dead-beat dads, and make them pay. You see it on TV all the time. Back then, nobody cared."

"But when Kaithlin married R. J.," I protested, "the stories said she'd been raised by her widowed mother."

She snorted in derision. "You of all people should know better than to believe everything you read in the newspaper. Jordan's mother told that story, said *widowed* sounded better than *divorced*. She was concerned about what her friends would think. For Kaithlin's sake, Reva didn't argue, but she swore she'd tell the truth if anybody asked. Reva wouldn't lie for anybody."

I stared as she sipped her weak tea, her eyes unfathomable. Were any of these people what they pretended to be? How did they keep track of the truth about who was really dead and who wasn't?

"Reva's divorce embarrassed Mrs. Jordan," Myrna Lewis continued. "Well, what goes around comes around." She smiled in grim triumph. "I wonder what her friends think about her son on death row?"

"But he didn't do it," I said quietly. "He'll be released."

"He shouldn't be." She rubbed her swollen knuckles. "It's not right."

Reva, she said, had remained unmarried until she was forty. Eric Warren, a handsome charmer, swept into her life abruptly. He left the same way, after depleting her modest savings and impregnating her. When her only child arrived late in life, she was all alone.

"Wait here." Myrna hobbled into the next room. "I have something to show you." She returned with the framed photo of a tiny blond posed gracefully in a pink tutu and ballet slippers. Her mother sat stiffly in a straight-backed chair behind her, graying hair pulled tightly into a severe bun, her eyes on her daughter, palms together in silent applause. Kaithlin looked about nine, which made her mother at least fifty in the photo.

"Look at them," Myrna Lewis demanded. Her eyes watered. "They're both gone now, and he did it. He's responsible, whether he killed them with his own hands or not."

I studied the strong lines of the mother's face. "Was she a strict parent?"

"Maybe, but she had to be. She was a religious woman. Saw only right and wrong, with not much in between. Reva wanted Kaithlin to concentrate on her schoolwork, but she wasn't well and Kaithlin insisted on helping. She said she didn't want her mother to work so hard. So Reva let her take a part-time Christmas job at Jordan's. They put her on the cosmetics counter, because she was beautiful, I guess. But she didn't need paint and powder to stand out from the crowd. Everybody who saw her knew she had something special. Reva most of all.

"She sent Kaithlin white roses on her sixteenth birthday. She admitted it was extravagant, but she said her daughter deserved it. Later, Kaithlin would send white roses to her mother on her birthday and every Mother's Day."

So it *had* been Kaithlin at the cemetery.

"Kaithlin changed after she took that job and met him. She became defiant and ungrateful. She broke her mother's heart, but it was him; he was the one responsible."

"R. J?"

She nodded, fingers wrapped around her empty cup as though for warmth. "He was a grown man twice her age, with a bad reputation. He changed her, turned her head. She started to stay out and come home late. Reva never had another peaceful day. She was able to stop it for a time, when Kaithlin was still underage. But they started up again as soon as she was eighteen. That man knew how to manipulate a young girl. Reva worried, she cried, she prayed to St. Jude. She begged me to pray with her—but all the prayers in the world couldn't save Kaithlin. That girl was all she had."

"But surely," I said, "her mother must have been relieved and happy for her when they got married."

Myrna Lewis's eyes flickered. "The husband was spoiled, a jealous, selfish man. Reva could never forgive him for all he . . ." Her voice faded. "They hated each other."

"But they both loved Kaithlin. Why didn't they work at getting along?"

She shook her head. "There are some sins only God can forgive."

"But St. Jude came through," I said persistently. "Kaithlin was alive long after R. J. went to death row."

"If Reva's prayers were answered," the woman said, leaning forward to jab an arthritic finger, "she died never knowing it. She made me promise that if she went first she'd be buried properly. She wanted her daughter's body found so she could have a decent burial, too. She bought a double plot and a fancy stone for her and Kaithlin. She wanted her girl with her, the way it was before him. She wrote letters to the prison, even had the parish priest write, begging R. J. to say where he put her. He never answered.

"The day Reva died, she was going to the church to talk to Father O'Neil about a special mass. She had them twice

80

a year, on Kaithlin's birthday and the anniversary of the murder.

"They said she stepped off the bus in front of St. Patrick's and fell down in the street. While she was lying there, somebody stole her purse. By the time she got to the hospital, she had no identification. But the maintenance man from this building had been driving by; he saw the ambulance take her and phoned me to find out how she was. I kept calling but the hospital kept denying she was there. Finally they put me through to a social worker who said they had an unidentified body.

"I had to go down to identify her." She gazed out the window, eyes flooded.

"You saw her body?"

She nodded. A single tear trickled down the wrinkled cheek.

"You're sure it was her?"

"What sort of question is that?" she snapped, frowning in confusion. "Of course. Why would you even—"

"I'm sorry," I said. "Do you still work at Discount Office Supply?"

She shook her head brusquely and blinked. "That's gone too. The big chains, Office Depot and Office Max, both moved in. Ran my boss right out of business. He packed up and moved north, think he opened a convenience store somewhere. The good Lord knows I keep trying to find something. Social Security goes only so far. Most people won't hire a woman my age."

She let me borrow the photo, as long as I wrote her a receipt and promise to return it.

"He should stay where he is," she said, as she saw me to

the door. "Look what he's done. Years ago, Reva and I made a pact. We were both alone and promised to be there for each other if anything happened. I did my part. Now who will be there for me?"

I made a pit stop at home to shower and change. Bitsy bounced out as I opened the door and I nearly missed the business card that fluttered to the floor. It bore the familiar Miami city seal with McDonald's name imprinted. Scrawled on the blank side were two words.

"Who? Why?"

I frowned, puzzled, as I pushed the PLAY button on my answer machine.

"Britt, what's up? Did you pick a fight with me because you had a late date? Who the hell was that guy?"

Distracted by the loves and lives of the clan Jordan, I paused to consider the question.

Then I realized what must have happened.

After driving off in a snit so long ago last night, McDonald must have reconsidered and returned just in time to see Rychek, arriving or departing. I winced, envisioning me, silhouetted in the open doorway, smoothing the rumpled detective's collar and delivering intimate sartorial advice at 2 A.M. in my robe.

"Oh, for Pete's sake!" I murmured as Bitsy grinned, pranced, and wagged her tail.

Did I have the time, energy, and patience to explain to McDonald right now?

Dutifully, against my better judgment, I hit his number on my speed dial.

"It's me," I sang out cheerfully.

"Hey." He sounded calm but chilly.

"Just got home and heard your message."

"Oh?"

The inflection in that single syllable set my teeth on edge as I contemplated all I still had to do in so little time.

"If you came back last night," I said, "you should have knocked."

"I saw a Beach detective's car, an unmarked."

"That was Rychek, remember? You met him once."

"Didn't realize you two were so tight."

"The man's pushing retirement." I resisted the impulse to add K. C. Riley's name to the mix. "He's good people, a source. He had information on a story."

"So he delivers news tips personally, at night?"

"For Pete's sake! McDonald. You never had an informant, a CI who was female?"

"Sure, lots of them. But I never served them drinks at my place after midnight."

Drinks? "So you were lurking in the bushes? Prowling and window peeping? Scaring my landlady? She's eighty-two, her husband is eighty-eight. One of them could have had a heart attack." Actually, Helen Goldstein would have brained him with her broom. "I'm damn lucky he did think of me. The story I'm working on is the big secret you wouldn't tell me last night. R. J. Jordan, right?"

"It's another department's case. It wasn't up to me to release information."

"Why not? The entire world will know tomorrow. I could have had it in this morning's paper."

"I was being professional."

"Sneaking around in the bushes is professional?" Ha, I

thought, he's on the ropes.

"Stop saying that," he said, voice reasonable. "I wasn't sneaking. You should keep your drapes closed."

"Why? I have nothing to hide. If you'd knocked, you would have seen how innocent it was."

"I tried that once."

Damn. A low blow, I thought, my face burning. He had dredged up ancient history. After the hurricane, the big one, when the phones were out, along with the electricity, the water, and the roads, when misery reigned and people were willing to kill for a bag of ice or a hot shower, McDonald came to my rescue—and found me with someone else. The look in his eyes that night haunts me still.

"That was long ago," I said quietly. "I thought the statute of limitations had run out on it. I'm sorry."

"So am I." He sounded weary.

My shoulders sagged. I felt fatigued and yearned to be with him, to relax in his arms. I fought the feeling.

"Have to go now." I tried to sound upbeat, to pump up my energy level. "I've got an early deadline. Talk to you later."

A terrible thought slowly took form after I hung up, materializing like something ugly in a horror film. All it lacked was a spooky score in a minor key. I'd heard those words, that tone, before. That was my mother talking. Was I becoming my mother?

I stepped into the bathroom, undressed, and stared into the mirror. No. No way, I told myself. It's the story, the deadline, my brain as overloaded as a computer about to crash.

When I finish this story, I promised, I will make it all up

to him. Make him forget K. C. Riley. I will lovingly whip up a succulent meal, some of my Aunt Odalys's exotic Cuban concoctions, a creamy midnight-black bean soup— or a green plantain soup thickened with ground almonds— and her *malanga*-encrusted snapper with olives and pimientos. I will massage his back, lure him into the shower, wash his hair with my scented shampoo, and smother him with kisses. Yes, I thought, stepping into the shower. I closed my eyes and realized I was not alone in that warm and steamy cubicle. The presence with me was not McDonald, it was Kaithlin.

How did a woman "dead" for ten years reappear, only to die again? Had she been kidnaped? Comatose? Suffering from amnesia? What triggered her return on the eve of her husband's execution? Did the execution lure her back? Or did she return belatedly to mourn her mother's demise? And if the M.E. was right, where was Kaithlin's child? And who was its father? If her first "murder" was not what it appeared to be, what about the second? Who killed her, and why?

Fresh-smelling body wash streamed like satin across my naked body, as I scrolled a mental list of possibilities and listened to whispered questions in the hissing flow of water.

5

Fortified by strong hot coffee, my brightest lipstick, and a favorite blue blouse, I filled in Fred Douglas, the news editor, by phone as I drove north on Collins Avenue. I needed no help, I told him. I had everything under control and was still reporting.

Unlike Myrna Lewis's modest abode, my destination this time was lavish and beachfront, with valet parking, a huge pool, cabanas, and a four-star restaurant. I used the gold-and-white house phone under a gleaming crystal chandelier in the marble lobby.

"I'm downstairs," I said, introducing myself.

Without hesitation, he invited me up.

A high-speed elevator whisked me to a spacious sixteenth-floor hallway with thick seafoam carpeting, ornate molding, and elegant gold sconces.

When I knocked, the door to 1612 buzzed, unlocked, and swung open, but the room appeared empty. I stood waiting.

"Hello?" My voice echoed in the silent apartment. "Is anyone here?"

No radio or TV played. No carpeting, little furniture. Lots of open space. The sea-and-sky colors of the walls and narrow drapes, all shades of marine blue and bottle green, were reflected in the expensive tile floors. The overall effect was one of being submerged in the sea instead of in a needlelike high-rise in the sky. Schools of fish would seem more natural outside these enormous windows than swooping pelicans or seagulls. One paneled wall concealed an elaborate entertainment center. Another, mirrored from floor to ceiling, reflected blue sky and water.

"Hello?" I called again. "Mr. Marsh?"

"In here." The computerized voice came from an overhead speaker. "To your right."

My heels clicked eerily on the tile floor.

A lock disengaged as I approached another door.

"Hello?" I hesitated, then pushed it open.

I gasped, suddenly face-to-face with myself, shocked at my mirror image, life-size and in full color, on a huge TV monitor. I hadn't even seen the hidden cameras. Bluish light flooded the room, which seemed even more sterile than the others; a slight odor of antiseptic was in the air. A man sat facing the screen, with his back to me. He touched the controls, and his motorized wheelchair spun in a hundred-and-eighty-degree turn.

His body looked shrunken and shriveled but his eyes glittered, dark and intelligent, and his thick salt-and-pepper hair looked absurdly healthy in contrast to the rest of him.

"I'm Zachary Marsh." He nodded briskly, in almost military fashion. "So you're Montero. I've read your stories." He eyed me approvingly. "Younger and prettier than your picture."

The man hadn't seen my picture, I decided, unimpressed. He had confused me with the columnists whose head shots appear with their work. But I didn't correct him. I was more interested in his toys.

At the oceanfront windows, two powerful telescopes stood on low tripods, adjusted to accommodate a seated viewer. Neatly arranged on an adjacent and immaculate glass-topped table were a moon-phase calendar, a NOAA weather radio, a police scanner, a cell phone, a cordless, two cameras, several sets of high-powered binoculars, and a remote-control device that looked sophisticated enough to operate every piece of electronic equipment in the apartment.

"Are those night vision?" I indicated a set of bulky black binoculars.

"Correct. But," he cautioned, "don't touch them! No one

else handles my equipment."

"Sorry." I stepped back. "I'm impressed." The National Guard used the night-vision glasses, originally developed for Israeli commandos, when much of South Florida was plunged into total darkness after the big hurricane. Now narcs and undercover cops used them for surveillance.

"How did you start . . . all this?" I said, still gaping at his array of equipment.

"Always wanted to watch the sky," Marsh said, "but never had the time. Too busy running the biggest Rolls-Royce dealership in the Northeast. Then my condition got worse, put me in this chair, and sent me south for the warm weather. Bought my first real telescope when I moved in. Studied the heavens for months. Then one day, by chance, I set my sights lower."

His lips curved into a half smile, his eyes roved to the windows, and his voice dropped to a near whisper.

"You have no idea what happens out there at night." He nodded toward the sea, awash in golden sunlight and sparkling innocently. "Everything from sea turtles marching out of the surf to lay their eggs, to beached whales, to cruise ships illegally dumping garbage. I've seen it all: incoming rafts, mother ships, smugglers in action—but none of it compares to the bizarre religious rituals and mating habits of the human species."

His hands, the left slightly clawed, turned palms up.

"To one in my position, the earthbound is far more intriguing than anything out there beyond our reach. Better than anything on television."

"You called in that floater," I said briskly, "a couple of weeks ago." I stepped to the window to gaze down at the stretch of sand where Kaithlin lay after being dragged from the water.

"Absolutely correct," Marsh replied, with a casual wave. "But that was nothing. Remember when those Haitian boat people began washing up dead on the beach last year?"

I nodded.

"That was me." His bony thumb jabbed at his sunken chest. "I spotted them first and informed the Coast Guard and the police. And when that dope plane cartwheeled into the sea last October? Dispatch even called me back, kept me on the line until the choppers were directly over the crash site."

I nodded, even more impressed.

"Remember when your own newspaper reported that 'the Coast Guard spotted' a fourteen-foot sailboat full of Cuban refugees who tried fighting them off with machetes? That," he said, voice rising, "was incorrect! The Coast Guard didn't spot them. Me—it was me. And when all those packages of cocaine washed ashore during that big music convention and people began picking them up off the beach? Guess who?"

"I remember, that was when the seven kilos washed up."

"Twelve." He inched up taller in his chair. "Twelve kilos. I saw who 'salvaged' the other five." He rolled his eyes toward a zoom-lensed camera on the table. "Even caught them in action."

"Wow." Though he hadn't invited me to sit, I assumed it was an oversight and dropped into a modern sculpted chair facing him. "What did the cops say when they saw the pictures?"

"They didn't see them." He shrugged. "Don't ask, don't

tell. They didn't ask, I didn't tell."

"But—"

"You know," he said accusingly, "you are the only one who has come to see me, to acknowledge what I do."

"But I'm sure—"

"I'm sure," Marsh snapped, "that they take the credit to justify their existence, to make it appear they're earning their pay. I see what they do down there at night, on duty, in their official cars, parked at the street ends on the beach in the dark. Not one has ever called to thank me, even though I'm the one who makes them look good."

"Perhaps they feel you'd rather remain anonymous, protect your privacy."

"Right," he said sarcastically. "The incompetents protect themselves. If they gave me credit, the public and their own superiors would soon question how I manage to see so much while the able-bodied men and women paid to protect our borders and our civilian population see so little."

"I'm sure Detective Rychek would like—"

"Oh, that one." He waved the name away with a dismissive gesture. "Called the other day, wanted to come by. Told him I was too busy."

"Why?"

"Did he ever call to thank me? Apparently he's too busy. Well, if he wants my help on something now, *I'm* too busy." His pout was petulant.

"The woman was murdered." I leaned forward intently. "Didn't you see the story? Someone killed her."

He looked bored. "I knew that—long before anyone else. You were there, on the beach that day. I saw you. When I read the story in the *News* the next morning, I realized that was you."

The look in his eyes gave me a sudden chill.

"Let me see here." He pressed a lever on his chair's control panel, maneuvering it across the narrow room to a low two-drawer file cabinet. Inside were dozens of folders, precisely labeled and color-coded. "Here we are," he said cheerfully. He removed a folder, thumbed through a sheaf of eight-by-ten photos, then motored back to where I sat, stopping his chair so close that his knees nearly touched mine. I wanted to push my chair back, but it was blocked by the table behind me. He selected a photo, studied it for a long moment, then presented it to me, his eyes meeting mine.

For an instant, I didn't recognize the woman in the picture. Hair and skirt caught in the wind. Sunglasses, notebook in one hand, pen in the other, my mouth open, speaking to someone, probably Rychek, who was outside the frame.

My legs looked good, I thought in a moment of vanity. He handed me another print and I reacted as though slapped. His long lens, that one-eyed voyeur, had zoomed in on Kaithlin's naked breasts wet and glistening in the sun. The close-up was so intense, the focus so sharp, that the individual grains of sand clinging to her skin were clearly visible. The small bare feet in the foreground had to belong to the boy, Raymond. His pail lay forgotten in the sand nearby.

"You never know what treasures the sea and Mother Nature will deliver next," Marsh said crisply. His lips curled in an unsettling smile. "Quite attractive, don't you think? I do my own darkroom work as well." As he reached for the photos his hand brushed my knee—deliberately, I was sure. The man is disabled, I reminded myself, swallowing my indignation.

"Did you photograph the murder?"

"Unfortunately, no." His smile faded. "My fault entirely." He gestured a mea culpa. "I'd been shooting a unique cloud formation at first light. Cumulus, with a vertical buildup. A huge geyser of red, orange, and purple, astonishingly like a mushroom cloud. Looked like Armageddon, the goddamn end of the world. Shot the whole roll. Emptied the camera. Not only would I have had to go to a hall closet for fresh film"—he made a small irritated sound—"in order to reload, I would have had to open that infernal cellophane wrapper, the cardboard box, then the film canister. My fingers don't work well some days. Had I tried, I would have missed it all. It happened lightning fast. But I have the pictures," he assured me, gnarled forefinger tapping his temple, "right up here."

"What happened?" My voice sounded faint, perhaps because my heart beat so loudly.

"Savage. It was savage." His eyes burned with the light of a boxing fanatic reliving a particularly brutal bout. "I couldn't tear myself away. The bugger popped her right square in the mouth. Punched her out, though the water did slow his swing somewhat."

"What did he look like?"

"Dark-haired white man is all I can say. From way up here, heads look like coconuts down in the water. Not much you can tell. He faced the horizon. I did catch her expression briefly in my binoculars. Total amazement, then horror. By then he was all over her. Didn't take him long at all. I couldn't see which way he headed once he swam ashore. I went to my bedroom for a better view but I had to unlock the door to the terrace. By the time I got out there, he was gone."

"Why didn't you call the police then?"

"To say what?" he demanded, rearing back indignantly. "To report a body somewhere in the Atlantic? She was no longer visible." He frowned at my naïveté. "I take pride in my word. When I say something is out there, it is in my sight. I can direct the authorities right to it. What if they didn't find her? What if they never found her? Sometimes they don't, you know. You can't cry wolf, not once, and ever expect to be taken seriously again."

"But," I protested, "they would have known hours sooner. The police might have stopped him or found other witnesses, maybe even someone who knew him."

Marsh stared as though I was the lunatic.

I gazed back, at a loss for words.

"I've acquired a backup," he offered, his tone conciliatory. "A second camera, always loaded. And I've ordered a video cam as well. Compact, lightweight, the newest, most sophisticated model on the market. Next time I'll have it all on video." He paused suggestively. "I see things before anyone else. Sometimes it's big news. Perhaps you and I can come to an arrangement. . . ." His fingers brushed my right knee again. This time they lingered. "So I call you first, give you the news tip." His chair pressed closer.

"You live here alone?" My eyes roved the premises hopefully, for signs of a caretaker with a net.

"More or less." He studied my breasts. "Don't like live-in help. I intend to stay independent as long as I can. A service sends somebody in twice a day, helps me bathe, makes sure I eat. Cleaning woman comes two days a week. Other than that, I'm on my own, doing whatever I like, thank you." He pushed a button on his remote, and hidden stereo speakers instantly responded, piping mindless elevator music throughout the apartment. He leaned forward, lips wet, eyes still focused just below my neckline. "We are alone," he said softly, "if that's what you're asking."

"Hate to leave, but I've got to go. Deadline," I sang out cheerfully, as I shoved his chair back and sprang to my feet.

"Thank you for coming," he said stiffly. "By the way, did they ever find out who she was?" His words were sly, his eyes bold.

"Yes," I said, halfway to the door. "I'm working on the story for tomorrow's paper."

"Then I suppose they also know where she was staying, correct?"

"No. Neither do the police. So much about her is still a mystery." I paused. Something in his expression made me ask, "Do you?"

"It's probably not important."

"It is," I said quickly.

"Don't ask, don't tell." His chair whirred and the music played as he swung back toward his windows. He raised the binoculars, as though I had already gone.

"I'm asking." I resumed my seat, after angling the chair so I could not be cornered again. "If you want your name in the newspaper, I'll spell it right, I swear."

He slowly lowered the binoculars and turned to me, clearly pleased to recapture my attention. "I saw her walk onto the beach. She was lovely," he said. "Simply stunning. Slim, yet feminine and shapely, not like the scrawny models who look like adolescent boys."

"How would you know where she stayed?"

"Simple. It was the Amsterdam." The name dropped lightly from his lips. "She had one of their beach towels draped over her arm. Can't miss the logo, big initial in a trademark scroll. She also carried one of those matching blue-and-white beach bags they comp to their guests. A status symbol. You see tourists with them all the time.

"She spread her towel on the sand and sat gazing at the horizon, at that same cloud formation I photographed. There was something about her. . . . I wondered if she, too, thought it looked like the end of the world. Then she stood up, all of a sudden, trotted down, and dove straight into the surf. She wasn't one of those people who tiptoe gingerly into the waves. She didn't hesitate. The sea was silver around her, all streaked with pink."

"You saw him arrive?"

"No. I was watching her. He surprised us both. Neither of us saw him until it was too late."

"Anything else I should ask you to tell me?"

"That's it for now," Marsh said thoughtfully. "I'll do better next time."

He maneuvered his chair along behind me. I beat him to the front door but it wouldn't open. I turned to him and frowned. "What's wrong with . . . ?"

Smiling, he touched a button on his remote. The locks disengaged with a series of metallic clicks.

I shivered in the corridor after his door swung shut behind me. Why are these buildings always so cold? I wondered. It was a relief to escape into the fresh warm air and gentle February sun.

6

Fuller G. Stockton peered around the massive mahogany door from his inner office, his florid face flushed a deep red. He was containing his absolute outrage at the condemnation of an innocent man until all the lights were in place and the cameras rolling. The lawyer looked especially dapper in a pinstripe suit that must have set him back thousands. His tie was silk, his attitude pugnacious. Satisfied that the television news crews packing his comfortable conference room, now chaotic and crisscrossed by tangled cables and wires, were nearly ready, he ducked back inside.

Lottie was crouched down in front with her cameras. I kept my distance, the only defense against being smashed in the snoot by heavy video equipment during a media stampede. Once the story was out and took on a life of its own, this crowd would multiply into a mob. By the time R. J. walked off death row, it would be a media circus.

Rychek walked in shortly before they began, accompanied by a stranger. Well-built, light-complected, and handsome, the newcomer had serious gray eyes and wore his blond hair short. They squeezed into a space near me, against the back wall.

"I have to talk to you," I whispered to Rychek, with a questioning glance at his companion.

He nodded, then jerked his head at the stranger. "Dennis Fitzgerald, investigator from the Volusia State Attorney's office."

"What are you doing here?" I murmured to Fitzgerald.

"Nice to meet you too." His cool smile had a playful edge.

"Sorry." I rolled my eyes at the media pack.

"Our office," he said softly in my ear, "prosecuted Jordan. They sent me down to find out where we went wrong."

"If this turns into a zoo," I whispered to Rychek, "let's meet later, somewhere close. I have to go back and write soon."

"How 'bout the parking garage under the *News* building? It's on our way back to the Beach," he said.

"Got some interesting info," I promised, hoping he'd be interested enough to show up, even if distracted by TV reporters.

Dennis Fitzgerald raised his blond eyebrows and smiled. Nice teeth. He smelled good, too.

The media parted like the waters for Stockton as he strode to the cluster of microphones. A spokesman from the Catholic archdiocese, longtime opponents of capital punishment, accompanied him, as did Eunice Jordan, who must have arrived through a back entrance.

Stockton dramatically recounted "this classic near-fatal miscarriage of justice," citing the irrefutable proof of his client's innocence, which he claimed he'd never doubted. His nose didn't grow at all.

"Police power is absolute," he boomed, working up to a rant, "and this is yet another example of its abuse. A shocking case of an innocent man railroaded onto death row. We're fast becoming a fascist state." He wagged his index finger in warning.

Eunice Jordan nodded and clutched a lace-trimmed handkerchief. Tall and striking in black, a single silver streak in her dark hair, she looked as though she'd just stepped out of a beauty salon. The man from the archdiocese fidgeted during the lawyer's attack on police but perked up considerably when Stockton reported that R. J. would be the eighty-fourth innocent man released from death row since Florida reinstated the death penalty in 1976.

"During that same time period," the lawyer said, fist clenched dramatically, "the state of Illinois has executed twelve prisoners while releasing twelve others as innocent. That means that Illinois has a fifty-fifty chance of executing the wrong person!"

He paused for effect, then said his client "was pleased and relieved, but not surprised" by the good news. "What surprised him was that it took so long. R. J. has always maintained his innocence."

"Is your client bitter?" a reporter asked.

"How would you feel? Losing a decade of your life, coming so close to death? But R. J. . . . he looks forward to coming home, spending time with his mother"—he gently rested his manicured hand on Eunice's slim shoulder—"and properly mourning the father he lost during his wrongful incarceration."

Eunice dabbed delicately at her eyes, careful not to disturb her makeup.

"What is Jordan looking forward to most?"

"You can ask him that question yourself on Monday," Stockton said, checking his watch. "We hope to have him free by lunchtime." The lawyer planned to fly to Daytona for an emergency hearing, he said. Rychek would also go, to present the forensic evidence, proof that the recent murder victim had been positively identified as Kaithlin Ann Jordan.

"What was Jordan's reaction to his wife's murder?"

"Naturally, he's devastated," the lawyer said glibly. "Kaithlin was the love of his life."

"Where has she been since she disappeared? And who killed her?"

Not a sound in the room. "There's the man to ask!" Stockton announced. He flung his arm at Rychek in a theatrical gesture, his diamond pinky ring winking under camera lights. "He's investigating her murder. Hopefully, this time, they'll manage to arrest the right man."

"If they do, will you defend him?" Wayman Andrews of Channel 7 asked. Other reporters sniggered.

"I think that ten years of this case is more than enough," Stockton said. "My client's innocence has finally been established, and I'm sure my partners would agree it's time to quit while we're ahead. This has been a long and arduous process for everybody involved, especially R. J. and his family."

With that, Eunice briefly took the floor. "Thank you for coming." She spoke graciously, as though this was her party and we her guests. Her joy was tempered, she said, by the anguish of their ordeal. "It killed my husband," she said softly, "and almost cost me my son. I will be thrilled to have him home again."

I wondered. R. J. had always brought trouble home. Now she would be dealing with it alone. Unless, of course, death row had been a character-building experience.

"Do you think your daughter-in-law deliberately framed your son?"

Eunice glanced for guidance to the lawyer, but he was busy smiling for a photographer.

"I have no idea," she said slowly.

I think I know where Kaithlin was staying," I told Rychek when we met in the *News* building's parking garage.

"You're kidding me," he said. "On the Beach? In the seventeen hundred block of Ocean Drive?"

"How did you know?"

"Found the cabbie who mighta taken her to the cemetery. Says she walked up to him at a cabstand there."

"I wasn't going to share it with you," I said, disappointed, "unless we made a deal that we could check out her room together."

"This is a homicide." He scowled. "A high-profile homicide."

"I promise not to touch a thing, not to tell anybody I was there," I pleaded, ignoring my persistently beeping pager. "We've worked on this together from the start."

He sighed. "I get called in on this, I deny everything and arrest you for criminal trespass. What d'ya think, Fitzgerald?"

"You know her better than I do." The Daytona detective shrugged. "If you trust her, wouldn't bother me. Your turf, your call."

I knew I liked the man.

"So where is it?" Rychek asked.

"The *Amsterdam*," I said. "One of the places I canvassed. The desk clerk lied to me."

"Or you just talked to the wrong clerk," Fitzgerald said.

"Ha," Rychek said. "They all lie. It must be in the employee handbook. That place has got a track record for it. That's exactly where I was gonna start, the priciest address on the block."

I quickly told them about Marsh. "Totally creeped me out. I feel sorry for the guy, at least I did till he grabbed my knee."

"Can't fault his taste in knees." Fitzgerald winked.

"That son-of-a-bitch," Rychek growled. "I called the guy and he had nothing to say."

"You have to ask right," I said.

"Nice knees help," Fitzgerald said.

"He's just a lonely lech in a wheelchair, into word games." I smiled at Fitzgerald in spite of myself. "Wait till you see his toys and the size of the chip on his shoulder. He wants to be appreciated, and he resents everybody taking credit for his vigilance."

Rychek sighed at the news that Kaithlin's father did not die, as believed, but had disappeared.

"What the hell is it with these people?" he grumbled. "Only way to be sure any of 'em are dead is to put a shovel in the ground, dig up their ass, and positively identify it."

"Or shoot 'em yourself," Fitzgerald offered helpfully.

The news desk beeped me again, and I told the detectives I'd catch them later at the Amsterdam.

I blew into the newsroom psyched into deadline momentum. The elevator ride had sent my blood pressure sky high.

"Where ya been, Britt?" Fred scowled at his watch. "We

need the story."

"Then do something about that damn elevator," I complained. "I break the sound barrier getting back here, burst through the door at a dead run, and that thing clanks and grinds and takes forever."

"Try taking the stairs." He grinned. "Good for your heart."

I rolled my chair up to the terminal. There is something exhilarating about the immediacy—the urgency—of news deadlines. Excited, you pump adrenaline and fight the clock, fatigue, and fear of failure. The high when you defeat them all is amazing—and addictive.

Tubbs edited my copy as Fred read over his shoulder. They questioned identifying Marsh as a witness to murder.

"It's safe," I insisted. "He can't identify the killer and he wants recognition. I didn't use his street address, and he's well insulated. He has excellent security, all kinds of electronics, and he's not out and about."

"What's this guy do?" Fred rubbed his chin thoughtfully.

"Sits in a wheelchair and scans the horizon. That's it. He'll be a great source. He'd make a good profile, too, when I have the time. You know, unsung hero still finds way to contribute despite physical challenges."

"If his security is so excellent, how the hell did you get in there?" Tubbs's round face screwed into a skeptical frown.

"Because I'm good, really good," I said sweetly.

The newsroom was abuzz about the story. Janowitz was writing a first-person reprise of the trial for Monday's paper, and the editorial board was meeting to ready a hard-hitting slam at capital punishment.

This case would fuel the controversy. Personally, I support the death penalty in certain cases. Rabid dogs are put to sleep, and I've met people far more dangerous. Those who claim the death penalty is no deterrent forget that it definitely deters those to whom it's applied. They kill no more.

"Great package." Fred stood at my desk. "Nice work, Britt. Keep it up. A helluva story." He squinted through his thick glasses and ran his fingers through his thinning brown hair. "Where the hell has the woman been hiding all these years?"

"With any luck," I said, "we'll know in time for tomorrow's street edition."

7

I t was nearly dark when I arrived at the Amsterdam, hoping the detectives hadn't already finished their work and departed. Hot pink and blue neon halos ringed the royal palms outside. Whose bright idea was it, I wondered, to embellish something as perfect as a palm tree with neon?

I was relieved to see Rychek's unmarked on the ramp. The four-story oceanfront low-rise provides intimate high-style pied-à-terres for the wealthy who like to keep their playtime private. His car's dents, dings, and yellow city tag made it easy to spot among the gleaming luxury sedans and chauffeured limos.

I saw no sign of cops in the elegantly understated lobby.

The woman behind the desk was not the clerk I spoke to the day I canvassed. I flashed my photo ID, my thumb covering the word PRESS.

"Where can I find Detective Rychek?" I asked, my tone official.

She said nothing, but her furtive eyes darted to the small office. I heard raised voices as I approached. The short swarthy manager was wringing his hands as I stepped inside. Rychek was shouting into the phone.

". . . exactly the way it was, or I'll charge you personally and every member of your staff with obstructing justice and lousing up a homicide scene. If I hafta shut this joint down, I'll do it. Go ahead. Call the mayor, the governor, call the pope if you want. I don't give a rat's ass. Do that, and I call every reporter in town, along with Geraldo Rivera, who happens to be a close personal friend-a mine."

According to Fitzgerald, who filled me in, Rychek was talking to the hotel's owner in New York. The detective was demanding that the hotel staffers, who had packed up Kaithlin's belongings, unpack them and return them to her room to re-create the scene.

"And may God help you all if a single bobby pin or Tampax is missing," he warned.

These people oughta be kicked to the curb," Rychek grumbled, as we waited in the small office for the staff members he wanted to arrive from home. Only after he had flashed his badge and persisted, he said, had management reluctantly acknowledged that Kaithlin had been a guest. She was registered as Kathleen Morrigan of 7744 Epona Drive, in Chicago. She never checked out.

After her corpse surfaced only blocks away, management had her room stripped and her belongings placed in storage, even though they claimed ignorance of the tragedy. Image is all in South Beach.

"They hadda know all along," Rychek griped. "Guest goes to the beach. Doesn't come back. Her bed never slept in again. Woman of identical description turns up drowned nearby. And nobody here put two and two together?"

Her death did not involve the hotel. She was not murdered in her room, didn't drown in their pool—yet it was entirely possible, I thought, that worried management had sent someone to retrieve her telltale towel and beach bag. That dreaded phrase "The victim, a guest at the Amsterdam" was negative exposure.

"Bastards did the same thing last year," Rychek muttered. "Remember the honeymooners who crashed their moped into the electric bus?"

I did, but was unaware of the postscript.

Distracted by the sight of Madonna jogging near Flamingo Park, the young Canadian couple on a rented moped had broadsided one of the city's new electric buses. He died instantly. She suffered only minor injuries.

The widowed bride returned from the hospital emergency room to their honeymoon suite at the Amsterdam but found the lock changed. Their luggage waited in the lobby. In lieu of sympathy, management offered a cab. Reporters who called were told the couple was not registered.

Death was a turnoff to their target market.

Chicago," I murmured. "What was Kaithlin doing there?"

"She was probably never there at all," Rychek growled. "Chicago PD has no record of a Kathleen Morrigan and no such address. No Epona Drive."

"Told 'im," Fitzgerald said happily. "Minute I heard the name. My grandmother used to spin stories from the old country. The Morrigan was an Irish goddess of war."

"Well, if she showed up here to do battle," Rychek said, "she sure as hell lost this one."

"What about her credit card?" I asked.

He shook his head. "Checked in three days before she's killed, paid for five plus in advance, with traveler's checks, issued at Sun Bank, right here on the Beach."

The hotel manager, still wringing his hands, reappeared with a request.

Could Kaithlin's room be "re-created" on another floor? Her suite, he explained, was currently occupied by a Swedish industrialist and a model from Brazil.

"Move their asses outa there. Now," Rychek said. "I want you to put *that* room back exactly like it was. And I need a list, names and addresses of every guest who's been in there and every employee who's serviced it since the occupant in question disappeared. We need to fingerprint 'em all for elimination purposes."

The manager reacted as though Rychek had announced plans to detonate a small nuclear device in the lobby. He scurried off to use the telephone.

"You think the killer was ever in her room?" I asked.

"Who knows? Fat chance we'll find anything now, but I'm doing everything by the book. Don't want nobody asking me later 'bout all the things I coulda, woulda, shoulda done. The assholes running this place sure as hell could have saved us a lotta time and trouble. All they hadda do was pick up the phone and say they had a missing guest."

The manager grimly returned with a metal box, the room safe.

"Where's the key?" Rychek demanded.

Guests retained possession of the sole key, the manager explained. A $250 charge was added to the bill if it was not returned.

"Open it," the detective ordered.

A maintenance man punched out the lock, and the detective spilled the contents out onto the manager's desk.

Greenbacks, a flash of gold, the fire of diamonds, but not a single valuable we sought. No passport, no driver's license, no ID.

The cash totaled nearly $10,000, with an additional $5,000 in traveler's checks bearing the name Kathleen Morrigan. The gold was an intricately carved wedding band. The diamonds studded a gold Patek Philippe wristwatch.

Head back, squinting through his reading glasses, cigar clenched between his teeth, Rychek scrutinized the timepiece beneath the light of a banker's lamp on the desk.

"Engraved?" Fitzgerald asked.

"Yeah," the older detective grumbled in disgust, and handed it to him.

"What does it say?" I demanded.

Fitzgerald passed it to me.

For all time. Somehow I doubted it was a gift from R. J.

"What about the ring?"

The slim gold band looked small and delicate in his

rough fingers. She was the last person to touch it, I thought, imagining her as she slipped it off. "See if you can make it out." He handed it to me.

The ring was custom made, with carved hearts entwined. The inscription was a promise. I read it aloud: *You and no other.*

"That's it? Nothing else?" Rychek groused. "Didn't these people ever hear of engraving initials, dates, social security numbers?"

"Oughtta be a law," Fitzgerald agreed.

Her suite's drapes were cheerful and flowered, the wallpaper gold-flocked. Her terrace faced the sea. The housekeepers were sisters, two small round women from Honduras. The bellman who had assisted them was from El Salvador. None spoke English.

"What's the similarity between these people and cue balls?" Rychek muttered, out of their hearing. "The harder you hit 'em the more English they pick up." He and Fitzgerald seemed amused at his bad joke.

I tried to translate, but nobody seemed to comprehend until Rychek began to talk residency and immigration status, asking for green cards and work permits.

Instantly, all three employees became animated. They smiled eagerly, nodded, and fired machine-gun rapid Spanish at one another. Yes. Yes. Of course! They remembered the woman now, the room, her belongings. Yes! They would restore them precisely, just as they had been.

The sisters placed objects just so, stepping back to study their work, rearranging them again, disagreeing as passionately over artistic differences as temperamental Hollywood set decorators. They folded silky lingerie in the hand-painted chest of drawers, arranged toiletries and perfume on the mirrored vanity table in the dressing room adjacent to the bath. Standing on tiptoe, they hung high-fashion designer garments in the spacious closets.

They restored a lined legal pad, its pages blank, to the night table next to the bed, along with a pen and a telephone message memo pad bearing the hotel's trademark logo. With a final flourish, one hung a lacy cream-colored bra, embroidered with tiny seed pearls, from the bathroom doorknob. Are they improvising? I wondered, eager to please, or did the room's prior occupant leave it dangling at just that rakish angle? Did she really leave the bed rumpled just so?

She had, they swore. They had re-created the room exactly as she left it. A crime-scene technician snapped photos as the detectives and I watched.

The rumpled bed with its soft pillows and flowered coverlet beckoned. I suddenly yearned to crawl between its silky sheets for a nap. How long since I had slept?

"What'sa matter, kid?" Rychek asked, "you crapping out on me?"

"No way." I stifled a yawn. "Let's look around."

"She had a helluva view," Fitzgerald said from the terrace.

Kaithlin's makeup was Christian Dior, her perfume Chanel. I inhaled the fragrance, feeling her presence. I imagined her wearing the clothes, all finely tailored in luxurious fabrics. Her cashmere sweaters, silk blouse, soft suede jacket, all looked as though they'd fit me. But there was no way to be sure. Because everything, even her lacy intimate apparel, shared something in common. The labels were missing. Every clue to the designer, owner, size, or origin had been methodically snipped away. The name tag and what must have been a monogram had been cut from her leather luggage, probably with the manicure scissors on the marble counter in the bathroom.

The crime lab technician was tweezing hairs from her comb and brush set, for comparison to the corpse. Fitzgerald lingered over the nightstand while Rychek examined the pockets and linings of her clothing and I studied her shoes, size six medium, practically new. Two pairs of pumps, a pair of leather boots, and casual sandals, all expensive, but all major designer names in mass distribution.

"Hey." Fitzgerald tipped the bedside lamp, spotlighting the top sheet on the legal pad. "Will ya look at this?"

We did. The page was blank.

"What?" Rychek demanded.

"Looks like somebody used it, wrote on the top page," Fitzgerald said. "You can barely see faint handwriting indentations. Might be a letter. Maybe the lab can raise something off it."

"That would make me a happy man," Rychek said. "She musta mailed the original. It sure ain't around here."

The manager provided a printout of Kaithlin's bill. Room service charges indicated that she had dined alone in her room with one exception: dinner for two, served in her room along with a bottle of wine, the night before her death.

"Now we're getting somewhere," Rychek muttered, chewing his unlit cigar. The server, from Ecuador, recalled her meals on the terrace, but that night he had set up a table in her sitting room. He lit candles, opened the wine. He remembered her well. She was an excellent tipper. No, he never saw her guest, who must have been elsewhere in the suite. No one in the busy hotel admitted seeing the guest arrive or depart.

The sisters recalled cigarette butts in the ashtrays just that once. Both they and the room service waiter also remembered stacks of papers and file folders on the desk. None remained among her belongings. Had Kaithlin destroyed the missing documents, were they stolen, or had they been inadvertently discarded by employees?

The bill also revealed that she had sipped vodka and orange juice from the minibar but never touched the snacks. The second night, she had ordered a film, my own favorite, *Casablanca*, that timeless classic of lost love and war. Surrounded by Kaithlin's possessions, her perfume, her presence, I felt I was beginning to know her.

"Yes, sir, we are certainly getting somewhere here," Rychek muttered, as he scrutinized her phone bill at the desk in her suite. "Yes, *sir*." The lengthy bill included more than a dozen international calls, all to points south. As his thick index finger roved down the list of dates and times that calls were placed, he paused. "Uh-oh."

I peered over his shoulder at the charges, then glanced at the sisters and the bellman, clustered close to the door. Conspicuously nonchalant, they looked everywhere but at us. I exchanged glances with Rychek, who nodded.

"Let's talk." I steered the youngest sister into the bedroom and closed the door. "So, you still have family in Honduras?"

She nodded. Her relatives there had been left homeless

by the flood, she said, staring at the floor.

"You must be very concerned about them. It is troubling, a big worry," I said. "Staying in touch is so important. So many who work here are worried about families back home."

Sí, she agreed. Reynaldo, the bellman, had a cousin and an uncle injured in a bomb blast in El Salvador. The election strife in Peru was affecting other employees, as was the financial crisis in Ecuador.

I learned that, despite management's claims of ignorance, word had swept among employees shortly after the body was discovered that the lovely occupant of this suite had drowned. By the time her belongings were packed up and moved out, numerous telephone calls had been placed from her room.

The callers, she said tearfully, needed their jobs.

I went back to Rychek. "Emery, I think you can disregard the international calls. It's a mistake."

"Yeah," he said. "It did seem amazing, being dead and all, how our victim managed to call south so often."

In a stunning transformation, hailed by Fitzgerald as a "true miracle from God," the sisters were now able to speak relatively understandable English and offered an intriguing detail. When sent to strip the room, they had found shreds of plastic, fabric, and tiny bits of paper on the floor around the toilet, apparently the detritus left by someone who stood over it, to cut up and flush away the evidence of her very existence. The debris, the housekeepers insisted, sucked into a vacuum cleaner, long since emptied, had been too shredded to identify or piece together. Had the killer erased her identity along with his own?

"Probably all her ID, driver's license, credit cards, maybe even a checkbook," Rychek said morosely. "You're absolutely sure?" he barked at the sisters, who cringed and insisted, big eyes terrified.

The local calls, apparently Kaithlin's, included half a dozen to the same Miami number. Rychek punched it into the desktop speakerphone.

"You have reached the law offices of Martin Kagan Junior. Office hours are nine A.M. to five P.M. Monday through Friday. If you have an emergency, leave your number after the beep and your call will be returned."

"Bingo!" Rychek sang out. "Not gonna leave no message. I gotta see this guy in person." He chewed with gusto on his stogie. "What was a classy broad like her doing with a two-bit slimebag like him?"

"I think his father used to do a lot of pro-bono appeals for death row inmates," I said. "He specialized in death-penalty cases, got a lot of press."

"But the old man ain't been around in years and his kid's a loser. Didn't even know he had an office. He must be coming up in the world. I thought he worked out of a phone booth at the jail."

Kaithlin's possessions were repacked and the boxes labeled and removed, bound this time for a police evidence locker.

"You look beat, kid," Rychek said. "Why don't you go home and get some sleep?"

"What about you?" I said. "Are you going to see Kagan?"

"Not tonight. I got other fish to fry."

"Like what?"

"She always has to know everything, huh?" Fitzgerald said.

"Always. I'd swear she never sleeps. You, kid," Rychek demanded, "you stay away from Kagan. Don't you tip 'im off till I get a shot at 'im. Hear me?"

"When will that be?" I said reluctantly.

"Probably not until Monday late, even Tuesday. I gotta get all my shit together to fly up to Daytona to spring R. J. Jordan. Whadda joke. Who'da thought I'd ever be up there getting some asshole *off* death row."

Fitzgerald caught up with me as I left the lobby.

"Where you headed?" I said.

"Emery's going back to the station. I'm gonna catch a cab to my hotel."

"Where you staying?"

"Shoulda got a place on the Beach. Instead, I'm over at the Sterling, near the medical examiner's office."

It was out of my way, across the bay, but it doesn't hurt to do a source a favor. Besides, I liked him.

"Come on, I'll drive you," I offered.

"No, no, you live here on the Beach, right?"

"No sweat," I insisted. "It'll just take a few minutes. You'll wind up going by way of Connecticut if you get a cabbie who makes you as an out-of-towner."

So," I said, as we merged into Collins Avenue traffic, "have you always worked for the state attorney's office?"

He hadn't. After the Gulf War, he'd served as a military policeman. Later he joined the Volusia County Sheriff's Office, rose from road patrol to detective, and worked in robbery, narcotics, and child abuse units until he became one of the elite, a homicide detective. He'd been on loan to the prosecutor's office for the past year.

"How come?" I asked.

He shrugged, staring out at passing traffic and throngs of scantily clad pedestrians. "Long story. Short version is a bad case of burnout. Thought I could use some R and R."

"So they sent you to Miami," I said. He obviously didn't want to talk about why he left homicide. "When they couldn't find her body," I asked, "why didn't anybody suspect that Kaithlin Jordan might be alive?"

"Nobody doubted she was dead at the time," he said, "not even her mother, and you know how mothers are; they always refuse to believe the worst."

"You're right," I said. "They always say . . ." I put my hand over my heart as he joined me in reciting that all-too-familiar refrain: "If my child was dead, I'd know it."

"Exactly," he said. "In this case it didn't seem unusual not to find her. So many possibilities existed. R. J. grew up hunting, fishing, and camping all over the state. Where do you start, with more than six hundred thousand acres of Florida's state forests, all within range of his plane? There was also a good chance he'd left her in a swamp or dumped her at sea. Dropped in the Gulf Stream, she'd never be found. Do me a favor, would you?" he said. "Stop at that minimart up ahead, so I can pick up a paper and some cigarettes?"

I slowed down, then recognized the minimart. "Don't buy the paper now," I said. "Wait for the final, for my story."

"I'll get some magazines then, to tide me over. I still need the smokes."

Reluctantly, I parked in front.

"Want to come in?"

"I'll wait here," I said.

I saw Fitzgerald through the store's plate-glass window. The place, recently reopened by new owners, looked clean and well run. Uneasy, I watched other customers come and go and leaned over to unlock the glove compartment. I keep my gun inside.

He came back with several magazines, a crossword puzzle book, cigarettes, gum, a bottle of aspirin, and what looked like a pint of whiskey in a paper bag. I unlocked the car door.

He spotted the key dangling from the glove box. "This neighborhood make you nervous?" he said.

"Oh, I come here all the time," I said casually.

His gaze was knowing and curious.

"I've been here before," I acknowledged. I nodded at the storefront. "Used to be a ma-and-pa grocery. 'Bout a year ago, just before Christmas, a teenage gang burst in, a nasty bunch. They'd done a rash of other robberies. At nearly every one they killed a security guard or an owner and took his gun. They were well armed when they got here. They jumped up on the counters, laughing, yelling, shooting, having so much fun they forgot to take the money.

"They killed the owner, wounded his wife and a customer, and kept shooting the butcher in the back. I saw him dead on the floor in the bloody sawdust behind the counter. He still wore his white apron. He had eleven children."

"Yeah. Some sights you don't forget." Fitzgerald gave a great heavy sigh. "Did they get them?"

"Oh, yeah." I sighed, too, and pulled out into traffic.

"Juveniles?"

"Yeah."

We did not speak again until I pulled up onto the ramp at his hotel a few blocks away. About to say something, he didn't. He hesitated instead, pushed my hair back from my face, gently touched my cheek, and ran his thumb along my jaw line.

" 'Night. Thanks for the ride." He got out of my car.

We hadn't said much, but in that moment I was sorry he was gone.

Numb with exhaustion, I drove home, walked Bitsy around the block, and tumbled into bed. In my dreams, Kaithlin Jordan sat on her terrace watching a shadowy sea. Her hair streamed in the wind, or was it the tide?

I awoke in the dark before dawn. My head ached and the inside of my mouth felt fuzzy. I rummaged numbly for my jogging shorts and a T-shirt, then staggered into the bathroom, reached for my toothbrush, and stared.

If detectives were to scrutinize my personal possessions, trying to re-create the final hours of my life, what would they make of this? Bristles littered the sink. My new toothbrush was shedding.

8

I walked two blocks to the boardwalk and the dark sea, then ran. Fine droplets of dew or sea spray evolved into a chilly drizzle that cooled my feverish face and throbbing eyes. The beach stretched as gray, wide, and vacant as a dead woman's eyes. The boardwalk was deserted except for an occasional diehard jogger. Most regulars were still asleep or taking the day off. A vague feeling of dread stiffened my spine as Casa Milagro loomed ahead.

Was Zachary Marsh awake? Watching me now? When did he sleep?

Eyes could always be watching, from any or all of the thousands of windows that face the beach. But that wasn't what was so disturbing. It was the watcher himself.

Never again could I swim, sunbathe, or melt, totally relaxed, into the warm sand within range of the high-powered lenses he wielded like weapons. How unfair.

Thoughts of Marsh made me uneasy. And then there was the murdered mermaid. Would I ever gaze at the sea again without thinking of Kaithlin?

No one else knows the landmarks that confront me daily in this steamy and mercurial city. On deadline, energy high, racing to a shooting, I experience a sudden rush of recognition, like the sight of a modest green house on a corner, flower beds in bloom. There were no flowers the day I saw them carry out the bodies: a woman, two small children, and their little dog. The husband intended a murder-suicide, he said, but failed. He blamed his hands. They shook too much to reload and use the gun on himself. He will be free some day; they will still be dead.

Buildings, businesses, even expressway ramps, all strewn with corpses from the past. Life is a battlefield, yet the more casualties I witness, the more committed I am to this place that I love. What is a city but its people? Who else is there to remember them, write about them, and keep track of the dead? Otherwise they would be truly gone forever.

But I had owned my secret retreat. This beach, and the solace of its limitless horizon, was mine. Now it too had been violated, my final sanctuary haunted by a murdered woman and spied upon from above.

I limped home, wet, cold, and nursing a sore hamstring, stopping only at the corner drugstore for a new toothbrush. The Sunday paper waited like a gift on my doorstep. It's like Christmas morning for a reporter to open the newspaper and see his or her big story. First, unfortunately, you have to unwrap it.

Bloated by scores of sections all tightly squeezed into a snug plastic bag, the weekend paper was a blunt object. Hurled onto a suburban lawn, it was a deadly missile, heavy enough to kill a small animal or knock a human being senseless.

Where the hell was the news? When did the newspaper become all things to all people? Even free samples of shampoo and hair conditioner were tucked inside. Sunday was once the best showcase for a great news story. Now readers are lucky if they can locate the news among all the sections devoted to boats, cars, coupons, comics, child rearing, music, entertainment, sports, food, gardening, home and design, tropical living, glossy magazines, the television guide, pop psychology, opinion, gossip, advice, classified ads, neighborhood sections, and real estate.

I impatiently flung sections into a bin earmarked for Billy Boots's sandbox. Reporters are constantly disheartened by editors who insist that we have no space, that the news hole is small and our stories must be kept brief, tight, and cut to the bone. That's what television news does. Print is supposedly superior, since we can dig into background and deliver information in depth. But apparently that only applies if the topic is how to prune a poinsettia, evaluate an antique, or remodel a home.

I finally found the A-section, the story of the "woman who died twice" and the resulting death row drama stripped across the front. It was accompanied by the backgrounder I had put together, including profiles of the players and a chronological account of the case. Lottie's press conference and cemetery photos completed the layout, along with head shots of R. J. and Kaithlin.

Another photo made the jump page inside: Kaithlin's covered corpse on the beach, the ubiquitous Raymond clutching his tiny shovel.

Suddenly shivering, I drank hot coffee, stripped off my wet clothes, took a hot shower, and dressed. Sweater weather had arrived with the rain, and even lower temperatures were predicted in the first real cold snap of the season.

I dug out my blue cashmere pullover and a pair of light-weight wool slacks and hit the office early. I love an empty newsroom.

Determined readers had somehow managed to locate the news section. My voice-mail box was already full. The phone rang nonstop. My most faithful callers, the lunatic fringe, offered theories. One frequent caller declared that Kaithlin was obviously in the witness protection plan and was probably still alive, relocated yet again. Another insisted that her corpse undergo painstaking examination for space alien implants. A tearful caller, once an unwed teenage mother, claimed her life had been turned around by Kaithlin's mentoring program.

"She was an inspiration," she said, "an angel."

"She was a conniving bitch!" railed a male caller, who claimed to be an old hunting buddy of R. J.'s. "She tried to have her husband murdered by the state! That man's the salt of the earth," he added. "Real people."

As I scrolled through old stories on Martin Kagan, I was interrupted by a high-pitched squeal, as though somebody had stepped on a puppy dog's tail.

"Britt! What are you doing here?" Angel flung both arms around me as though we were long-lost sisters.

"I work here," I mumbled.

"I mean this early! The kids are so excited!" She pushed her long blond hair out of her eyes. "I was so thrilled when Rooney said you'd be in the wedding!"

Bewildered, I stared over her shoulder at the prospective bridegroom, who smiled happily. Had he misunderstood our conversation?

With her rosebud mouth and big eyes, Angel still looked too young and pretty to be mother to so many. She wore the same black leather jacket she had on the day we met, when she angrily slammed her front door on an intrusive reporter, me. The same tiny gold angel dangled from a chain around her swanlike neck. She was still slender, except for her protruding stomach. She had come to pick up her betrothed, whose shift was about to end, she said. Was her radiance the glow generated by pregnant women or simple joy at the opportunity to somehow screw up my life again?

"Well, I know you probably want to keep it small," I

said, backing off, "and I wouldn't want to intrude on—"

"Oh, Britt, there's nobody I want more as my maid of honor. I'm thrilled!" She hugged my waist. "Thank you, thank you. I have a Sears catalog," she added, "with pictures of dresses I want you to look at."

"Dresses?"

"Bridesmaids' dresses! Do you like a sort of salmon pink? It's got the cutest little bustle."

Bustle. Salmon pink. Sears. Words that would induce a migraine in my mother.

"I'm not even sure I'll be in town then," I lied blatantly.

"We haven't set the date. We can build it around your schedule. We'll know more about that when the baby comes."

Lottie and a new shooter, named Villanueva approached down the hall from photo, carrying coffee and a sack of doughnuts.

"Lottie!" Another puppy-dog squeal made my ears ring as Angel rushed her. I shook my head in warning, a high sign to Lottie, but, too late, her arms were open. She hugged back, exclaiming over Angel's bulging belly as though it were a badge of honor.

My phone rang again. An agitated caller claimed to know the answer to the Jordan mystery. R. J. must not be released, she warned. He was dangerous, a killer. Both murders had happened. Kaithlin, she announced, had been twins.

"Twins? Did you know her family?"

"No, I never met any of them. But I'm sure of it. I saw a movie like that once. I think it was Meryl Streep. . . ."

By the time I said goodbye, Angel and Lottie were knee

deep in wedding plans and it was too late to escape.

I'd rather do a hundred hours of community service than be in Angel's wedding," I moaned, after the happy couple's departure.

"It'll be fun," Lottie said. "Hell-all-Friday, I'm doing it, and you know her lots better than I do. I'm gonna be a bridesmaid." She wrinkled her nose and grinned. "You love her kids and it's a happy ending, fer God's sake. They sure ain't common around here. Ain't it great to see a happy ending once in a while?"

"Sure," I said. "I'm all for happy endings, but with Angel . . . I swear to you, Lottie, it'll turn into one of those weddings where the FBI arrests the groom at the altar or somebody winds up dead, face down in the cake."

Lottie rolled her eyes. "Sometimes I swear you've been on the police beat too long. They're kids in love. Ain't it nice to see normal, happy people for a change?"

"Normal?" I said. "What about all those kids?"

"Not her fault," Lottie said.

"I beg to differ."

"Okay. She was Catholic and he was careless," she said, "but they're great kids."

That, I couldn't argue with. "Please," I begged, "just promise me we will talk her out of the salmon pink. With your hair and my tan? No way." We both winced at the image.

"You're right," she said. "I've been busting my ass on the Stairmaster to git rid-a my own built-in bustle."

She offered me a doughnut, which I declined.

"I'll leave one anyway," she said, "a cruller, your favorite."

She placed it on my desk, despite my protests, then disappeared around the corner of the wire room. Two minutes later she reappeared.

"Hey, what do you think we should get them for a wedding present? Should we chip in together?"

I couldn't answer, caught with my mouth full of cruller.

I'd seen Martin Kagan Jr. hanging around criminal court, where he was a familiar figure, hoping for appointments from judges who had known his dad. The senior Kagan founded his own firm and served for a time as a highly respected circuit court judge. Late in life he won national recognition as a fierce crusader against capital punishment, often working pro bono to save death row inmates. His lawyer son inherited the name but somehow missed out on the character and ethics that went with it.

Junior had been involved in several scrapes, including a ninety-day suspension from practice for misusing a client's funds. After his father's fatal stroke, the partners had forced the son out of the firm.

Down on his luck, Kagan Jr. operated a one-man practice out of a small converted duplex near the Justice Building.

What, I wondered, was his connection to Kaithlin? Did they know each other before she disappeared? Nothing in our files linked either Kagan to the Jordans.

I called Myrna Lewis. "It's really true," she whispered, still stunned. "I saw it in the newspaper this morning and it was on the radio news. How could it happen? I still don't understand. . . ."

"Ms. Lewis, is there any possibility that Kaithlin had a sibling, a sister? Maybe a twin?"

"A twin? What are you talking about? Of course not."

"I didn't think so." I sighed. I asked if Reva had ever mentioned Kagan and if he had any connection to her meager estate. She said no to both.

Fred stopped by my desk at ten to discuss my follow-up story before the morning news meeting. Almost as an afterthought, he added, "You're going to Daytona for the hearing tomorrow, right?"

"I didn't know it was in the budget," I said, startled.

"Of course," he said, "for a story of this magnitude."

"Well, thanks for letting me know." The trip would have been routine a few years ago, but budget cutbacks in the newsroom had put a moratorium on reporters' travel.

I paged Rychek to see what flight he'd be on, but he was traveling in style, aboard Stockton's private jet. The press wasn't invited.

Gloria, the newsroom receptionist, booked me on an Atlanta-bound flight that stopped in Daytona that evening and into a hotel room near the courthouse.

I called my landlady, Mrs. Goldstein, who said she'd take care of Bitsy and Billy Boots. She had read the story and had her own theory.

"The husband beat her up and left her for dead. She came to, with amnesia. Ten years later, she remembered who she was and came back to Miami. But somebody who wanted R. J. dead recognized her and killed her to keep her quiet."

"But who?" I said.

"Oh, the man had lots of enemies. Rich people always do. He was always in trouble, always in the newspaper.

Some man whose wife he schtupped, somebody injured in a car he wrecked, or angry that he stole all that money from Jordan's—"

"Not bad," I said. "I'll pass it on to the detective."

My overnight bag is always packed. I travel light, but threw in a long-sleeved dress so I'd look presentable in court, then wore a T-shirt and jeans to the airport under a blouse, a sweater, and a navy blazer.

We boarded on time and I thanked God for Gloria, who had booked me on a big jet instead of a commuter flight for the forty-minute trip. When it comes to planes and me, the bigger the better.

Safety experts say aisle seats are safer but I love to see the twinkling lights of Miami, the shadowy Everglades, and the mountainous clouds from above. I found my window seat. A young black woman on crutches, her right foot in a cast, had boarded early and sat in the row in front of me. A mother with two little girls took the seat across the aisle, one child next to her, the other beside the woman on crutches. I settled in, hoping the flight wouldn't be full so I could spread my notes into the space beside me. No luck. My seatmate towered in the aisle, stowing his bag in the overhead.

"We have to stop meeting like this," he said.

"What are you doing here?"

"Why do you always ask me that?" Fitzgerald shrugged. "Everybody's got to be someplace. I heard you say that to Emery yourself."

"This is no coincidence."

He grinned, looked innocent, and slid into his seat. "Only

so many commercial flights stop at Daytona. We're both headed there tonight." He shrugged. "What are the odds?"

"That we would be seated next to each other on a flight with more than a hundred passengers?"

"Damn." He paused, eyebrow raised. "That's right. You must be stalking me."

He bought me a drink and we discussed the upcoming hearing, serenaded by a screaming baby several rows back. I asked about Circuit Judge Leon Cowley, who had sentenced R. J. and would preside in the morning.

"Interesting guy, his honor." Fitzgerald smiled. "A rock-ribbed conservative who transcends mortality, at least in his own mind. Circuit judges do have godlike powers, but Cowley's at the next level. He thinks he *is* God. You know the type."

I did, although for most Miami jurists it's a mere job. They preside for six or eight hours, take off the black robes, and are just Bob, Paul, or Frank again—probably because they are acutely aware that they themselves might become defendants at any moment. There are always a few in trouble, indicted, or being investigated.

"What's he look like?" Fleecy white clouds raced by our tiny window as I sipped my drink.

"Six foot, stocky, still in good shape, proud he never let himself get soft. Likes bonefishing and a few drinks. Played football for the University of Florida. Got through law school back when it was easy. No intellectual, but very responsive to the people of his district, who want everybody hanged, everybody put away, everybody locked up."

"So he's tough."

"The man played smash-mouth football and he's a

smash-mouth judge."

"This case must be giving him second thoughts."

"Doubt it." Fitzgerald munched an airline pretzel. "A lotta people up there will never believe Jordan is innocent."

"How can they not? There's a dead body to prove it."

"In this age of conspiracy theories," he said, "there'll always be doubt. Betcha a good thirty to forty percent of the population will swear that the gal who showed up dead in Miami was an imposter, not the real Kaithlin Jordan but a lookalike, maybe even the victim's sister, who had her fingerprints altered and plastic surgery to look like her."

How odd, I thought. More speculation about a fictional sister. Would it become a popular theory among amateur sleuths? Real life is stranger than fiction. Who could prove without a doubt that Reva Warren, dead for years now, did not give birth to a second child more than three decades ago?

"Nope," Fitzgerald was saying, "you'll see no contrition from Cowley about sentencing an innocent man to die. He'll be defensive of the jury, the people of his county. Criticize the verdict and you criticize them. Damn." Fitzgerald squinted disapprovingly over his shoulder at the infant, still howling nonstop. "What a set of lungs on that kid."

"Well," I said, "the judge still has to offer R. J. and his family some sort of apology. The guy lost ten years and came within a week of execution."

Fitzgerald shrugged. "Cowley won't be overly apologetic. Count on it. You'll see tomorrow."

The FASTEN SEAT BELT sign went on, and the flight attendants prepared for landing at Daytona International Airport.

I saw the lights of the runway and the nearby Speedway, home of the Daytona 500, as we began the final approach. The cabin was brightly lit and full of chatter, passengers preparing for landing amid the wails of the screaming baby.

The crew's intercom dinged four times.

Fitzgerald reacted. "Uh-oh."

"What?" I said.

He shook his head and watched the chief flight attendant go to the cockpit. She returned moments later, and all four flight attendants convened in the forward galley.

Fitzgerald leaned close and spoke softly in my ear. "Looks like we've got ourselves a problem."

"What? No." I twisted in my seat, firmly rejecting the suggestion. Everything looked fine. The flight attendants had returned to their stations, composed but not smiling.

The public address system crackled to life.

"This is your captain."

I heard Fitzgerald's sharp intake of breath, or was it my own?

"Got a little problem, folks," the captain said genially. "A cockpit light up here is telling us our landing gear didn't drop and lock. Nine out of ten times that warning light is a false indicator. So we're gonna circle around for a fly-by of the control tower. The folks there will attempt a visual, try to tell us if the landing gear is actually down and the cockpit indicator is malfunctioning. We'll keep you posted."

The young mother across the aisle straightened in her

seat, eyes alert, her fingers resting lightly on her little girl's hair. The cabin chatter continued.

"So, we get to spend a little more time together." Fitzgerald smiled.

I enjoyed his company but yearned for a bed, the TV news, and a good night's sleep. I fretted, annoyed, as we swung back over the airport.

"Okay, folks," the captain said. "Unfortunately the control tower confirms that our cockpit indicator is correct. Our landing gear has not come down. So we're gonna fly out over the Atlantic for a while to use up some fuel while we try to correct the problem."

Impatient groans swept the cabin as we soared into a silken sky over dark water. A passenger who'd probably already imbibed too much asked loudly for a drink. The flight attendant declined, saying she couldn't block the aisle with the cart.

He exploded angrily. "I didn't ask for the damn cart, just one goddamn drink!"

"How long do you think this will take?" I asked Fitzgerald uneasily.

He shrugged. "They'll probably try to lower it manually."

"What if they can't?"

"These guys are good; they know what they're doing," he said.

I had my doubts as the co-pilot emerged from the cockpit. Carrying a flashlight, he stopped midway down the aisle to check something at the emergency exit over the wings.

This would make interesting dinner conversation back

home, I thought, as the man returned to the cockpit. It was thrilling in a superficial way. I hate delay but there are worse things than being stalled in the sky with a handsome man.

"Okay, folks, keeping you posted as I promised. This aircraft is equipped with a crank-down system that can manually lower the landing gear. So far, our attempts to do so have been unsuccessful. The gear is apparently jammed, so we're gonna exert some pressure on the aircraft, up and down, to try to jostle it loose. Please remain in your seats, seat belts fastened. We'll try this, then fly by the tower again for another look-see."

Nervous laughter swept the cabin. The pilot's voice resonated with confidence, but that's what he was trained to project. Suddenly I found it difficult to swallow. What if . . . ?

"Hope you like roller coasters." Fitzgerald sounded nonchalant. He took my hand in both of his.

The plane climbed, then suddenly dropped. I caught my breath as my stomach rose, the way it does during rapid descent in an express elevator.

"It's the g force." He squeezed my fingers. "Hold your breath as we go up. When he pulls back and climbs, positive g's force you down in your seat. On the way down, your body becomes lighter because there is less g force. Like a roller coaster."

The young mother across the aisle had protective arms around her daughter. Her other little girl, in front of us, laughed aloud, unafraid and giddy at the ride.

While she enjoyed herself, I relived plane crashes I had covered. I bitterly blamed the *News* for this development and vowed to charge a lavish room-service meal to my expense account if I reached the hotel alive. If I was killed or severely maimed, they would publish my photograph. They'd use the humiliating one on my ID card, when the camera caught me in mid-sneeze. That was not how I wanted to be remembered.

Stomach churning as the plane lurched and bounced, I asked silent forgiveness from everyone I'd ever hurt. Who would adopt Bitsy and Billy Boots if this flight was doomed? Who would love them? I wondered. How unfair for Bitsy, that dear little dog, to be orphaned again.

"Everything's okay," Fitzgerald murmured.

Not reassured, I imagined my mother alone, like Reva Warren, and cringed at the thought. In the sudden rush of departure, I hadn't called her. My mother didn't even know I was flying. Too late now. The attendant said no in-flight phones were in service. I wanted to scribble a note, but what note would survive a crash I didn't?

One small consolation. If we don't make it, I thought, I don't have to be in Angel's wedding. But now I didn't want to miss it. I didn't want to miss anything.

The roller-coaster ride smoothed out and we circled Daytona airport again. The chief flight attendant revisited the cockpit, followed by another huddle in the front galley.

"What do you think?" I asked Fitzgerald.

"I believe," he said, eyes alert, "that he's gonna bring us down without it."

"We'll be okay?"

"They'll follow all the emergency procedures," he said calmly.

"You've seen it done?"

"Sure. During the Gulf War, we had a B-Fifty-two come in with a jammed gear. Two of our choppers trailed it right down the runway, moving in fast to rescue survivors. The plane slowed down so much that the crew was able to jump out onto the foamed runway before the plane ran off it, skidded onto the tarmac, and exploded. They all survived. But both choppers got sucked into the flames. Those guys didn't make it."

"Thank you very much," I whispered sharply. "As if I needed to hear that story."

"You asked," he said mildly.

"Ladies and gentlemen," the pilot said, "our maneuvers were not able to shake the gear loose. Please listen carefully to your flight attendants. They will instruct you on preparations for an emergency landing."

Shit, I thought. This is happening. It's really happening.

"Don't worry," Fitzgerald said. But I saw the fear in his eyes.

"I'm okay," I lied. Sure. As our lives spun totally out of control, in the hands of strangers, dependent on a malfunctioning machine.

"If we do go down," he muttered out the corner of his mouth, "I'm glad that screaming brat goes with us."

He wanted me to smile, but I was too busy fighting panic.

"If this works out," I swore aloud, "I will rent a car and drive back to Miami. Nothing will ever get me on another plane."

"Statistically," he said, "it's more dangerous to drive."

"Yeah," I said, "but you can always park and walk."

The scenario was surreal, as we were instructed to

remove and stow high heels and loose objects, even big earrings, and shown how to assume the position: head between the legs, hands on the back of the head, fingers locked, or as Lottie always described it: "put your head between your legs and kiss your ass goodbye."

The lights will go out, the attendant said. Take nothing with you. Follow the emergency lighting system in the floor. Evacuate fast. We needed to be out in ninety seconds.

We were warned not to use the overwing emergency exits, only the front and back.

"Why?" I whispered aloud.

"Because if there's fire, that's where it'll be," Fitzgerald muttered.

"Why don't they just tell us that?"

"They don't use the F word," he said quietly. "If anybody panicked, things could get out of control fast."

In a sudden revelation, I realized I should have married Josh, my college sweetheart. My mother would have had a grandchild, a child already ten years old. A week ago, I had wondered if I ever wanted to marry and have children. Now I lamented that I never did.

Belts were checked, infants secured in baby seats.

Our flight attendant stopped and spoke so softly in Fitzgerald's ear that I scarcely heard her words.

"We have some handicapped, unescorted minors and other passengers who may need assistance." Her eyes moved toward the mother, her two little girls, and the young woman with her foot in a cast. "Are you available to help?"

"You've got it," he said. "I'm a police officer, former military, familiar with the procedure."

The attendant spoke quietly to the young mother, who looked wary, pale, and terrified, then informed the woman in the cast, who now clung to the other child. Fitzgerald nodded reassuringly as each made eye contact.

The captain's voice interrupted my silent prayers. "Just wanted to warn you folks about the screeching sound you'll hear. That'll be the bottom of the aircraft on the runway. We have an experienced crew up here and we expect to be able to control the aircraft to some degree. We plan to set down on foam, on the center line of a ten-thousand-foot runway. Emergency vehicles are standing by. Your flight attendants will assist you."

"Okay," Fitzgerald said calmly. "I'll be outa your way as soon as we're down. You go straight to the exit, hit the slide as quick as you can, and don't hesitate at the bottom. Get away fast, so you're not rammed by the next guy coming down. Run from the plane, as far as you can. I'll find you after we get the others out."

"I can help with the kids," I said. "You take the mother and the little one. I'll take the one on this side. Then we can help the woman with the cast."

He hesitated. "You're sure?"

"Yeah." I nodded, beyond scared as the plane swung into its final approach.

"Hear that?" I croaked, clinging to Fitzgerald as we began our descent.

"What?" he said, face tight.

"The screaming baby. It stopped."

We hugged as close as our seat belts allowed; even our legs were intertwined.

"It'll be okay," he promised. His face, color drained,

belied his words.

I saw the flashing red beacons of the fire trucks and ambulances waiting below, then assumed the position.

9

The engines roared like jungle animals as the plane shuddered, skidded, and scraped, hurtling dead ahead. Forty-five seconds seemed endless. The pilot killed the engines, and the lights went out. Floor lights bloomed along the aisle. The aircraft vibrated violently, but we slowed only slightly. Where would we stop? Would we run out of foam? I sneaked a look. Fire engines raced alongside, lights flashing.

As we screeched to a jolting stop, doors opened, slides deployed, and a shock of cool air swept through the cabin. The flight attendants' shouts cut off a smattering of applause.

"Go! Go! Go! Jump! Jump!"

Fitzgerald was gone before I released my belt. Our eyes met for an instant as he lunged past, the little girl under one arm, the other locked around her mother's waist, propelling her forward. She was screaming, reaching back for her other child. I darted ahead, fumbled to free the girl, no more than six, from her belt, then scooped her up as she cried out for her mother.

People pushed and shoved; someone sobbed aloud. Passengers were pushed out the open doors. A middle-aged man blocked the aisle as he tried to remove something from the overhead. A male attendant hit him like a linebacker, forcing him into the moving tide. I stumbled to the door. "Look, look, it's okay," I told the little girl, and swung her onto the slide.

Bright yellow, about four feet wide, it resembled a giant play toy in a kiddy park.

Pushed forward, I struggled to go back. Then Fitzgerald appeared, half carrying the woman in the cast. He sent her flying onto the slide. As she went, he swept me off my feet and sent me after her, hurtling down into foam and chaos.

I tumbled off and out of the way at the bottom, then ran, looking over my shoulder for him. Where the hell was he?

Firemen shot foam onto the belly of the plane. Metal glowed, red hot. Or was it only the reflection of their lights?

I blinked, confused, ankle deep in cold wet foam.

"Move away from the plane! Away from the plane." People in uniform tried to herd us away. A paramedic carried the young woman with the cast. I turned back to the flashing lights, shouts, and shadows to find Fitzgerald.

Someone whisked me away, into the dark. I resisted, then saw it was him.

Mercifully, there was no fire, no death, only a few injuries: a broken ankle, heart palpitations, back pain, and vertigo. Amid the noise and excitement I glimpsed the formerly screaming baby, now sleeping peacefully in its mother's arms.

Airline officials insisted that medics take our vital signs. Airline reps briefed us. Our bags would be delivered. We were advised to make no statements to the press. Ha, I thought, knees shaky, as I looked for a phone.

We were bussed to the terminal. I rested my head on

Fitzgerald's shoulder. From a pay phone, I called the city desk collect to unload. No crash. No deaths. But since the flight originated in Miami, I knew they'd want a brief story. I was fine, I told Tubbs. No, I would not write it. I was busy. Fitzgerald waited, with a cab. We climbed in and our bodies collided, lips fused. The rigid tension in my neck and shoulders melted into that smoldering kiss. The cab stopped before we did.

We fumbled our way into his dark apartment without turning on the lights. His hands were so occupied he had to kick the door closed. I had no idea where we were. I didn't care. The piece of furniture we first made love on may have been a sofa. I'm not sure.

Fear and near-death experiences lead to sex. That's a fact. So easy: no complications, no history, no problems. Until I awoke next morning in a strange bed with a strange man in a strange city. I sat up, staring numbly at my clothes strewn across the carpet.

Fitzgerald blinked awake. If seeing me was a surprise, he hid it well. "Good morning," he said, voice sleepy, and drew me to his warm, broad, comforting chest. The room was chilly. How tempting to simply pull the blankets over us and stay the day.

"Wait a minute," I said. "What time is it? What time is court?"

"Jesus." He looked at his watch and hurtled out of bed. "I'll make coffee," he said, as I dashed for the bathroom.

I stared guiltily into the mirror, expecting shame. Instead, my color was excellent, my eyes bright. I never felt more alive. "You are a bad person." I denounced my reflection.

"If this gets back to the *News* you'll be disgraced, could lose your job." Why was I smiling?

The man whipped up a killer omelet, with onions, peppers, and mushrooms. I wore one of his shirts and we gazed at each other across the breakfast table like any domesticated couple.

"I guess you're not married," I said.

"No." He poured orange juice. "Was once, but not anymore."

In daylight, his apartment was scrupulously neat for a bachelor pad. Even stacked newspapers were precisely lined up in military fashion, as were the files and papers on his desk.

The airline had delivered his duffel bag. My overnighter probably waited at the hotel. I borrowed a toothbrush and did the best I could to look neat in the clothes I wore the night before, once I found them.

The morning was cold and windy as we walked to the courthouse for the 9 A.M. hearing. We parted discreetly outside the building. Judge Cowley's courtroom was crowded, with a substantial electronic presence: cameras on tripods in the back of the courtroom, cords and wires taped to the floor all the way out to the sound trucks and aerials outside. Laws allowing cameras in the courtroom specify that they be unobtrusive, which is impossible. This was a main event. I was glad to be covering it.

Rychek was at the defense table up front, wearing his blue shirt and conferring with Stockton. He glanced up, saw me, then squinted slightly, brow furrowed, as though puzzled. Then Fitzgerald ambled in. Rychek nodded, then did a double-take: to me, then back to Fitzgerald. His expression changed. He knows! I thought. How? But he knew, I read it in his face. Were we that transparent?

I gave a little wave. He responded with a look of weary resignation, then resumed his discussion with Stockton.

A batch of handcuffed and shackled prisoners shuffled in as I found a seat. R. J. was not among these drunk drivers, thieves, street wanderers, alcoholics, and homeless people who had run afoul of the law. Jailers herded them into the empty jury box, a bumper crop, a motley cross section of major and minor criminals. A few immediately began to mug for the cameras, which were not yet turned on.

A half-dozen handcuffed hookers paraded in next. They sashayed into court as saucy as they had apparently been on the street, eyes bold, smiling and winking.

Judge Cowley made his entrance a short time later, black robe swirling. His shrewd eyes flew straight to the cameras as he strode into his courtroom, stalwart and impressive. His posture relaxed visibly when he saw they were not yet in operation.

Cowley sped through his morning calendar with brisk efficiency. Prosecutors and public defenders clearly accustomed to a more leisurely pace were cut off mid-sentence and defendants whisked offstage before settling into the spotlight. Scant repartee was tolerated. The judge, like all of us, was eager for the big case, but for different reasons. We faced deadlines. He just wanted it over.

As the prisoners straggled out, their various lawyers and relatives left and I managed to snag a seat up front, behind the defense table. More press arrived, filling the gallery.

During a five-minute recess, two jailers brought in R. J., handcuffed and in prison garb. Ten years on death row had taken its toll. Still handsome at fifty-two, his features were harder, more craggy. A visible scar creased his pale forehead. His thick dark hair, now shot with silver, had receded only slightly. Reports were that his smart mouth and bad attitude had kept him in constant trouble with both prison personnel and fellow inmates. Much of his time had been spent on X-wing, the harshest section of Florida's toughest prison.

Rychek beckoned and I leaned forward, hoping for some profound insight on the proceedings.

"Jesus Christ," he muttered. "I can't leave you two alone for five minutes."

My face burned as he turned abruptly back to the defense table.

The lanky silver-maned prosecutor who had convicted R. J. entered through the chambers door. To his credit he showed up; he could have sent an assistant and tried to distance himself for political reasons. Cowley returned, called the case, and the cameras rolled. The prosecutor requested that the conviction and sentence be vacated, citing extraordinary circumstances.

Rychek presented proof that the alleged victim, Kaithlin Jordan, was alive until February 6, 2001, and that her corpse had been positively identified. Stoic until then, R. J. reacted for a moment at the sound of her name. Was it pain or something else reflected in his expression? Guilt? Satisfaction?

"The obligation of the state attorney's office," the prosecutor boomed, grandstanding as though he himself had ferreted out and brought this miscarriage of justice to the court's attention, "is to find the truth and make full disclosure. My job is to seek justice. That's why we're here today."

The judge had already examined affidavits from finger-print experts and the Miami–Dade County medical examiner and conferred with them by phone. Stockton sat beside his client. Unusually subdued, he had little to say. The evidence spoke louder than words.

"The system did work well," Judge Cowley intoned, "the way it's supposed to, based on all the available evidence at the time." He ordered R. J.'s release. "I wish you well," he said, and abruptly adjourned. Cold and correct, he swept out quickly, eager to end the mess in his courtroom and his nice good-old-boy town.

No one even asked who killed Kaithlin, or why, I thought, as the jubilant lawyer and client embraced.

I caught Fitzgerald's eye and nodded. He was right. No apologies from this judge, not in this jurisdiction. He nodded back, the look in his eyes igniting a heat that made my mouth dry. Nervously, I licked my lips, then caught Rychek watching us both.

I joined the press clamoring for comment from R. J. and his attorney. His lawyer looked more elated than the freed man, who was led off to retrieve his personal belongings and complete some final paperwork.

"This is one of life's greatest events," Stockton crowed. "There is no feeling in the world that compares to freeing an innocent man from death row. It's better than arguing before the U.S. Supreme Court."

As bailiffs asked us to clear the courtroom, Stockton promised he and his client would meet the press on the courthouse steps in twenty minutes.

I caught up with Rychek on the way out. "Look," I said. "You're tight with Stockton. Can you help me get a one-on-one with R. J.? There's no way I can interview the man in the middle of that mob scene."

"I'll see what I can do," he said.

I called the city desk, went to the court clerk's office to pick up a copy I had ordered of the trial transcript, then dashed outside. Stockton was alone, holding court on the steps. R. J. had pulled a fast one and made his getaway from another exit.

His client, the lawyer apologized, would not talk to the press until he returned to Miami. R. J. wanted out of Volusia County ASAP. Who could blame him?

The media stampede fought, jostled, and shouted their way down the sidewalk after Stockton. As I tagged along, lugging the transcript, Rychek sidled up, a purposeful look on his face.

"Don't say it," I warned, expecting a rude comment on my sex life.

"Okay, okay," he muttered. "I talked to Stockton for ya, kid. But if you don't wanna hear it—"

I broke stride. "What did he say?"

"No interviews here. We're headed for the airport now . . ."

I sighed.

". . . but there's room on the plane. May be a little rowdy, a lotta celebrating, but hey, kid, wanna hitch a ride?"

I stared. He was serious.

"Sure," I said. "I'd love it."

10

What an emotional experience, walking out of prison with an innocent man saved from execution!"

Champagne glass in hand, as his sleek jet streaked home to Miami, Stockton retold his story. "They kept me waiting. Other prisoners were cheering when they finally brought him out. They had to give him a pushcart for all his books, his legal papers, and ten years of correspondence."

Good quotes. I took notes, but this flight was short and what I needed was time with R. J. He'd shown such interest in the late-model jet, with its computerized cockpit and sophisticated controls, that for a moment, when we boarded, I feared they'd let him fly it. He was the man of the moment. Now, however, as Stockton continued to crow, as though his genius and persistence had freed his client, R. J. was quiet, immersed in thought.

I seized a chance to slip into the seat beside him when one of Stockton's assistants went to the rest room. R. J.'s rugged good looks were more impressive close up. Prison garb flatters no one. He had changed into a soft leather jacket over a sweater and twill slacks, garments Eunice must have sent to Volusia with his lawyer.

"What are you thinking?" I asked.

I withered under the close scrutiny of his dark eyes, wishing I'd had the chance to change clothes, comb my hair, and freshen up.

"That I can walk down the street," he finally said slowly,

"and feel the sun on my face. I couldn't do that yesterday. Today the grass is greener, the sky bluer. I can even appreciate a raindrop. I can take a drink." He raised his champagne glass. "I can sleep in a real bed tonight, use a real bathroom. Is that what you wanted to hear?" he asked arrogantly.

"If those are your true feelings," I said softly. "I know this is an emotional time for you. I'm sorry to intrude, but everybody is interested in your story, in this miscarriage of justice—"

"Where were they," he snapped, "ten years ago when I was railroaded by a kangaroo court in a redneck county?"

"It had to be terrible," I said, "that no one believed you."

He nodded, his smile ironic. "She nearly got what she wanted."

"Your wife?"

His granite eyes flickered dangerously at the word, but he said nothing.

"This is such a happy time for your mom," I offered.

"For me too," he said, eyes still grim. "The woman who put me behind bars got what she deserved. Had the state succeeded—if they had walked me down that hall to the electric chair—she'd be as guilty of murder as somebody else is now."

"But you loved her. . . ."

"Let me tell you something, Miss Reporter." He leaned close, his face inches from mine, speaking swiftly, sotto voce. "On X-wing I lost whatever fondness I had for the woman. Let me tell you about life in Cell X-3323. Let me tell you about the open metal toilet, the total lack of privacy, being told what and when to eat, when to sleep, when to take a shower. Let me tell you about the chemical spray, the 'electrical restraint devices,' and the pepper-gas grenades." He smiled with no humor. "The guards refer to them as 'foggers.' Kaithlin"—he paused and sighed—"no day went by that I didn't think of her. I'd have killed her with a smile on my face, Miss Reporter."

His cold words sent a chill rippling between my shoulder blades. "It's Britt," I said softly. "Britt Montero, from the *Miami News*."

"Well, Miss Reporter, I'm sure you're eager to ask how I *feel* about her death. Let's just say relieved, with a new appreciation of poetic justice. There is some balance in the universe after all."

"Who do you think might have killed her?"

"I don't know, but I'm grateful. Her killer saved my life. His timing was excellent, but I wish he had done it a hel-luva lot sooner." He leaned back in his seat. "Now they're both where they belong."

"Both?" I glanced up from my notebook.

"Her mother. She's dead too. Did you know that? The witch who stirred up all our troubles."

"How so?" I asked.

Dark and sullen, he shook his head, then turned to respond to Stockton, who interrupted to discuss how to handle the press at the Miami airport.

"One more question," I said hurriedly. "Did you have something engraved inside Kaithlin's wedding ring?"

He refocused on me, eyes narrowed. "How would I remember?" he said curtly. "It was a long time ago."

I reluctantly relinquished my seat to the lawyer. It was his plane.

I sat next to Rychek.

"So." I sighed. "How did you know?"

"You and Fitzgerald?"

"Yeah."

"I ain't been a detective all these years for nothing, kid. Hey, he's a cop, and he don't know any better. I keep telling the young guys to keep their eyes open and their pants zipped, but they keep getting it backwards. But you . . . I'm surprised."

"Do me a favor?" I asked, suddenly weary. "Don't tell anybody, at least until this case wraps up. Okay? It wouldn't look good, with me working on the story and all."

" 'Course not. He ain't a bad guy, but I thought you wuz otherwise involved."

"I don't know, Emery." I shook my head. "I guess I'm not."

We didn't mention it again.

R. J. stopped by my seat, shortly before we landed.

"The date," he said. "June twelfth, nineteen eighty-five, and initials. Hers and mine." As I jotted it down, he leaned over and spoke softly in my ear. "Did you see her?"

I blinked. "Kaithlin?"

"They said you were there, on the beach the day they found her." His words were casual, his eyes were not.

"I was there."

"How did she look?" he whispered, Adam's apple working.

"Pretty much like she did before," I said awkwardly, remembering her features in the water. "Judging from old pictures, she hadn't changed much. She was a beautiful woman."

He winced, as though in pain.

"Why?" I said.

He straightened up abruptly, shook off the question, and moved on to rejoin Stockton.

His remorse, if that's what it was, was apparently fleeting.

Facing the press in an airport meeting room, R. J. morphed into the flamboyant charmer, still the spoiled bad boy of Miami society, high-fiving his lawyer for photographers, hugging his mother, Eunice, who met the plane elegantly attired in—white, a stunning designer suit.

"I got what I wanted," R. J. told the press. He knew how to step back into the spotlight and hold center stage. "I was determined to walk out of that hellhole a free man—or die. No compromises." His eyes roved the room, searching each reporter's face. "That's why I refused to plead guilty. Prison is no place to spend your life."

A Channel 7 reporter asked if R. J. now planned to crusade against the death penalty or for reforms in the system.

"Hell, no." R. J. grinned. "I'm no poster boy for prisoners. I never related to any of them. They all claim to be innocent. The difference is, I really was."

Stockton stepped up to blame the state for ruining the life and reputation of an innocent man.

"He can never retrieve what they took. You know the old story. Take a pillow to a mountaintop, rip it apart, and fling the feathers to the four winds. Then try to retrieve each and every feather. It's impossible," he drawled. "That's exactly what it's like to try to regain a ruined reputation."

I exchanged skeptical glances with Lottie, who was

among the photographers. R. J. was no innocent bystander. What about the domestic abuse? The restraining orders? The mistress? The lies? The missing millions and his renegade past? The world might not have been so quick to believe he was a killer had he not ruined his own reputation first.

"What would you say to your wife's killer?" a reporter asked as the press conference wound down.

"Thanks, pal," R. J. quipped, without hesitation. Even Stockton winced at his client's heartless smile.

"That R. J., what an SOB," Lottie said, as we headed to the parking garage. "He's hot, ain't he?"

"Bad boys are always attractive to women," I muttered. "I wish I knew why."

"Speaking of bad boys," Lottie said, "you look like hell."

"Thank you. Haven't seen my lipstick, comb, or a clean pair of underpants since I left Miami. Nice to see you too."

"Heard the flight up was rough."

"Tell me about it."

"Heard you never checked into your hotel. Gretchen was trying to hunt you down. She got so mad she wanted to twist off your head and shit down your neck."

"Oh, swell. Any more good news?"

"Yeah, Angel showed me the catalog. The one with the bustle?" She sighed. "It's the best of the lot."

Cool, crisp, and dressed for success as always, Gretchen Platt, the assistant city editor from hell, scrutinized me from head to toe when I breezed into the newsroom. "What happened to your shoes?" She looked aghast.

"Foam," I said, checking my mailbox. She dogged my

footsteps, trailing behind me as I searched for my chair, which someone had appropriated in my absence. I recaptured it from another desk and rolled it back to my terminal.

"Don't disappear again," she said tersely, "until your story is in and we can review it together."

My face must have reflected my thoughts, because she backed off and had the sense not to harangue me while I worked. But I knew I'd pay the piper later.

Whew." Fred gave a long low whistle as he read R. J.'s quotes in a printout of my story. "He really said that?"

"I didn't make it up."

"He's cold," Fred said. He sat on the edge of the desk next to mine.

"Stone cold," I said. "As stone cold as any killer. Who could blame him? He admits he would have killed her himself, given the chance."

"Think he did?" Fred asked thoughtfully. "Killers for hire aren't hard to find behind bars."

"Who knows?" I said. "But that poses another question. If he did hire somebody, could he be prosecuted? He's already been tried and convicted for killing her once. Does double jeopardy apply?"

"Interesting thought. Check into it." He took off his gold-rimmed glasses and massaged the inner corners of his eyes with a thumb and index finger. "In the meantime, where do we go from here on this one?"

"The next feeding frenzy is to find out where she was all these years. That's the big, burning, searing question. It's probably only a matter of hours before all the TV news mags and tabloids—*48 Hours, 20/20, America's Most Wanted*—zero in on it. Somebody who knows her will see the mystery aired and expose her secret life. We can try to beat them, pull it off ourselves. I'd like to give it a shot."

"How do you propose to do that?"

"I've got the morgue picture . . ."

He frowned.

". . . and a stack of old file photos of Kaithlin before she disappeared. I'd like the art department, with all their new computerized equipment, to do a really good lifelike drawing of how she looked recently. We can fax it to missing persons bureaus in key cities. And I'd like Onnie, the best researcher in the *News* library, to do an exhaustive computer check, see if we can match her to recent reports of missing persons all over the country. She's been dead for weeks now. Somebody somewhere must be looking for her. If there was a short or even a classified ad in her current hometown paper, I'd like us to find it first.

"Meanwhile, I'll track down as many people from her old life as possible. Somebody might have heard from her or know her well enough to say where she'd go to start over."

"Sounds like a plan," Fred said. "Maybe we'll get lucky. I'll get the art department on it. You talk to Onnie."

"Ask for a full front and a profile," I said, handing him the morgue picture.

He looked at the photo and winced, then put his glasses on and stared at it more closely. "If she had a whole new life somewhere, why the hell you think she came back?"

I shook my head. "You know how Miami is; it gets under your skin. Maybe she just couldn't stay away. Or maybe she had second thoughts and wanted to save R. J. Maybe she came back to find the missing money. Maybe, though it seems improbable, she just learned that her mother was dead."

"A lot of maybes," he said tersely. "Give it your best shot. So far we're ahead of the pack. It'd be nice to stay there." He frowned at me. "Why don't you go home and get some sleep."

I shook my head again. "I want to start tonight. I'll just go home, shower and eat, and come back."

"If you're up for it," he said. "One thing more." He paused, as though hesitant to broach the subject. "The desk had a problem last night. They had space out front, so Gretchen wanted more reporting on the emergency landing. The airline stonewalled, aware that we were close to deadline. She wanted you to work it from that end, but you were unreachable. The hotel said you never checked in. She even tracked down Stockton's people at their hotel. They said they hadn't seen you."

"It was a frightening experience," I said, annoyed that I'd been checked up on, like a truant schoolgirl. "I immediately called the desk, unloaded all I knew, then stayed with a friend who lives there. I didn't even have a toothbrush or a nightgown. My bag still hasn't caught up with me."

He peered skeptically at me through his bifocals.

"I'm going home now, to brush my teeth. I'll be back in an hour or so."

He nodded.

"Good job," he called, as I left the newsroom.

I hurried down the stairs, rather than risk being cornered

by Gretchen or having Fred shoot more questions at me while I waited for the damn elevator.

I called the library from the car as I emerged from the building. Onnie had escaped an abuser herself. She'd relate to Kaithlin.

"Onnie, if you had to flee, disappear forever, change your identity and start over, where would you go?"

"Trouble with the desk?" she asked breezily. "Come on, Britt. Nothing's that bad. It's that bitch Gretchen again, isn't it?"

I explained what I wanted and we brainstormed, agreeing that Kaithlin would probably run as far from Miami as possible. Onnie said she'd start checking West Coast newspapers, California, Washington, and Oregon—and Colorado—then work her way east.

"She was probably smart enough not to go to a resort city," I said, recalling a homicide I'd covered. The victim, on the witness protection plan out of New York, insisted on opening a small bar in South Beach, ignoring the feds, who warned that Miami was too high-profile and he'd be seen and recognized. They were right. He was shot dead two weeks later.

Kaithlin didn't need the feds; she had created her own witness protection plan. It kept her safe for ten years, until something went wrong.

"Try to get somebody else to handle routine requests from the newsroom," I said. "Fred wants to give this priority."

"We're swamped and short-handed as always," she said, "but I'll do my best. So you saw R. J. Jordan, today, huh? How'd the man look?"

"Not bad for a guy past fifty. Lottie thinks he's still a stud."

"Hey, that's not old. Look at Newman, Redford, Poitier, Sean Connery."

"Yeah, but this guy's only talent is trouble."

"Talking talent," she said lightly, "you got yourself a new sweetie you didn't tell me about? Heard you went AWOL in Daytona."

"Have to hang up now, talk to you later," I said, and turned south on Alton Road.

I had been gone for only twenty-four hours. As I parked outside my apartment, it seemed longer. It was already dusk. Mrs. Goldstein, in a heavy sweater and gloves, was watering her banana trees. Her face lit up. "I just saw you on TV! They showed the press conference at the airport." She dropped the gurgling hose into the grass and hugged me. "You looked so tired, I made you some soup. Where's your bag, Britt?"

"I don't know," I murmured, then surprised us both by weeping on her soft shoulder, big snuffling sobs and scalding hot tears.

She walked me into my apartment, heated the soup, brewed tea, and listened. Slumped in my favorite chair, Billy Boots purring in my lap, I told her that McDonald was out of my life and recounted the frightening moments on the plane.

"I thought he was the one," she said sadly.

"So did I." I sniffled, hugging Bitsy, who sat up, eyes concerned, her eager paws on my knees.

"I'm glad you're home safe," my landlady said kindly. "No wonder you're upset, after such an experience. You're having a delayed reaction. You need to eat something good, take a shower, and go to bed. Then tomorrow take a book and go lie on the beach—"

"I—I can't." I hiccuped. "I have to go back to work tonight."

Shocked and indignant, she castigated my bosses as "insensitive and unreasonable" men who constantly take advantage of my loyalty and good nature. It wasn't true, of course. I am a willing volunteer when it comes to trouble. But I needed kind words and sympathy from someone who cared.

"Take a shower," she instructed, "and I'll bring you a bite to eat. Oh, honey," she said at the door. "I bought you a new toothbrush, too. I saw yours when I came to take the dog out and change Billy's sandbox." She shook her head. "You should replace it every six months, at least."

"They don't make them like they used to," I said numbly.

By the time I'd showered and dressed, she had brought a plate of warm beef flanken with horseradish and potato latkes.

The food, comforting and sustaining, didn't fill the empty place where my heart should be, but it was fortifying. I put on warm clothes and filled a thermos with strong Cuban coffee. I felt stronger as I drove back to the paper through the chilly night, as though I'd found my second wind. Who needed sleep? How did the words of the song go?

I'll sleep when I'm dead.

How novel. A great argument," Jeremiah Tannen said. The former boy wonder from the public defender's office was the first person I called. Now in successful private practice, he specializes in criminal law. "But it wouldn't work," he said, "and I'll tell you why.

"You can't be tried twice for the same crime. That's double jeopardy. But a man wrongfully convicted of his wife's murder the first time could, indeed, be charged with her recent murder. It's not the same crime. It's a different murder, at a different place, on a different date, in a different jurisdiction.

"However," he continued, "it would be fascinating, if he was convicted, to try to persuade the court to grant him credit for the time he served for the first crime, the one that never happened."

R. J.'s anger at Kaithlin's mother haunted me, as I cleared my desk of mail and messages. Why did he detest Reva Warren so? After all these years he was still furious at a sad senior citizen, now dead, whose only sin seemed to be working all her life to raise the woman he had once loved.

Did she do more than meddle? Was it because she had testified against him?

I called my mother, who had left multiple messages.

"Britt, darling. Were you out of town? Someone said something about a plane . . . ?"

"Yes," I said, "but it all turned out fine. Mom, when you

worked for Jordan's—"

"I just heard the news, dear. R. J.'s free!"

"I know, I was there."

"I can't believe it! I was shocked. Did you see what Eunice was wearing? Chanel! She looked like an absolutely different person. She's worn nothing but black since it all happened."

"I guess it was sort of a celebration that she has her son back. Mom, did you—?"

"Eunice always had style," she said, "but no business sense. Con was brilliant, generous to a fault. He led everyone to believe she was an asset, when in reality she was nothing but a self-centered clotheshorse."

"Mom, I'm at work, trying to piece it all together. Maybe you can help. Did Kaithlin ever discuss personal problems with you, the animosity between her mother and R.J?"

"That was all very long ago," she said, suddenly less talkative, "and I'm just on my way out. Nelson and I are attending a cocktail party for the Dade Heritage Trust; then we're off to dinner." I tried to place Nelson. She'd had frequent escorts since she began dating after only recently, belatedly, coming to terms with my father's death.

"I won't keep you," I promised, "but there are so many theories, so many possibilities, and I have to work fast. I need some direction."

"What are they saying?" She sounded wary.

"Oh, a thousand and one stories." I pulled out the witness list and flipped open the thick trial transcript. "People are even speculating that there was another child, that Kaithlin wasn't the—"

"Maybe that's not so far from the truth," she broke in.

"What? You mean there was—"

"Darling, I really can't say any more." She seemed instantly to regret saying as much as she had. "There's the doorbell. Got to go. Love you."

"Mom, wait—" She hung up.

I pushed the redial button. Her number rang and rang. I hung up, hit it again, and it rang some more. Even her machine didn't answer.

In the course of my job, I can often draw out intimate, even damning information from reluctant, even hostile strangers. Why then can't I connect with my own mother? Did R. J.'s sudden freedom shock her because she knew something more, something important?

I scanned the witness list again and highlighted a name: Amy Hastings, Kaithlin's childhood friend, one of the last people she spoke to before the murder that didn't happen.

I drew more bright yellow highlights through the names of Dallas Suarez, the mistress who had testified against R. J., and the Jordans' live-in housekeeper, Consuela Morales. The housekeeper had testified through an interpreter about the couple's domestic strife and R. J.'s rages. She said she once saw him push Kaithlin against a glass table, and she witnessed another quarrel when he slapped her until she sobbed. The housekeeper said she had applied ice to Kaithlin's bruised cheekbone so she could attend an important business meeting the following morning. She had also testified that she so feared R. J. she would have quit her job but was afraid to leave Miss Kaithlin alone with him. She, too, had wept on the stand.

No wonder the jury wanted to hang him.

The housekeeper was fifty-one at the time, her name

common. I suspected that if still alive and working in the United States, she would probably be in the same neighborhood. Non-English-speaking household workers are usually hired via word-of-mouth by employers who are acquainted with one another.

I found the blue book, the city cross-reference directory, and began with the house on Old Cutler where the doomed marriage of Kaithlin and R. J. fell apart.

A precocious child answered, then gave up the phone to his harried mother, who said she'd never heard of Consuela Morales. Neither did the next-door neighbor, who had recently moved in. But a longtime neighbor on the other side thought she remembered the woman.

"I believe she's somewhere over on the next block now, working for a doctor and his wife."

I found her on the tenth call.

"I would like to come and talk to you," I told her in Spanish.

She was too busy, she protested. When I persisted, she reluctantly agreed to see me in an hour and a half.

Until then, I searched the Florida Department of Motor Vehicles database. No current driver's license for Amy Hastings. Her old license, issued at age seventeen, gave me her date of birth and physical description. Records revealed that, in 1993, Amy Hastings had renewed her license as Amy Sondheim. Bell South showed no Amy Sondheim, listed or unlisted. I called the apartment complex where she had lived at the time. The manager did not remember her but gave me the names of four longtime residents. The second said Amy had divorced and moved to Baltimore. No phone listing there. Maryland driver's license records showed she had renewed her license and changed her name to Tolliver. New residents at her old address said she had moved to San Jose, California, in 1997.

Was it to be near Kaithlin? I nearly called Onnie to suggest she focus on central California, but Amy wasn't listed in San Jose. Her trail dead-ended. Then I managed to tap into a credit bureau report, not the confidential file, only the header on the top page that identified the individual in question. Amy had been busy: divorced and apparently remarried once more. Her new address? Miami. She had returned in late 2000, now using the name Salazar.

I should have known. An itch afflicts natives who leave this place. Live elsewhere, as I learned to my dismay in college, and an uneasy sensation nags, as though you went to bed forgetting to brush your teeth. Suddenly wide awake in the dead of the night, you sit up, slap your forehead and say, Oh, yeah, I forgot something today. I forgot to go home, to go back to Miami.

Her number didn't answer. If she'd been reading the newspaper, I wondered why Amy hadn't called me. I hoped no other reporter had found her first.

I checked the time. I only had fifteen minutes to meet Consuela Morales.

No wonder R. J.'s fury had made Consuela cower. She stood less than five feet tall, petite and solemn with huge spaniel eyes. We talked in her room, a sparsely furnished cubicle with a private entrance, surely smaller than some closets in the big house where she now worked. She would not like her current employers to know of this, she said.

There was no trouble here. It was an excellent position.

She had been afraid but had testified despite threats, pleas, and even offers of money and lifelong employment from Eunice Jordan. She testified for Miss Kaithlin, she said, an angel who had helped the rest of her family emigrate from Guatemala, sponsored them herself, and found them jobs. It had been difficult to work for the couple. They loved each other passionately, their housekeeper said solemnly. They fought. Always. It grew worse and worse, until she was afraid R. J. would kill Miss Kaithlin. Though she had detailed his rages for the police and lawyers, no one ever probed into what triggered his anger. The prosecutor didn't need to and the defense didn't want more on the record about R. J.'s bad temper.

Consuela's English was not good then; it wasn't now. But one thing she understood. Always, when they fought, it was for the same reason.

R. J. would shout, demand, and curse. He even wept. Always the same thing: "*¿Dónde está mi hijo?* I want my son!"

"They had no children," I said.

"I know." Consuela shrugged and rolled her dark eyes, as though the peculiarities of her employers were not her business.

"You're sure that's what he was saying?"

She was. Kaithlin often called her mother during arguments, she said. R. J. would shout. Sometimes they struggled over the phone. "He very mad," she said in English.

She had never seen Kaithlin pregnant, never saw a child or even a child's photo.

The medical examiner said that Kaithlin had given birth.

But if she and R. J. had had a baby, where was it?

Back at the office, I called R. J. He wasn't home, and Eunice was "unavailable."

I dialed Amy Salazar. This time she answered. "You're the former Amy Hastings," I announced flatly, giving her no opportunity to deny it. "I need to talk to you about Kaithlin Warren." Then I identified myself.

"How did you find me?" She sounded soft and girlish, though she had to be at least thirty-six or thirty-seven.

"It wasn't easy."

"What about Kaithlin?"

"I guess you're aware of the story about her recent death and R. J.'s release."

"Yes, but you're all wrong," she said cheerfully. "Kaithlin isn't dead. She wasn't dead then. She isn't dead now."

"What do you mean?" I gasped.

"I don't like to talk on the telephone," she said slowly.

"I'll come out there," I said. "Right now."

She lived in Coconut Grove, a historic Miami suburb of small houses, big trees, and narrow streets named Avocado, Loquat, and Kumquat. The address was difficult to find: a cottage scarcely visible from the street, dwarfed by towering oak and poinciana trees. It looked dark, but luminous eyes watched from the porch as I carefully picked my way along a fern-lined path. Several cats retreated into the anthuriums as I approached the wooden steps. Clove and cinnamon scents from night-flowering plants perfumed the air, and water splashed against stone somewhere nearby.

The interior light was so dim that I shivered, hoping she was still there.

Her almost musical voice responded to my knock. "It's Britt Montero," I called, and she opened the door.

She was barefoot despite the chill, her hair and clothes loose and flowing. White candles burned as she ushered me into the living room, where wind chimes and planters hung from the ceiling. The furniture was wicker and the floor Dade County pine. The flickering candlelight glinted off a crystal suspended from a ribbon around her pale throat.

"Is the power out?" I asked.

"Oh, no." She laughed and switched on a brass lamp in the corner. "I prefer to meditate by candlelight."

I sat on a canary-yellow sofa and declined her offer of a fruit drink. She sat in a wicker rocker opposite me. She was thin, with a wide, generous mouth and thick dark eyelashes.

"You startled me when you said that Kaithlin isn't dead."

"Of course she isn't," she murmured confidently, her smile benevolent. "There is no death, only change."

I stared, not sure whether to laugh or cry. "If it is only change," I said, "you must admit, it's a pretty drastic one." What I had hoped was a major break in the story was nothing but new-age babble.

"The soul never dies," she said serenely. "Kaithlin lives on in spirit." She gazed around the room. "I feel her presence often."

"So do I," I said, surprising myself, emotions mixed. "I wish she could tell us what happened, enlighten us about her last ten years. Did you ever hear from her in all that time? In real life? Did you know she was still alive on this plane?"

"No." She looked hurt. "When I testified at the trial I believed every word I told them. I believed she was in spirit. I felt like I'd lost a true sister."

"Were you and she always close?"

"We met in kindergarten." She smiled. "Miss Peters's class. We had a fight the first day and wound up in a hair-pulling match. I can't remember why, but Miss Peters had to pull us apart. We were both crying and in trouble. From that moment on we were inseparable. Like, I was her shadow. Kaithlin led, I followed. I was totally shy and backward. I adored her. She was smarter, ran faster, and told better jokes than anybody else in school.

"We shared all our secrets. We were always together," she added, twirling a lock of her long hair, "until she met R. J."

She suddenly bounded over to join me on the couch, tucking her bare feet beneath her, skirt billowing. She had bounced up so abruptly that the chair she vacated continued to rock, as though occupied by an agitated ghost.

"We were sixteen," she said softly, eyes aglow. "From the moment their eyes met, it was all fire, passion, and excitement. It was the most romantic thing we'd ever experienced. First love for her, and on his part, I think, a rediscovery of innocence. She wasn't allowed to date, but we had done a little experimenting with boys our own age. R. J. was different. Like, he kept coaxing and teasing her. On their first date, when she was supposed to be studying at my house, he drank too much—so she walked out and took a bus home. He didn't see her go, didn't even know her phone number. He showed up, furious, the next time she worked at the store. But she was good, God, she was good. Like, she turned it around so he was furious at himself." She leaned on one elbow, hand in her hair, eyes dreamy. "From that moment on, he was hooked; he had to have her. Kaithlin knew how to get what she wanted. She wanted R. J. and she got him."

"I thought she and her mother were very close."

"Nah." Amy frowned and plucked at her skirt. "I think Kaithlin was a change-of-life baby or something. Her mother was, like, older, strict, some kind of religious nut, absolutely dumpy and old-fashioned. Kaithlin had to wear all these positively stupid, freaking clothes the woman sewed. She never fit in with the rich kids at school until she started to mature. Then everybody wanted to hang with her.

"I was in the wedding, you know." Amy's expressive eyes darkened. "She and R. J. were so blissed out, despite everything else that had happened."

"Where did it go wrong?"

"They were definitely soulmates," she responded vaguely. "So high on each other, like birds mating in flight. The sort of relationship that's made in heaven but can't survive on earth. Like, there must have been a shitload of bad karma to work out. Kaithlin said it would take them both to hell—and it did."

"What about the baby?" I asked.

She stirred, eyes uneasy. "It was the baby," she acknowledged, in a whisper. "It was all about the damn baby.

"A couple months before her seventeenth birthday, Kaithlin was late, afraid she was pregnant. Turned out she was right. She trusted him, but R. J. freaked at the news, said the baby probably wasn't his. I mean, Kaithlin was under age, still in high school. He didn't want anybody, especially his parents, to know. He backed off, dumped her. She didn't want her mother to know, they'd already been fighting because of R. J., but there's no way to keep a pregnancy secret for long. When her mom went to see R. J., he called Kaithlin a lying tramp and walked away."

Myrna Lewis's words about "sins only God can forgive" made sense now.

"What happened then?" I asked.

"Officially"—she shrugged—"Kaithlin missed a semester to take care of her sick mother. She had the baby but only saw him once, the day he was born. Her mother wouldn't let her keep him. She arranged a private adoption.

"Once the baby was out of the picture, R. J. started calling, trying to see her. He wouldn't stay away. Her mom threatened to have him arrested and Kaithlin committed to juvenile hall as incorrigible. It got really ugly. It was like Kaithlin was in prison, with her mother the warden. The day she turned eighteen, she and R. J. started to date openly and she went back to work at Jordan's. Her mother couldn't stop her then, though she tried.

"You almost had to feel sorry for the woman. It was like trying to stop a whirlwind with your bare hands." Amy hugged her knees, face awash in memories.

"When did R. J. decide he wanted the baby back?"

"He didn't get on that kick until years later, after they were married. Like, his parents were hot for a grandson. It meant a lot of money to R. J. He was impatient, always wanted everything right now, couldn't figure out why

Kaithlin didn't get pregnant." Amy smirked. "She didn't trust him yet. I mean, she'd seen him in action the first time. She wanted a solid marriage first, to know he'd hang in and be a decent father. She wanted to keep working, build a career, until he was ready. She never told him she was on the pill.

"But when Kaithlin didn't get pregnant, R. J. decided to take their baby back. He had the money and all to do it. But Kaithlin's mother refused to tell them any details about the adoption. R. J. went nuts, accused Kaithlin of knowing where the boy was and deliberately keeping him from his son, all kinds of shit like that. Poor Kaithlin knew nothing. She was a kid. Like, all she did was sign the paper her mother put in front of her."

"A mess," I said.

"Sure was." Amy nodded slowly. "Her mom hated R. J. Guess it was her chance for payback, big time. R. J. hated her too. He was vindictive; it was all he thought about. Kaithlin got caught in the cross fire, all that hostility, negative energy, all those bad vibes." Amy hunched her shoulders and shivered as she stared into the empty stone fireplace.

"Trapped between the two people she loved most," I said.

"Right. They made her miserable. Like, her only joy was her job. She loved it. She was so good at it, she had a way with people, and it was her escape from a husband and a mother who wanted to kill each other." She glanced up, eyes bright. "You know what I mean? Like, she threw herself into work to escape the pain in her personal life."

Oh, I knew.

"What finally brought it all to a head?"

"She found out R. J. was seeing that Suarez woman. A real slut. We even followed them one night in my car, saw them together. God only knows what else he did. He had it all, the cars, the boats, the plane. Nothing was enough. There were rumors, even in the newspaper, about missing money at Jordan's. Kaithlin suspected R. J. and some accountant friend he'd hired. But she knew in the end she'd be blamed. His parents would defend him. They always had, you know. He was blood; they always found somebody else to blame when he fouled up."

I nodded, imagining how Kaithlin felt. She'd lost her relationship with her mother, she'd lost her baby, and she was on the verge of losing her marriage and her career.

"The day before she went to Daytona," Amy was saying, "she said she had to make it work. I told her to bail. Like, the world is full of men. But she wanted to persuade R. J. and her mom to see a shrink with her. She'd tried before, but they'd both refused. She didn't like failure. When R. J. asked her to go away for the weekend, she went, to do whatever she had to to make it work."

"You knew her best," I said. "During that last call to you, from the motel, was she really frightened?"

"I offered to drive to damn Daytona to get her, and I didn't even have a decent car at the time," Amy blurted, voice rising. "I would've rented one, or hailed a goddamn cab. That's how sure I was that he was out of control and she needed help.

"See"—she leaned forward, eyes plaintive—"we were always there for each other. Kaithlin would have done the same for me. That's the great thing about her. Like, she never forgot her friends, never forgot her roots, always reached out to the underdog, always wanted to help other women. So what I want to know is, How could she just run off like that, never even call me to say she was okay? I was her best friend our whole lives." Tears skidded down her pale cheeks.

"You knew her so well," I said. "Where would she go?"

Amy wiped her eyes and lifted her shoulders. "She never talked about going anyplace else. Miami was home. She grew up here. All I know is she wanted to stay here and live a normal happy life."

"Don't we all?" I said sadly.

"I made a lot of mistakes," Amy said earnestly, tears still flowing, "and moved around a lot. But I'm enlightened, I finally found nirvana, the bliss I was seeking, right back where I started. Like, it was waiting here for me all along."

"I'm glad."

I was grateful that someone was happy and content with her life.

"Your husband lives here too?" I said, as she saw me to the door. "His name is Salazar?"

"No." She looked vaguely troubled. "I think he's still in San Jose. I have a restraining order."

12

I drove away on streets as dark and shadowy as the past. The woman I had so identified with *was* dead. I had seen her corpse. Why had I been so elated when for a moment Amy led me to believe that Kaithlin might still be alive? Utter madness or wishful thinking? At least I'd learned one of her secrets. Perhaps now the others would follow. If I could understand her and her demons, perhaps I could understand myself.

Miami's population, huge and uncountable, is swollen by tourists, fugitives, and undocumented illegal aliens. Yet Kaithlin and I had to have crossed paths many times. When we were growing up, those of us born and raised here, who lived in Miami year round, had not yet become lost in vast urban sprawl and dense downtown development. People our age frequented the same movie theaters, shopping centers, and skating rinks. I had shopped at Jordan's, a local institution, and my mother worked there. I nearly joined her one year for a summer job, opting instead to intern at a small weekly, on the recommendation of my journalism teacher.

Kaithlin and I had surely seen each other, perhaps even spoken. We shared so much in common; both fatherless, raised under difficult circumstances by working mothers, we were both conflicted by love and work. But how could she walk away from family, friends, and career and simply disappear? Could I do that? I wondered.

Instead of taking the downtown exit, I accelerated, driving north to the old apartment house in North Miami, hoping she wasn't asleep.

"Mrs. Lewis," I said into the squawk box, when she answered the bell, "it's Britt, from the *News*. I need to see you for a moment."

She wore a tatty bathrobe and slippers, her thinning hair in plastic curlers.

"Did you bring back the picture?" she asked, blinking.

"No, sorry. It's on my desk. I'll mail it when I get back to the office."

I answered the question in her eyes.

"I'm here to ask you about Kaithlin's baby."

She grimaced and limped to the stove to light the burner under the ever-present teakettle. "What about him?" she asked brusquely.

"You knew?"

"Of course. I was Reva's best friend."

"You didn't tell me when we talked."

"I didn't know you knew."

Was everybody in Miami suddenly practicing Don't ask, don't tell?

"I wish you had said something," I told her, exasperated.

She faced me, the burnt-out match still clutched between arthritic fingers. "Reva asked me not to tell anyone."

"But she's dead; so is Kaithlin."

She looked startled. "Death doesn't mean you don't keep a secret. A promise is a promise."

"But that information might have some bearing on the case," I protested.

"It doesn't."

"How do you know?" I said.

"It was too long ago," she said, with a wave of derision. "It couldn't."

"Knowledge is power," I countered. "It helps to have all the facts."

"Helps who? Your newspaper?" she challenged. "When I was young, journalism was all about the five double-yews: Where, When, Why, What, and Who. Today it's about the gees: Garbage and Gossip."

"You may be right to a degree," I acknowledged bleakly, "a large degree. But not in my stories. Solving the murder is what's important."

"Breaking promises won't help," she said.

"Don't you value justice?"

"I do," she said solemnly, and aimed a gnarled index finger at the cracked ceiling. "A greater justice."

"But you have to admit it would be a comfort to see some here on earth."

Her small smile conceded that much. "I dropped a hint," she said, cocking her head, "when I told you some things can't be forgiven."

"Sorry, I should have picked up on that sooner. So Reva took her revenge out on R. J. by refusing to reveal his son's whereabouts."

"No!" she cried, taken aback, eyes wide in shock. "That's not how it was at all! I thought giving up her only grandchild would kill her. It nearly did. But she made the sacrifice because he deserved two responsible adult parents. What chance would he have had with a teenage mother and a playboy who denied being his father?

"She couldn't bear to watch Kaithlin sacrifice everything to raise a child alone. She had tried it, did everything any woman could do, and failed. She spent hours with the priest, seeking the strength and courage to give him away. He said adoption was best."

"But she could have forced R. J. to pay child support. Hired a lawyer, called the Jordans . . ."

Myrna shook her head as she poured steaming water over fresh tea bags in cups for us both. It was chamomile. "The law didn't work for her, and she knew it wouldn't for

Kaithlin. The Jordans were too powerful. She tried to talk to R. J., but he was crude and humiliated her. She had her pride. She always made her own way and never asked for help. It broke her heart to lose him, but Reva said her grandson went to a wonderful home."

I stared down at my notebook. "But if it wasn't revenge, why wouldn't she help them find him?"

"Because, by the time R. J. changed his mind, there was no baby anymore," she said indignantly. "He would have been a little boy in school. Six years old. You don't uproot a child, take him from the only family he knows. You don't do that to the parents who love him. How could Reva let R. J. change his mind on a whim? What if he changed it again later? You can't play with human life that way."

"So Reva was protecting the boy?"

"Her grandson, at all costs," she said solemnly. "She destroyed the paperwork on the adoption so it would never be found. If something happened to her, she didn't want her grandson's life ever disrupted by strangers with briefcases. Later, she suspected that was why R. J. killed Kaithlin, to take her child away, the way he accused her of taking his son. I can't tell you all the times she sat right where you're sitting, crying her eyes out."

I closed my eyes as the image evoked a shiver. "Do you remember Amy Hastings?" I asked. "She testified at the trial."

"Kaithlin's little friend." Myrna nodded. "Always had their heads together, whispers and giggles. Not as smart or as pretty as Kaithlin, but she promised she'd stay close to Reva afterward, even swore she'd be her surrogate daughter, because they'd both loved Kaithlin. I thought she might be a comfort, but after the trial Reva never heard from her again. Not a call, not so much as a Christmas card. She was a flighty little thing. Ditzy, if you ask me."

I drove along Biscayne Boulevard, bathed in the cozy glow of anti-crime lights, wondering why everyone but her own husband felt loyal to Kaithlin. Back at the office, I went to the trial transcript and found the address of the condo R. J. had bought for Dallas Suarez, the mistress who later testified against him. Beachfront, in Key Biscayne. No phone listed for her there, or anywhere else in Miami-Dade. The high-flying adventuress and flight instructor could be anywhere by now, I thought. Her public image at the time of the trial was that of a sensation seeker, an expert pilot, diver, and skier who also thrived on the thrills of illicit romance. I got out the trusty city directory. The building had only twenty-five units on five floors. I lied through my teeth, posing as an old friend in search of a long-lost chum.

"She's my neighbor!" trilled the first woman I spoke to. "She's still here! Married now, to a lovely guy. Lives here with her husband. Want me to tell her you called?"

"No, please don't." I checked the time. Too late to drop by tonight. "I want to surprise her."

I called Eunice, but her answering service picked up. I left messages for her and R. J., then addressed an envelope to Myrna Lewis. Before dropping the photo of little Kaithlin and her mother in the outgoing mail, I again studied Reva Warren's solemn face and plain appearance, in contrast to Kaithlin's lively beauty and mischievous charm. Who would believe they were mother and daughter? When had I thought that before?

I checked my mailbox and found a copy of the art department's sketch of Kaithlin, along with a glossy page torn from a catalog. The sketch was excellent. To my dismay, the salmon-pink bridesmaid dress on the catalog page appeared iridescent, with flounces, the bustle far larger than I had imagined.

"Don'tcha love it?" Rooney startled me, peering over my shoulder.

"Don't ever sneak up on me like that again!" I protested.

"Sorry," he said, his expression wounded. "I thought you saw me."

I sighed. "How are Angel and the kids?"

"Great," he said, his grin returning. "We thought the baby was coming the other night, but—false alarm." He focused on the page in my hand. "Misty already got her dress."

"This one?" I asked, hoping to be wrong.

"She loves it. Angel says she looks adorable."

Damn, I thought, too late now to change Angel's mind.

"You might think it's silly for us to be having a nice church wedding now. You know," he said self-consciously, "with the kids and all. But it's my first time and Angel never had one. Her parents signed for her to get married the first time and some clerk down at the marriage license bureau officiated. She was only a kid, didn't even have a flower to hold.

"This time," he said, dreamy-eyed, "is special. It's for good." His smile wasn't the usual goofy grin. It was almost appealing.

I checked the library on the way out, surprised to find

Onnie still working. The lenses in her computer glasses glowed green as she squinted at the screen.

"Got involved," she explained, her smile tight. "Called my sister to give Darryl his supper and put him to bed."

"Find anything promising?"

"Lord have mercy." She pushed away from the screen, her expression weary. "I never knew how many folks disappeared, or wanted to. Forget milk cartons. I've got enough right here to print them on toilet paper, a new face on every square. You 'member that big, fiery, high-speed rail crash in London a while back? The death toll started out high 'cause of all the passengers missing and presumed dead. It dwindled after they cut apart the molten wreckage and the bodies weren't there."

I looked at her quizzically.

"Where were they?" she asked, blinking up at me, her coal-black eyes intent. "I mean, if you narrowly escaped a deadly disaster, what would you do first?"

"Have sex," I said truthfully, "maybe a stiff drink, kiss the ground, hug loved ones, say a prayer, call the newspaper. Not necessarily in that order."

"Me too," she agreed, nodding thoughtfully, " 'cept maybe for the sex."

"Trust me," I said.

"Is that experience talking?" She coyly arched an eyebrow. "You'd think all of the above," she went on, when I did not answer, "but noooooo. Weeks, months after the crash, there were sightings of people presumed dead and gone. Turns out dozens of commuters seized the moment and made a run for it, to disappear and launch new lives under new names."

I pulled up a chair and read the story on her screen. "Amazing," I said, "how many people are willing to walk away from everything in a heartbeat."

When disaster struck, as fellow commuters died, survivors didn't run for help, they just ran, to shed their pasts as snakes do their skin. They saw misfortune as an escape route. That crash was accidental. How many others deliberately create their own disaster? Maybe Kaithlin was ahead of her time.

I drove home, the radio off, the windows open to the serenade of boat whistles, wind, and night birds on the causeway.

The courtyard patio was dark, the exterior light burned out. A car door slammed somewhere on the street behind me, and I picked up my pace. I usually have house keys in hand before leaving the car, but this time, my mind cluttered, I wasn't thinking. I groped hurriedly for the keys as quick footsteps gained on me.

I had warned my landlady and fellow tenants about a recent rash of nighttime robberies, motorists followed home and accosted at their own front doors. I had urged caution, then failed to heed my own advice.

I glanced fearfully over my shoulder. A man moved fast through the shadows, directly toward me. Too late to find the key. I flung my open purse into the thick shrubbery, scattering the contents, then whirled to face him, heart pounding.

"You son-of-a-bitch! Don't even think about it! Get the hell out of here!"

He stopped short. "What's wrong?" he said. "Britt? Are

you mad at me?"

Lights bloomed in other apartments. Inside mine, Bitsy yapped frantically, hurling herself at the door.

He stepped closer.

"Oh, jeez," I said. "Help me find my keys before somebody calls the cops."

We were on all fours in the bushes retrieving my possessions when Mr. Goldstein appeared in pajamas, brandishing a baseball bat in his best Mark McGwire imitation. His wife, close behind him in her bathrobe, waved her broom.

"Careful, Hy, he might have a gun! Britt, are you all right?"

"He's one of the good guys," I said, embarrassed. Fitzgerald apologetically explained that he was delivering my overnight bag, which he had tracked down from the airline.

We said good night, went inside, gazed at each other, and grinned. "So that's how you welcome visitors. No wonder you're not married."

"Sorry, I thought you were a robber."

"Well, you scared the bejesus out of me. I was ready to assume the position, spread my legs, and give you my wallet."

"Keep the wallet," I said, and walked into his arms.

"I know you have somebody," he murmured, voice husky in my ear.

"Where'd you hear that?"

He stopped kissing me long enough for his lips to shape the word. "Emery."

"He's got a big mouth."

We stayed stitched together at the lips for several minutes. "I'll make some coffee," I said, pushing him away as we came up for air.

"Uh-oh," he said. "Not exactly the words I hoped to hear."

"I'm sorry. It's just that . . . what happened in Daytona was due to the intensity of the moment. We don't even know each other."

He sighed. "That other guy?"

"No. That's over," I said. The words sounded shockingly final to my ears. "It's you and me, our jobs, this story, us both being involved in the case. It's unprofessional."

"We could low-key it."

Where had I heard that before?

"Just until the case is closed or pushed onto a back burner. Looks like that's happening sooner than later. Emery's not on the case full-time anymore," he explained. "They've already got him shouldering a full workload again."

"You're sure?"

"Hey, no new leads, nothing's panned out. The department's spread thin, the brass can't justify the manpower. Lousy for the victim, good for us. No story, no problem."

"Right. But when that happens, you go home," I said, "three hundred and fifty miles away. How romantic."

"That's not so far." He took my hand. "Why not just go for the ride and see where it takes us?"

"Maybe," I said. "You want decaf?"

"Naw." He sighed. "Gimme the hard stuff."

The crime lab, he said, tried using fiberoptic light sources to shadow, then photograph, the handwriting impressions on the bedside notebook from Kaithlin's room. No luck. The legal pad had been sent on to the FBI lab in Washington in the hope that more sophisticated techniques could decipher something legible.

"Those guys up there are good," he said hopefully. "They've got a machine made in England, originally designed to detect fingerprints on paper. In some cases, they've successfully raised handwriting impressions from six sheets down."

Rychek had also run a check on Zachary Marsh. "Emery was pissed off at 'im. Wanted to see who the hell he was."

"What's his story?"

"Ran a Rolls dealership, like he said. Married for eighteen years. She dumped him when he got too sick to work. Ran off with an old high school boyfriend, taking most of his bank account and their two teenagers with 'er."

He and Rychek had talked to Kagan, the lawyer whose office number appeared repeatedly on Kaithlin's hotel bill. He denied knowing her.

"Lots of people call his office every day, he said. Swore he never met her, never talked to her."

"A guy like him would remember somebody like her," I said.

"Emery also ran the names of the hotel housekeepers and the bellmen by him, on the off chance they made the calls."

"They wouldn't bill local calls to her room," I said, "and any of the hotel employees who needed a lawyer would look for somebody bilingual who handles immigration cases. It wouldn't be him."

"I agree." Fitzgerald paused as we carried our coffee

mugs into the living room. "What's that? You hear something?"

I stopped to listen, then heard it too: a low familiar singsong rumble accompanied by a faint grinding sound. Fitzgerald gingerly pushed open the bathroom door.

Billy Boots sat in the sink, eyes closed, chewing contentedly on my toothbrush, still in its wall-mounted holder.

He stopped the loud purring and opened his eyes to stare.

"You let him do that?" Fitzgerald frowned.

"Of course not." I snatched my cat out of the sink, plucking bristles from his whiskers. "This can't be good for him."

"Or you," Fitzgerald said. "Or me." He grimaced and licked his sexy lips, so recently pressed to mine.

"Very funny," I said, clinging to Billy, whose tail lashed fitfully as he fixed a baleful, yellow-eyed stare on Fitzgerald.

"You plan on using that toothbrush again?"

"Only before dates with you."

He kissed me good night gingerly and worked his mouth in the manner of a professional wine taster. "A hint of catnip," he said. "That must be what turns me on."

"Either that," I agreed, "or the hair-ball medication."

We made a date for dinner the next night. "See you then." He gently ran his thumb along the line of my jaw the way he did the first time. Was it him I wanted, or a warm, friendly body next to mine? I searched his eyes for the answer, found none, and let him walk away, out into the night. I immediately regretted that he was gone.

I called Rychek first thing in the morning.

"I'm up to my ass in alligators here, kid."

"What's this I hear about Jordan being pushed to the back burner?" I asked. "Isn't this way too soon? It's a big case."

He sighed. "That's why the city commission and the chamber of commerce would be delighted to see it go away. It ain't the only open homicide we got. Plus, we got teen curfew biting us on the ass."

Rowdy teens had recently invaded the South Beach club scene, fighting, drinking, crowding streets, damaging cars, and strong-arming adult customers. A curfew had been set but largely ignored.

"The commission is pissed," Rychek said. "They want enforcement, so the chief assigned a lotta the young detectives to a special squad. They're sweeping South Beach every night. Their caseloads are falling on us."

"Kagan must be lying about the phone calls. Can't you lean on him, subpoena his files?"

"There ain't enough to get a subpoena and the man's a lawyer, for chrissake. This ain't the old days, kid."

"But you can't just give up," I argued.

"Never said I did. Something new surfaces, I'll be the first to run it down. But we got nothing right now, 'cept a lotta other cases we're more likely to close."

Already running late, I had a stop to make first.

"Has he been troubled about anything lately?" the doctor asked. "Changes or traumas at home?"

Billy Boots crouched sullenly on the examining table, cranky and glaring.

"I was out of town briefly, but that can't be it. He'd

already chewed through four toothbrushes before I left."

She listened to his heart with her stethoscope. "How's his appetite?"

"Fine. He steals the dog's food and the dog steals his. Each one wants what the other has, just like people."

"Do they get along?"

"I think they're friends."

"It could be," she said, studying his chart, "that he feels a lack of attention or just likes the minty taste left on the toothbrush. He may need to see a psychotherapist. I can give you the number of someone."

A shrink? If anybody in my household was in need of a shrink it wasn't my cat, it was me.

I held him all the way home, stroking his glossy fur, promising him more time, more toys, more treats. What kind of mother would I be? How could I expect to ever nurture a child when life with me had turned my own cat into an obsessive-compulsive toothbrush-gnawing neurotic?

The temperature had suddenly soared back to 80 degrees, catching by surprise people now sweltering in sweaters and long sleeves. Bright, bare limbs and colorful sails flashed in foamy green water on either side of the Rickenbacker Causeway to Key Biscayne. Ponce de Leon sailed into the bay to claim the island for a Spanish king five hundred years ago. What would he think today, I wondered, of this towering, multi-laned toll bridge favored by cyclists, windsurfers, kayakers, and divers?

A huge gumbo limbo, pines, and buttonwood trees shaded the oceanfront building where Dallas Suarez lived. About twenty-five years old, it was modest in size, unlike the soaring structures built today with hundreds of units.

I rang her doorbell at nearly nine, hoping she wasn't already gone or still asleep.

I heard scurrying, as a small commotion erupted inside. Did I interrupt something? I wondered. Did the femme fatale linked to murder, adultery, and big bucks still run true to form?

Someone peered through a peephole, then opened the door. The same black hair, the same woman in the ten-year-old news clips, but far from the sultry siren I was prepared to dislike. Her face looked sunny and free of makeup, with just a trace of lipstick. Large fawnlike brown eyes, freckles sprinkled across her nose. The eyes, exquisitely soft, contrasted startlingly with her hard body. She was fit and athletic, her black tights and oversized white shirt nearly hiding the fact that she was about six months pregnant. The commotion I'd heard had been a little girl, about three, scampering to the door. Her halo of curly hair was lighter, but she had her mother's eyes.

"Alexa." The mother collared the little one. "Stay in here with Mommy, you can't go out now." Her voice was throaty, her words warm, with the faintest trace of an accent.

"Dallas Suarez?"

"Svenson." She smiled. "Dallas Svenson. I've been married for some time."

Her eyes widened slightly at my name. "Can I talk to you about what happened ten years ago?" I asked.

She stepped back, took a deep breath, and glanced away for a moment, blinking, as though my appearance was painful. "I was afraid of this," she murmured. Her Bambi eyes refocused on me. "I was afraid the press might look me up."

"I have no plans to rehash old news," I assured her. "I'm just trying to piece things together, to find out where Kaithlin was all this time."

Polite but wary, she let me in. We sat in a sunny break-fast room, her little girl busy nearby with a coloring book and crayons.

"I almost didn't recognize you," I said.

She smiled and patted her stomach. "I'm not surprised. I guess it's obvious I'm not doing much skydiving, flying, or skiing these days. Life changes when you have kids, you know."

"But you look happy, as though you have no regrets."

"Happy? Yes," she said. "Regrets, sure. Have you seen him?" She lowered her eyes. "Have you see R. J.?"

I nodded.

"How is he?"

"Older," I said. "Bitter,"

"Who could blame him?" she said. "Even I didn't believe him. Oh, I did at first. But the police kept ques-tioning me. They were so sure. Everybody believed he did it. So, eventually, I believed it too. I should have known better."

"Why did he prefer you to his wife?"

"That was the hell of it," she said, smile rueful. "He didn't. He loved her. I knew he'd never get her out of his system, no matter what he said."

"What was she like?"

"Stupid," she said, without hesitation. "She had to be the

world's most stupid woman. He craved attention, needed love and affection, tender loving care. He didn't get it from her."

"His reputation and his press clippings seem to indicate that he never lacked attention."

She clasped her hands, taking a deep breath. An impressive diamond-studded wedding band and an oval amethyst winked on her long slender fingers. "I thought the same thing when we met. That facade of his masked a great many insecurities. He looked like a Greek god, larger than life, with a roguish, wild-Indian sort of charm. He never lied about being married. He had to qualify when he bought the plane. I was his flight instructor. We both loved to fly. What started as a harmless flirtation became serious for me once I got to know the man. When I saw his sensitive, vulnerable side, I fell."

She sighed, soft eyes caressing her little girl.

"He hated the family business," she said. "It was all his parents thought about when he was growing up. They gave him everything except what all kids crave; that's why he ran wild. Ironically, he finally married a woman he loved and she rejected him too, by becoming involved with the same rival, the family stores."

"But it all would have been his eventually."

"He wanted no part of it." She stopped to praise a picture colored by little Alexa. "They insisted he study business administration," she continued, lifting the child onto her lap. "He hated that. Did you know he wanted to study architecture?"

"No," I said. "I never heard that."

"You should see his sketches. He was so talented,

absolutely wonderful. He talked about it all the time. He dreamed of designing buildings, timeless structures to shelter people and their children. He had no interest in operating retail stores, selling cosmetics, clothes, and jewelry.

"It was a crazy time," she reflected, smoothing her little girl's hair. "It was the usual thing. The same sad story. You always hear it. I loved him, he loved her and she loved . . ."—her voice trailed off—"who knows? Her picture was always in the newspaper. She was a community activist, she helped women, was involved in civic projects that were good public relations for the company, but what did she ever do for him? She couldn't even get pregnant, and he wanted a family more than anything."

"It meant money," I said cynically. "His parents promised—"

"He didn't care about the money," she said derisively. The child abruptly wriggled off her lap and eluded her grasp.

"Wanna go out, wanna go," the little girl insisted, romping toward the door.

"She's so willful." Dallas rolled her eyes in mock desperation. "What will I do with her?"

"Wait till she's sixteen," I said, thinking of Kaithlin.

Recaptured after a minor skirmish and a few wails, the child settled down with a cookie and crayons to work on another picture.

"Where were we?" Dallas asked. "Oh, right. R. J. didn't care about the money. He believed a baby would save the marriage, make it work. That Kaithlin would stay home to be a wife and mother. She'd promised to work only until they had a family. But it didn't happen. R. J. had a wife, they slept in the same bed, but he was lonely. When they talked about it, she suggested he become more involved in Jordan's, to put on a suit and go to the office every day. He tried, but he hated it."

"What about the money?" I said. "The prosecutors and the jury believed he stole it, in part to lavish on you."

She looked pensive. "I don't want to be quoted." She paused again, white teeth gnawing at her full lower lip. "He might have," she finally said. "He was so jealous of the business. If he took the money it was because he felt they owed him. I admit, we spent a lot. He bought me presents. We took overnight trips when we could, to the islands, did some scuba-diving and gambling. We flew to Vegas a few times after they separated. Even went to the Kentucky Derby that year."

"Was he a big loser?"

"Actually, no. R. J.'s a good gambler, won big-time. Especially at blackjack. We had fun; he was generous. I took expensive gifts, but I was beginning to realize he'd never divorce her, even though he kept saying it was inevitable. I kept hoping, but I could see he thought about her, talked about her, all the time.

"My parents were humiliated when it happened. They didn't know I'd been seeing a married man. Once she was missing and he became a suspect, the newspaper stories were horrible. I was questioned, had to testify. My parents were furious. I was so ashamed. Now I'm ashamed that I testified against him. But, you see, everybody said he did it. They kept saying it until I believed it and was devastated, convinced I had unknowingly contributed to her death. Then he said all those hurtful things when he testi-fied, that I meant nothing to him. I was a basket case. I still loved him. I was a mess." She gave an ironic, self-deprecating laugh. "Took me years to get past it, to get myself grounded again.

"I wish him well," she said earnestly. "I wish all the hap-piness in the world for him. He deserves it. He married the wrong woman, he made mistakes, but he's not a bad man."

"Have you contacted him?" I asked, as we walked to the door.

"Of course not," she said emphatically. "He wouldn't want to hear from me after all that happened. And I'm a happily married woman now, with children."

"What does your husband do?" I asked.

She smiled. "He's an architect."

13

Martin Kagan appeared more successful than I expected. His shiny new midnight-blue Cadil-lac—bearing the vanity tag ACQUIT—was parked in the narrow alley beside his building. His thick office car-peting looked fresh and new, and the man actually had a secretary.

Well past middle age, tall and thin, she wore a simple, inexpensive business suit and a harried expression.

"Is he in?" I asked.

Startled, she stared up, mouth half open. Fumbling with her glasses, she peered curiously at me through the thick lenses. "Do you have an appointment?"

"Is that affidavit ready yet?" a man bellowed from an inner office. "What the hell is this? I don't have all day!"

She reacted as though dodging a bullet. "Right away, sir."

She shuffled through some papers and hurried into his office, document in hand.

The phone was ringing when she emerged. She spoke briefly to a wrong number whose Spanish she could not comprehend, then turned to me apologetically. "I'm sorry. Who shall I say is here?"

A door burst open and Martin Kagan hurtled out as though shot from a cannon.

"What the hell *is* this shit?" he demanded. Small and sallow-skinned, he had dark hair plastered so firmly in place that I doubted a hurricane-force wind could disturb it. He appeared to be wearing football shoulder pads under his expensive suit jacket.

"Can't you get anything right?" he bawled. "Doesn't that expensive machine have a goddamn spell check? Look at this! Look at this!"

He rudely pointed out a minor misspelling.

"Sorry, sir, but you were in such a hurry." Her hands shook as she took the document back to correct.

His furtive eyes flicked my way with what appeared to be a glimmer of recognition. "Can I help you with something?" he asked, thick fingers plucking fastidiously at the cuffs of his fancy monogrammed shirt.

"Yes," I said. "A few minutes of your time."

He checked his gold watch. "Sure, just let me make a call first."

He snatched the corrected page from his secretary's

uncertain hand, stormed back into his lair, and slammed the door.

"Is he always that obnoxious?" I asked softly. A light flickered in the phone set on her desk as he made his call.

She nodded, eyes glistening.

"Why do you put up with it?"

"I need the job," she whispered hopelessly.

"Right." A younger, bilingual secretary would walk in a heartbeat, probably land a better job the same day. But this woman, with no wedding ring, in her sensible support hose and homely, low-heeled, no-nonsense shoes, had no such luxury. Jobs are scarce in Miami for self-supporting Anglo women of a certain age, no matter how impressive their *résumés*.

Her name was Frances Haehle. "I have to hand it to you," I commiserated while waiting. "The stress factor must be high. You're the only one here? You do everything?"

"I'm it." She sniffed. "I'm used to it, but these last few weeks he's been—"

Kagan's office door cracked open. "Come in, Ms. Montero."

"I didn't think you remembered me," I said.

"Oh, I've seen you around the justice building, seen your byline. What can I do for you?"

My impressions of Kagan, as he darted from courtroom to courtroom, had been that of a man who embarrassed other lawyers. Never ready to proceed, never ready for trial, always unprepared, his defense weapon fired blanks. When he represented a client, everybody knew a guilty plea would follow. But today he appeared supremely confident as he motioned me to a leather chair.

"I'm sure you've heard about the Jordan case."

"Sure, who hasn't? Hell of a thing."

"Was Kaithlin Jordan your client?"

"No, no," he said vigorously, then cocked his head, as though puzzled. His sharp chin and bright dark eyes gave him a cunning ferretlike look. "You know, some detectives stopped by here the other day and asked the same question. I'll tell you exactly what I told them. Never met the woman. Never heard from her. My secretary will tell you the same thing." He picked up a file, dismissing me.

I remained seated. "Perhaps you met before her supposed murder ten years ago."

Leaning back in his shiny leather chair, he looked down his nose as though I was something nasty he had stepped in.

"Perhaps in school," I suggested. "You both grew up here. Maybe you knew her as Kaithlin Warren. Her mother's first name was Reva."

"Sorry." He shook his head. "I saw the pictures in the paper. Her picture. I'da remembered that."

"Your father would have loved this case," I continued. "It's right up his alley. An innocent man on death row."

Kagan's ferret eyes darted around the room.

"Too bad he wasn't here for it," I said.

He consulted his gold Rolex. "I hafta be in court in ten minutes," he said abruptly. "Sorry I can't help you." On his feet, suddenly a man in a hurry, he snatched his leather briefcase as he ushered me out.

"If you remember anything," I said, "please call me." I tried to hand him my business card.

"Yeah, yeah." He waved it off impatiently. "Leave it with

my secretary on your way out."

Frances was on the phone as I left, but I saw the other button light up. I parked down the block in the T-Bird, sat, and watched for forty-five minutes. The man in a hurry never left his office. He didn't go to court.

So I did. I went to the fifth-floor clerk's office. Each lawyer has an identification number. Using that number you can pull up every case assigned to any particular attorney in Miami-Dade. Kagan was attorney of record for defendants charged with robbery, possession of stolen property, lewd behavior, and resisting arrest. That charming clientele failed to reflect any sudden surge in business, nothing to account for his recent prosperity, new car, new suit, new carpet. Even his fine leather briefcase looked brand-new.

I called Onnie. "Anything?"

"Naw." She sounded dispirited. "Thought I nailed her first thing this morning. Successful real estate woman, right age, physical description, turned up missing at the right time, out of Baja California. Thought for sure it was her."

"Maybe it is," I said quickly.

"Nope. They found this one, in a shallow grave in the desert."

"Jeez," I said, disappointed. "What a shame."

"The shallow grave, or her not being Kaithlin Jordan?"

"Both."

"Yeah," she said bleakly. "I'm still on it."

I called Frances, Kagan's secretary. She said he was out. "Good," I said. "Let's have lunch. We can go somewhere close by."

"I can't leave the phones, I'm the only one here."

"Put them on service," I coaxed. "You'll be back in an hour."

"I really can't," she said regretfully.

"Okay," I said. "I'll bring lunch to you. We can eat at your desk."

"I don't think that would be wise," she said carefully.

"He wouldn't be happy to come back and find me there?"

"You've got that right."

"He was upset by my visit this morning?"

"Off the wall," she said.

"Well, you have to eat lunch sometime."

"I brought something. Some yogurt."

I sighed. "I just thought maybe we could talk, confidentially, about a story I'm working on."

"I have to go over to the justice building later, to file some motions for him," she offered hesitantly. "I could meet you for a quick cup of coffee."

Ten floors of misery, the Dade County Jail stands directly across the street from the justice building. A covered walkway links them four stories above traffic, so prisoners are protected from the temptations of fresh air, open sky, and outside influences as they are marched to court.

Frances completed her work at the clerk's office, called me, and walked to the far side of the jail, where I swooped by in my T-Bird to scoop her off the street corner. She scanned the block to see if anyone was watching before ducking into my car, as though we were engaged in some clandestine operation.

The first-floor coffee shop at Cedars of Lebanon Hospital several blocks away wasn't crowded. Frances leaned back, eyes roving the room with interest, as though it had been some time since she had sat in public with someone over a snack.

"The story you came to see my boss about," she said, after we ordered tea and pastries. "It's the Jordan case, isn't it?"

I nodded.

"I've been reading about it," she said, eyes downcast.

"It's a fascinating story," I said.

"I was sure that's why you came. Did you know the police came to ask him about it too?"

"Yes," I said. "That would be Detective Rychek."

"Right. How did they make the connection to him?" she asked, her expression intent.

"Kaithlin Jordan's hotel bill reflected phone calls to your office."

"Ah." She nodded slowly. "So that was it."

"But he denies they ever spoke. Said you'd confirm that."

"That's what he told me to tell the detective."

"Is it true?"

Her pale fingers toyed with her napkin. The nails were blunt, without polish. "I can't be quoted," she blurted out. "Whatever I tell you is background and you can't divulge the source. Is that agreed?"

I did so reluctantly, after trying without success to persuade her to talk on the record.

"Did she call him?"

"Many times. I could lose my job over this." She leaned forward, lips tight. "I'm in trouble if I lose this job, but I don't want to go to jail."

"If your boss did something wrong, why should you be implicated? You're just an innocent bystander, working for an honest living in a town where it isn't easy."

"I've never been in trouble," she said, "not even a jay-walking ticket." She used her napkin to blot away a tear with a quick embarrassed motion.

"I'm sure," I said. "How did he know Kaithlin?"

"She was the mystery woman," she whispered. "The one I was never supposed to see."

"But you did see her?"

"Once."

"What happened?"

"When she called, it was always a major occasion. I've never seen him as excited about a client. He even called in the Digger."

"The Digger?"

"You know, that private detective. Dan Rothman. Everybody calls him the Digger. He's the one my boss always uses when he has to hire an investigator."

The mystery woman first called Kagan nearly eight months earlier, Frances said. She left no name or number, but twenty-four hours later a manila envelope arrived, no return address. Kagan's new prosperity arrived with it, flourishing as more envelopes followed.

"He bought a new Cadillac, new suits, began to update the office equipment," she said.

"So he did some legal work for her?"

Frances shook her head. "Not that I saw. No legal documents were ever drawn up, no letters dictated, no official file opened. I don't think he knew exactly who or where she was. He kept urging me to try to get her name or number, but she always refused to leave it. Caller ID only indicated that her calls were from out of the area. Call return was blocked. Eventually he called in the Digger. But everything was secret. They'd stop talking when I walked in."

"Did they seem worried or apprehensive?"

"Quite the contrary." She gave a little laugh. "A couple of months ago, they were absolutely giddy, celebrating and high-fiving."

"There have to be records."

"There is something"—she lowered her voice—"a fat folder. I saw it open on his desk one day after the Digger came in. But he never sent it out to be filed. He keeps it locked in his desk."

The mystery woman often called Kagan for lengthy conversations. Envelopes arrived about once a month. Several weeks ago, Frances said, the routine suddenly changed. The mystery woman called and, for the first time, left a number, insisting he contact her at once. The number was local.

Startled, the lawyer canceled all other appointments and hastily summoned the Digger to a private conference. When the woman called again, a face-to-face meeting was arranged.

"So, that's when you saw her?"

"I wasn't supposed to. My boss sent me home early, something he never does. He insisted, practically shoved me out the door. I suspected something shady or a sexual liaison. That's happened before. But he usually doesn't care

197

if I'm there. He just says he doesn't want to be disturbed. After I left, I stopped at the post office and then, on my way to the Metro Mover, a storm began to blow up all of a sudden. The sky was getting dark. I have a long walk to make my connection and he'd rushed me out in such a hurry I forgot my umbrella, a little collapsible one that I keep in my desk. So I went back to get it, let myself in with my key, and heard them in his office. She was already there."

"What did you hear?"

"Quarreling; they were threatening each other. It was frightening, as though they might come to blows."

"What were they saying?"

"I didn't hear it all. But she was upset about something she'd seen on television. Called him a liar and a thief, said he could be disbarred or go to jail. He laughed, called her names, and said she was the one who stood to lose everything, not him. They accused each other of all sorts of things, extortion, blackmail, lying, stealing. It was horrible. I slipped out the door before they heard me.

"It was already raining. I was under the awning of the building next door, opening my umbrella, when she came out. She was upset, her face red, crying. She walked right past me, to a cabstand. She was putting on big sunglasses and a scarf, but I got a good look at her face first.

"A day or two later, they spoke on the phone again. I only heard snatches of what was said, but it sounded as though they'd calmed down and reached some sort of agreement. She refused to come to the office again; I heard that. He said he would see her, go to meet her, that evening. She never called again."

"What did she look like?" I asked.

"Very attractive. I never saw her in person again after that day," she said, "but I saw her in your newspaper, after they identified her as the dead woman on the beach. When I saw the story, I counted back the days. Her body was found the morning after he arranged to meet her. You realize what that means?"

She stared bleakly across the table at me, shoulders sagging, her fingers working nervously together.

"I didn't have my glasses on when you walked in this morning. For a moment I thought you were her. I knew, of course, that you couldn't be. I guess I was somehow hoping to be wrong . . ."

"Will you tell all this to the detective?"

"I can't." Her mouth quivered.

"Why? How important is keeping your job if—"

"It's more than that," she interrupted. "If he committed a crime, he won't go down alone. That's what he's like. I could be in serious trouble. If he even suspected that I talked to you—."

"That won't happen," I assured her.

"Oh, my God," she said suddenly, "look at the time! I have to get back. Remember, we never talked." She folded her untouched pastry into a paper napkin and gathered her things.

She carefully checked to be sure no one was watching before exiting my car two blocks from Kagan's office, then rushed away, nearly stumbling on the curb in her haste.

I walked into the newsroom, scooped up my ringing phone, and slid into my chair.

"I saw you," the caller said softly, "early the other

morning, jogging in the rain."

He *had* been watching. "Yes, that was me." I tried to sound cheerful.

"You demonstrate an admirable dedication to physical fitness, or you have trouble sleeping. Which is it?"

I didn't answer.

"Saw you start to limp. Hope you didn't pull a muscle. Looked more like a charley horse or a cramp," he said.

"Oh?" I said, as though I didn't recall.

"You never looked up," he said accusingly. "You knew I was there."

"Tsk, I forgot," I said lightly. "That's right, your building is somewhere along that stretch."

"I have something for you." He lowered his voice to a suggestive register. "A story."

"Oh?" I rolled up to my terminal and opened a file.

"Yes but, tsk, I forgot."

"Don't tease me, Zack. I'm in no mood for games. Come on," I coaxed, "spill it. I won't forget again."

"One of those big earthmoving machines the city uses for beach maintenance backed over a sleeping sunbather. An older man. Tourist, I think."

"Oh, no. How badly is he hurt?" I took notes.

"He didn't look good. The medics worked on him. He was trapped underneath. They had to jack up the whole damn machine to get him out. They took him away a little while ago. The cops and the driver are still there."

"You should have called me right away," I said.

"I did, but you didn't answer."

"I just walked in the door. Thanks, Zack. I appreciate it."

"Wave next time," he demanded.

I trotted up to the city desk and asked Tubbs to assign a reporter. He scanned the room. "You'll have to take it, Britt. I've got nobody else."

"But I'm working Jordan full time," I protested.

"Is there a new development for the street? I didn't see anything from you on the budget."

"No," I admitted, "but I'm working leads."

"Britt?" Gretchen glanced up from her editing screen. "If you're tired of your beat and want a change, say so. Until then, I suggest you take this story and follow your leads later."

She smirked as I left.

The scene was precisely as Marsh reported. The machine operator was distraught, either because of the victim's injuries or the joint the cops had just found in the cab of his bulldozer. His boss, his union rep, an assistant city manager, and a city attorney were present. None looked happy to see me.

The uniformed cop handling it said that the driver had been rearranging the beach, eroded by heavy winds and waves the night before. The driver insisted that as he pushed drifted sand, the tourist must have spread out his beach towel and reclined behind one of the artificial dunes being created. The operator was backing up and never saw the man, he said, until passersby screamed that someone was caught under the machine.

The victim's leg was broken and his pelvis crushed, among other injuries.

I ignored the creepy sensation that I was centered in the crosshairs of a zoom lens focused from above. At the first opportunity, I waved.

About to leave, I saw Emery Rychek trudging across the sand. "Hey, kid, it's *déjà vu* all over again."

"They have you working this too?" I protested, aware the city would require an intense investigation and mountains of paperwork due to the potential liability.

"I'm the man," he said grimly. "Looks like you're off the story too."

"They didn't have anybody else."

"Welcome to the club," he said.

Once greeted by the city hall staffers, Rychek was too busy to talk. Besides, I told myself, Frances had sworn me to secrecy, and neither Rychek nor Fitzgerald would consider a twenty-year-old news flash about Kaithlin's baby more than ancient gossip. That did not explain why I didn't tell my editors. Would the sordid story about the Jordans' secret love child interest them? I was afraid it might. Myrna Lewis's crack about garbage and gossip must have stung more than I realized.

I called the ER at county hospital on the way back to the office. The hapless tourist was still alive, en route to surgery.

As I drove toward Biscayne Boulevard moments later, my cell phone startled me.

"Britt! This is Onnie, in the library. I think I've got a hit! I think I found her!"

"Great! You're sure?" I hit the brake and swooped off the exit ramp, a red light ahead.

"Hell, no. No way to be sure. But she definitely looks good."

"I'm five minutes away. I'll be right there."

14

H er name is Shannon Broussard, a Seattle woman reported missing by her husband, Preston, three weeks ago!" Onnie handed me the printout, her face as excited as I felt.

"Is there a picture?"

"No, but her description fits Kaithlin Jordan to a T. Husband owns a software company. Two little girls, five and seven."

Shannon Broussard had failed to return from a three-day shopping trip to New York. She had boarded her flight in Seattle but never checked into her Manhattan hotel, the story said.

Onnie hovered behind my chair as I called Broussard's Seattle company, my heart pounding. His personal assistant said he was not in the office and not expected.

"I'm calling about his wife," I said.

"You have news?" she said quickly.

"I'm not sure," I said. "It's possible."

She took my number. He called in less than five minutes.

"You're in Miami?" He sounded bewildered. "My assistant said you called about Shannon."

"She hasn't been located yet?"

"No," he said, disappointed. He clearly hoped I had called with answers, not questions. "She disappeared in New York City. I just returned from there—with nothing."

"Was she originally from Miami? Did she ever speak of it?"

"No. She's from the Midwest." He sounded weary. "You have her confused with someone else."

"When did you meet your wife? How long have you known her?"

"What is this?" he said angrily. "What kind of question is that? We've been married for almost nine years."

"I'm sorry," I said. "I was just hoping to eliminate the possibility up front."

"What possibility?"

"A few weeks ago," I said carefully, "a woman was found dead in Miami Beach. We're trying to determine where she came from, attempting to match her to missing persons reports."

Silence. "Are you still there?" I asked.

"This . . . woman, she—she hasn't been identified?"

"She has and she hasn't. It's a long story that I won't burden you with unless the possibility exists that she might be your wife."

"How—how did this woman die?"

"She was murdered, drowned in the ocean."

"That's not my Shannon," he said quickly. "She was in New York, not Miami. She's an excellent swimmer. And she's not the sort of person anyone would deliberately hurt."

Children's voices clamored in the background. "Daddy, Daddy," one called, "is it Mommy?"

"Please hold on," he said. I heard him ask someone to take the children into another room.

"Sorry," he said, upon his return. "They miss her. We all do."

"Mr. Broussard," I said, "is there an inscription engraved

in your wife's wedding ring?"

"The same that's in mine," he said. *"You and no other."*

I felt no elation. Instead, my eyes blurred.

"Mr. Broussard," I said softly, "I think you should call our medical examiner's office or the police detective on the case."

"Oh, my God," he said. "No! It can't be."

He took down the names and numbers I gave him. "It's still possible," he said, voice cracking, "that this is all a coincidence. Isn't it?"

"I hope so," I said, certain that it was not.

I replaced the phone in its cradle gently, as though it was something fragile that might shatter.

"You did it," I told Onnie, who waited, eyes expectant. "The poor guy. I could hear the kids in the background."

We began a computer check of Seattle newspaper files for background on the Broussards.

The husband called back in less than thirty minutes, his voice shaky and distraught.

"I couldn't reach the detective," he said. "They left me on hold, then said he was out. The people at the medical examiner's office say they have the woman you mentioned under another name: Jordan. I don't understand. Can you please tell me what's going on? I'm on my way, but I couldn't get a direct flight so I won't be there until late. But I need information, some clue as to what's happening."

As I described the life of Kaithlin Jordan, "murdered" by her husband a decade ago, he began to sound relieved, repeating, "That isn't Shannon. That's not Shannon," over and over again.

"She wore an earring," I finally said. "A small open heart, in gold."

His breathing began to sound labored, as though he needed oxygen.

"Are you all right?" I asked.

"No," he gasped. "Last Mother's Day," he finally whispered. "I took the children to Tiffany's. They picked them out. She always wore them."

I had dozens of questions but he was rushing to the airport for the long flight ahead. He promised to call when he arrived, no matter how late.

"I hated it," I told Onnie later. "I could hear his heart break."

"We did him a favor," she said flatly. "It's better than never knowing, jumping every time the phone rings, searching faces in every crowd, always looking for his wife."

"But Onnie, he still doesn't realize she never was his wife. That it was all a lie."

"Nine years and two kids sounds more married than Kaithlin and R. J."

"Who, unfortunately, were never divorced."

The desk opted to hold the story until Kaithlin was positively identified as the woman Preston Broussard knew as his wife, Shannon.

Our computer search of Seattle society pages revealed that, though considered one of the city's best-dressed women, Shannon Broussard was notoriously camera-shy, a charming eccentricity which, in retrospect, made perfect sense. She raised funds for local charities and won trophies in amateur golf and tennis tournaments. Kaithlin the achiever, I thought.

A charming feature photo of her two children, Devon, then four, and Caitlin, age seven, with their father, a tall, lanky fellow, at a country club Easter-egg hunt indicated they had all been living the good life. What on earth brought her back here to a bad death?

I called Fitzgerald's hotel and left word canceling our dinner date because I had to work. Hopefully I'd be able to interview Broussard before police whisked him away and the media pack picked up his scent.

Lottie and I grabbed sandwiches in the News cafeteria. "Wonder if he's another R. J.," she drawled, as I filled her in. "You know how we tend to repeat our mistakes."

Was I oversensitive because the truth hurt? I wondered. I had confided to Lottie about Fitzgerald. Did she mean me?

"I doubt it," I said. "The guy sounds sweet. They have kids; apparently they were happy."

"If playing house with him was such a fun trip, what from here to Hades was she doing in *this* town? Lord knows, she'd been through enough to know you don't squat with your spurs on. Did ya see how good Eunice Jordan looked in some of the pictures I made at the airport? That woman's gotta be pushing seventy."

"She is elegant," I said. "In great shape."

"With a lotta help. Plastic surgeons have had at her like a Sunday roast." She glanced across the room and abruptly changed subjects. "Any brainstorms 'bout our weddin' gift for Angel and Rooney?"

I followed her gaze. The betrothed had finished dining at

a table across the cafeteria. Rooney, in his security uniform, reached out to steady the small blond as she struggled to her feet. Her belly bulged like that of a baby whale.

"Ain't they sweet?" Lottie said. "That baby's ready to see daylight any damn minute. Look at her, she can hardly waddle. You in on the office pool? She's already a week overdue."

"Stop looking at them." I wrapped the second half of my grilled-cheese-and-tomato sandwich in a paper napkin for later.

"Why?" Lottie reluctantly wrenched her eyes from the happy couple.

"They might come over." I drained my cup.

"Well, ain't you Miss Congeniality."

"I swear, Lottie, it's a disaster every time that woman crosses my path."

"Pshaw," she said, waving greetings their way. "That's all over. They're as happy as clams at high tide. Angel's got her act together now."

Our strategy, we decided, was to ambush Broussard at the airport. Until then, I returned to my desk to wrap up the story on the bulldozed tourist, who was still in surgery. Police had arrested the operator for marijuana possession, accident charges were pending, and he had been suspended from his job. Reached at home, he had no comment.

I called Marsh to thank him for the tip. "I saw you," he said playfully.

"I know, I know. I waved. Did you see me wave?"

"Oh, yes. In fact, I got it on tape. My new video cam arrived. The quality of the playback is excellent. I can count the buttons on your blouse."

Oh, swell. I grimaced. Why did the most innocuous conversation with this man always make me want to take a shower?

He asked about the Jordan story. "Looks like she was married," I confided, "living out west, with a couple of kids. The husband's flying in to make the ID. But don't repeat this to anyone till it's confirmed. Okay?"

He agreed, and I said I'd keep him informed. News sources love being kept abreast as a story develops.

I called Rothman, Kagan's private detective, and talked to his answering machine. The phone directory listed no street address. He probably worked out of his house. I also tried a second number, a beeper, then called Kagan's office and left my number on his emergency line.

Rothman called back almost immediately.

"Who is this?" His voice was loud, his brusque tone abrasive.

"I need to talk to you about Kaithlin Jordan," I said, and identified myself.

"You need to talk to me about who?" he said, even louder.

"Kaithlin Jordan."

"Don't know 'er."

"That's odd." I sounded confused, always easy for me. "I understood differently. I spent some time with Martin Kagan earlier today."

"*He* gave you *my* name?" He spoke the words distinctly and very slowly.

"Where else would I get it?" I said blithely. "I'm working on the story, this whole thing is about to hit the fan—"

Gloria signaled that I had another call.

"Whoops," I said. "Important call, another new development, have to get back to you." I hung up.

Good timing is rare. This was one of those golden moments. It was Kagan on the other line.

"What do you want?" he said rudely, realizing it was me.

"I'm working on the story," I said cheerfully. "The Kaithlin Jordan thing we talked about."

He gave a quick sigh of annoyance. "I told you. I never met her, never talked to her."

"I guess that's because you knew her by a different name," I said sweetly. "Shannon Broussard. From Seattle. Does that refresh your memory?"

"No idea what you're talking about," he said coldly.

"Well, that's odd," I said, perplexed. "See, I was just talking to Mr. Rothman."

He hesitated. "Who?"

"You know, your private eye, the Digger. You hired him to do some work on the case—"

"*He* told you that?"

"Well." I hesitated. "I'm sure I didn't misunderstand. I just spoke with him, not five minutes ago. He said that you—uh-oh, have to go now, the news meeting just started. Get back to you later."

The news meeting *had* just started, editors assembling in the glass office. As usual, I was not among them. Reporters are not invited.

Broussard's flight was on time, the airline said. Lottie and I left early. Miami International Airport was always bedlam at the height of the season, with parking spaces so rare that distant offsite parking lots use trams, trains, and buses to transport people to MIA from miles away. With patience and luck, we eventually snagged a spot in a short-term garage on actual airport property.

The cacophony of foreign languages added to the chaos and confusion as horns blared, exhaust billowed, and cabbies battled. There are those who are overwhelmed by it, those inured to it, and those who thrive and prosper: the pickpockets, the sharp-eyed thieves who loiter near airport phones to rip off credit card numbers as owners use them, and those who deliberately splash mustard, ketchup, or a drink onto startled travelers so they can profusely apologize, elaborately "assist," and otherwise distract them while accomplices steal their valuables.

Northern-bound travelers in heavy winter clothes rubbed shoulders with island-bound vacationers in shorts and T-shirts, as we staked out the concourse, hoping Broussard didn't change flights at the last minute. This one arrived thirty minutes late. The first to disembark strode by, rushing to make connections. The weary followed, loaded down with carry-ons, pulling hand carts, carrying babies.

"Over there, bet that's him!" I said. He resembled the man in the photo at the Easter-egg hunt. Tall and slender, with wavy brown hair and glasses, he looked about forty, distracted and fatigued. He wore a rumpled gray wool sports jacket over a white shirt open at the neck. His tie was loosened and he needed a shave. He seemed confused, almost a bit of a nerd, totally unlike R. J.

Though startled, he seemed relieved to be met by someone, even strangers eager to pick his brain. When I offered to drive him to his hotel, he agreed. He did not protest or even seem to notice when Lottie shot a few discreet photos. Instead, he eagerly asked questions, propounding his own theories.

"I thought about it all through the flight," he said, "wracking my brain. The dead woman isn't Shannon. Definitely. I'm positive. Shannon's jewelry must have been stolen and this other woman was wearing it."

Lottie and I exchanged dubious glances. "Anything is possible," I said reluctantly, trying not to encourage him. "Stranger things do happen."

I was tempted to display for him copies of Kaithlin's photos from the *News* library, in a thick manila folder tucked between the front seats. I didn't. He would live with the tragedy forever. Let him live with hope, I thought, for one more night.

"I called the detective again, from the plane," Broussard said, as I popped the trunk for his bag. "I have to meet him at nine A.M., at police headquarters. He said we'd go to the . . . to the morgue. We'll know then." His voice faded from hopeful to bleak.

We dropped Lottie off at the *News* building and drove across the causeway to the Deauville Hotel.

He checked in, asking me to wait while he went to his room. "I just need to call the kids," he said, "and say good night."

I sat in the bustling lobby wondering what it was like to learn the person you loved for years is a total stranger and gradually became aware that a disproportionate number of guests seemed to be statuesque African-American women in stiletto heels, short bright-red wigs, strapless tops, and neon micromini skirts. I remembered the hip-hop music convention in town as they strutted by, music blaring, to their various events, as a band in a nearby ballroom played a rousing version of "Hava Nagila" for bar mitzvah celebrants exuberantly dancing the hora. Only in Miami Beach, I thought.

Preston Broussard reappeared in twenty minutes. He wore the same rumpled shirt and jacket, minus the tie.

"Sorry I took so long," he said. "I hate leaving the kids again. I haven't even been to the office since Shannon disappeared. I wanted to be with Devon and Caitlin every minute. Shannon always talks about how important these formative years are. I don't want them to feel frightened or insecure, even if *I* do. Thank God my folks came up from San Diego to stay with them."

He had no appetite and wasn't thirsty, so we wandered out beyond the lighted pool area to the ocean beach. We sat on a wooden bench facing the starlit sea and a stretch of wet sand that smelled of salt and seaweed. Strolling couples laughed, and distant strains of music accompanied the tide's retreat beneath a full moon.

"I'm sorry to be the one who brought—"

"No," he interrupted. "I appreciate what you've done. I could have waited and come tomorrow, but I can't take doing nothing. I feel more alive when I'm looking for her. New York was horrible. The police—" He grimaced. "They were polite but disinterested. They seemed to think she'd never arrived there, so it wasn't their problem. And the Seattle police say she boarded a plane and left their jurisdiction, so it's not their case. They all took reports, but nobody really was doing anything."

Shannon Broussard's Seattle–New York flight had a brief stopover in Chicago, he said. "But she had no reason to disembark there."

If she did, I thought, she could have made a Miami connection without leaving the airport.

Shannon's trip to New York was not unusual, he said, a routine formed early in their marriage when she took buying trips for a small boutique she owned and operated until the birth of their first daughter. When business permitted, Broussard accompanied her, he said, to take in the Broadway shows. Women friends occasionally joined her, but she made the last trip alone. He hadn't been worried. "She's a sophisticated traveler," he said.

They met traveling, on a cross-country train ten years earlier. "I'll always be grateful to Amtrak." He smiled wistfully. "Heading home from Chicago on business, I like to take the scenic route, to see the big sky, reflect and recharge my batteries."

Both were aboard the Empire Builder, which traverses Montana, winding its way into Washington along the Canadian border. She appeared troubled, alone and withdrawn, when he first saw her in the dining car. That attracted him. "I guess I always want to be the rescuer," he said, leaning forward, elbows on his knees. "Even as a kid I brought home every sick stray animal, every sadsack misfit from school. Of course, Shannon was no misfit. She's an absolute knockout."

She was reluctant but he persisted and they were soon in the club car, where picture windows curved up into the ceilings surrounded by Montana's dramatic big sky, and he was pointing out the prairie dogs and silos, and then the stars. That's how it began.

"I assumed she'd been through a bad experience and I was right," he said. "It was obvious. She could scarcely speak about it. She was traumatized, shell-shocked by tragedy. She'd lost her entire family."

Her name was Shannon Sullivan, he said, from Stanley, Oklahoma, a small community devastated by a catastrophic class-four tornado. Twenty-seven had perished. "I remembered reading about it in the news at the time," he said. "A monster storm, a mile and a half wide, it left farm machinery twisted like pretzels.

"It was horrifying. Shannon's sister had an infant son. The twister tore the baby out of its mother's arms and killed them both. They didn't find the baby for days. Shannon was left literally alone in the world. Lost her parents, sister, best friend, everybody who ever meant anything to her. That's why family—our family—is so dear to her. That's why she would never willingly do this, never leave us."

They lived happily, he said, her past a tragic memory. Sometimes moody and melancholy, she always snapped out of it. He understood and supported her through the grief process.

I could see what drew Kaithlin to this sensitive and sympathetic man.

"Did you quarrel recently? Did she seem bored or restless?" I asked.

"Not at all." His words rang with the certainty forged by years of intimacy. "She loves being a mom, loves our life. I know it."

"Something must have changed recently."

He sighed. "I've thought a lot about it," he said. "Early

last summer, I saw something was bothering her. She seemed tense, less talkative, spent a great deal of time on the Internet. That's not like her. Shannon's a woman of action. Loves sports, taking the kids horseback riding, hiking, and boating. We live on Puget Sound."

"What was she doing on the Net?"

"I'm not sure exactly. I wish I'd paid more attention." He sighed and ran his hand through his hair. "I keep thinking of all the should-haves. She denied being troubled, said everything was fine, but I could see . . . I thought the kids were getting on her nerves, or maybe it was the pressure of all her volunteer work. She initially got on-line to conduct research for a charity campaign that would fund a program to assist young single mothers. That was one of her passions. Next thing I knew she was up there alone in her study for hours, often late at night."

"That's when she began to appear stressed?"

"That's right," he said thoughtfully. "At the time I didn't think the two were connected. Now I wonder. . . ."

"You have access to her computer, right?"

"I thought so. After she disappeared, a detective suggested I check her e-mail and computer files. I tried, even brought in a troubleshooter from my company. He had no luck either. The hard drive was wiped out. There must have been a crash, maybe a power failure."

"Perhaps it was deliberate."

He shook his head and glanced at me sharply. "That would mean that her disappearance—everything—was premeditated, that she planned to leave us. I'll never believe that."

Restless, he got to his feet, began to pace, then suddenly

turned to me.

"I'm already thinking ahead. What do you think of that?" he demanded, eyes wet. "Thinking ahead to the next lead after this one doesn't pan out. If Shannon was no longer on this planet," he said, his right hand over his heart, "I'd know it, I'd feel it. That means something, doesn't it?"

I murmured an encouraging sound but remembered all the similar words from people who refused to face reality.

Wide-awake, though exhausted, he wasn't ready to rest, so we walked south to the boardwalk.

"What was her financial situation when you met?" I asked. "Was she broke?"

"No, not at all. She had money of her own."

"Three million dollars?"

"Whoa." He smiled. "She was no multimillionaire, but she was comfortable. I think she had somewhere in the neighborhood of nine hundred thousand dollars."

"Nice neighborhood," I said. About a third of the missing money, I thought.

"Insurance and inheritance," he said. "From her family and the property that was destroyed. She invested. Shannon's a shrewd businesswoman. At first I wrote off her little boutique as an indulgence, a hobby, something to keep her busy, but she put it into the black in six months. Highly unusual for a small business."

"Did she keep her money separate after you married?"

He hesitated, as though debating whether to answer. "She mingled some with mine in our joint portfolio, kept a few accounts, investments of her own." He paused. "You know, discussing Shannon's personal business like this makes me extremely uncomfortable. If you're asking whether Shannon cleaned out her bank accounts when she left, she didn't. They're still intact. She's no Mata Hari, no schemer or swindler. You'd like her," he said hopefully. "I hope you two get to meet one day."

Casa Milagro loomed ahead.

"There's a guy up there," I said, "on the sixteenth floor. Sees everything down here. He's probably watching from a dark window right now with night-vision binoculars, telescopes, and zoom-lens cameras."

We stared up. "He witnessed the murder," I said. "He saw the whole thing."

Broussard looked startled. "So why didn't the police arrest the killer?" He gazed up at the high floor.

"He didn't call it in until much later, when the woman's body surfaced and began to float in on the tide. He was worried about his credibility. Wanted to be sure the cops wouldn't doubt his word. He's an odd guy."

"He must be. I thought there were good Samaritan laws," he said gravely. "When you see someone in danger, you have an obligation to help."

He stopped.

"Wait," he said, "if he saw it from up there, then this must be where it happened."

"That's where they brought her out of the water." I pointed.

"The poor woman, whoever she was." We both shivered in the cool night air. "What's that?" he asked.

Like a beating heart, the distant repetitive throb of a *bata* drum came from somewhere down on the beach, near the surf.

I strained to see in the darkness. "It's the full moon," I

said. "A salute to Chango, the Afro-Cuban god of thunder and lightning."

"So they actually practice that stuff here. What does it mean?"

"Chango," I said, "is a macho ladies' man and an avenger of evil."

"He must have his work cut out for him in this town," Broussard said bitterly.

We walked in silence for a time, listening and looking at the moon.

I gave him directions for his early appointment at police headquarters and said good night back at his hotel.

On the way home I checked my messages. Kagan and Rothman had left several each, some urgent. Let them wait until morning, I thought. Let them join the rest of us whose sleep would be troubled tonight.

15

I drank the liquid fire otherwise known as café Cubano after a restless night disturbed by thoughts of little girls far away and the father who would soon return to them with bad news and worse memories.

My mother finally answered her phone.

"You knew about Kaithlin's baby, didn't you?" I asked.

"Britt, darling, isn't this your day off?"

"No, Mom, I'm still working on the story."

"The same story? When do you take time for yourself? No wonder you have so little personal life."

"Thanks, Mom. You knew, right?"

"I'm weary of it, Britt." Her voice shook. "I don't want to hear any more about it, read about it, or even discuss it again. It's ancient history. Nothing can change the past."

"Mom, why is it, when all I ever ask is that you be honest and up front with me—?"

"Are there no other stories?" she asked sharply. "Why does this one obsess you so?"

"Good question."

"You sound exhausted, dear. Why not go back to bed, get some sleep, and we can talk later."

I went to the morgue instead. The winter day was breezy, the sky a hard bright blue, and the golden air so alight with promise that, as I waited outside the medical examiner's office on Bob Hope Road, I began to experience a heady unwarranted optimism. The coffee must have scalded my brain cells, but I began to wonder. What if? What if we were wrong and the woman inside was not Shannon Broussard? Real life and death are stranger than fiction. A sunny sense of wellbeing flooded my soul. Then they emerged. Broussard wore the same jacket. He was red-eyed and weeping.

"Hey, kid." Rychek's face was grim.

"It's her," Broussard blurted emotionally, his shield of false hope shattered. Tears streaked his face. "I should have known. I thought she'd been abducted or might be lying in a hospital somewhere, injured or ill, unable to speak, but the longer she was gone, the more my heart knew it would end this way.

"What can I tell our girls?" he pleaded, to no one and everyone, as he got into Rychek's unmarked. I heard him sob as it pulled away.

The apologetic guard at the Williams Island security gate said that neither R. J. nor Eunice was "available." I asked him to call and tell them that I knew where Kaithlin Jordan had been for the past ten years. He did, and the gate swung open.

R. J. lounged in shorts and an open cabana shirt at an umbrella table that held the remnants of a Bloody Mary and a leisurely breakfast. Immaculately groomed, his color was better, his skin aglisten with suntan oil. His table overlooked water that shimmered like shattered blue glass. Overhead, palm fronds shimmied in the breeze. His X-wing prison cell seemed a thousand light-years away. The young woman beside him wore a skimpy bikini and a deep and glorious tan she would probably regret in twenty years.

He turned triumphantly to her as I approached. "See? I told you, who needs to buy a paper? They deliver the news to me personally. So, Miss Reporter." He leaned back in his chair. "What's the latest?"

"While you were on death row," I said evenly, "Kaithlin was happily married, with two *more* children."

The color in his face faded, along with his smile.

"Go home," he said dully to his companion, without even looking at her.

She did a double take, startled by her summary dismissal.

"Go home," he repeated.

"But you—"

"Now! I'll call you later."

She arose reluctantly. The thin gold chain around her slim waist glittered cheerfully in the sun.

"Now!" he barked impatiently.

She quickly snatched up her things, glared daggers my way, and stalked off, her shapely buns an eye-popping sight from the rear in her high heels and thong bikini. R. J. didn't notice. It was as though he had already forgotten her.

"Two *more* children?"

"In addition to your son, the boy Kaithlin gave up for adoption."

"Where did you hear about him?"

"I've been working on the story, talking to people. Does Eunice know about her grandson?"

He gave a noncommittal shrug. "She wouldn't care if she did."

"Every woman yearns to be a doting grandmother," I said.

"Not every woman. Not the bitch I had for a mother-in-law. So," he said, "she won that battle. But the best revenge is living well. Isn't that right? They're dead and gone and look who's living well. *Moi.*"

His gesture embraced the ambience surrounding him, the lush tropical landscaping, expensive yachts, and uniformed employees.

"As for my mother, it might have meant something when my father was alive, when the business was intact, when they wanted to keep it all in the family. But now there *is* no business, no dynasty to preserve, and the time for caring is past. There'd be no point. We all have lives of our own."

He slipped his sunglasses off to inspect an oily smear on the lens. His words were casual, but the intensity in his eyes betrayed him. "What's the so-called husband like?"

"A nice guy," I said. "In the software business in Seattle,

where they lived. He was clueless, thought she came from the Midwest."

"He's here?"

I nodded. "He'd been searching for her for weeks."

R. J.'s small laugh was sardonic. "The man had better luck than I did. I never found her, or anybody who believed me, so I wound up screwed, blued, and tattooed."

"He identified her this morning. He's heartbroken."

"I'm sure he is." His voice sounded hollow. "Kaithlin had a way about her, something genuine, even as a teenager. You could see it in the way she carried herself, her mannerisms, the way she looked at you. Whatever it was made her hard to forget. I had any woman I wanted but, to my misfortune, she was always the one on my mind. How old is he?"

"About forty, I'd say, maybe a little younger."

"You see?" He nodded, as though age explained everything. "They were just four or five years apart. We had totally different backgrounds and a significant age difference; it doesn't sound like much now, but she was a teenager and I was already thirty when we met." He sighed. "Their children?"

"Two little girls," I said.

"So," R. J. mused, "she never had a son."

"Only yours."

He seemed pleased at that. "How long were they together?"

"Married nearly nine years."

"No." The word rolled like a bitter taste off his tongue. "She was *married* to me." He jabbed a thumb to his hairy chest.

He motioned for another Bloody Mary and ordered iced tea for me.

"I see you're readapting nicely to life outside," I said pleasantly.

"Beats lights on at six A.M." His eyes drifted to the baskets of flaky croissants, fresh fruit, and fluffy muffins. "Better than a metal meal cart rattling down a bare cement hallway and a tray shoved through a slot in the door. Yeahhh." He gazed across the blue expanse of water. "My existence was gray, bleak, and controlled for too long a time. I plan to make up for it now."

"I see you're already socializing." I indicated his companion's empty chair.

"Sure," he said. "I've been socializing nonstop, so much"—he patted his groin—"that I'm sore."

Dallas Svenson had sworn the man had a sensitive side. Either she was mistaken or he was doing a mighty fine job of concealing it.

"Eunice must adore having you back," I said mildly, sipping my iced tea.

"My sainted mother," he said sardonically, "didn't visit very often. The strip searches must have deterred her."

"Why do you think Kaithlin came back?" I asked. "Her husband says—"

"No, not husband." He waggled a warning finger.

"Okay. Her significant other says she became troubled about eight months ago, in June. She didn't discuss the problem, denied she had one, but it apparently escalated just before she disappeared and turned up here."

"No idea," he said sharply. "As I've said before, for publication, her bad luck was my lucky break."

He looked thoughtful, absently stirring his fresh Bloody Mary with a celery stalk.

"Eight months ago, in June," he finally repeated, "my social calendar was rather limited. I had an appeal denied that month and a wire service ran a piece about me—actually about half a dozen of us—due to die on death rows around the country. I made the cut, I guess, because I'm white and well off, not your typical death-row inmate. The reporter quoted my lawyer, who was delighted. Sent me a tearsheet. Here I am about to fry, and he's getting his rocks off over seeing his name in the national press."

"Speaking of lawyers," I said, "do you know Martin Kagan?"

He frowned, then seemed to place the name. "No, but I saw his name on a lot of old death-penalty pleadings, popular reading matter at my former place of residence."

"This one is his son. He had a private detective working for him, Dan Rothman, the Digger."

R. J. averted his gaze and slipped his shades back on, hiding his eyes behind the smoky lenses.

"You know him?"

He shook his head and checked the sailboats on the horizon. "You'd be surprised at the people popping out of the woodwork. I've had calls from *60 Minutes, 20/20, Dateline.* Even the medical examiner's office. Some clue-less clerk actually asked when I planned to claim my wife's body. Tried to talk me into it. For a decent burial, he said. As if she would have planned one for me. And some dick-head from the Volusia County prosecutor's office even had the gall to show up here."

"Dennis Fitzgerald?"

"I think that's right. Know him?"

"We've met."

"He never got past the gate. Never will. I'm not putting up with any harassment from those bastards now."

"They're doing a postmortem on the case," I said, "trying to figure out where they went wrong."

R. J. did not appear impressed.

"Is there anything else you'd like to say for publication about the latest development, Kaithlin's . . . significant other showing up?"

"What do you want to hear, Miss Reporter? That I'm sorry for his loss?" His smile was ironic, his eyes hard.

"I'd like to see Eunice," I said. "Is she home?"

"She's having her hair done," he said.

"Too bad, I hoped to catch her."

"You can," he said nonchalantly. "My mother has her own personal beauty salon."

That she did. The maid at their penthouse apartment ushered me into a spacious room equipped with professional upscale salon fixtures, a hair dryer, black marble sinks with gold faucets, and full-size makeup, massage, and manicure tables. I found her relaxing under the dryer, feet soaking in a foamy bath, hands resting on velvet cushions as her platinum-color nail polish dried. She turned off the dryer and excused the uniformed manicurist so we could speak in private.

I admired the room, with its soft lighting and softer music. Her hair stylist and manicurist visited as needed, she said, several times a week. "I'm so busy. It's so much more convenient than having to make appointments and go out to a salon."

I agreed, as though every girl should have one, then mentioned that Catherine Montero, my mother, had been a Jordan's employee for years.

"Oh, yes," Eunice said coldly. "I think I remember her. Conrad, my husband, knew her far better."

So much for breaking the ice.

"What's it like," I asked, smiling enthusiastically, "to have your son home again? It must be wonderful."

"It's what it was always like," she said, voice brittle. "People don't change. You said you had news about my daughter-in-law."

I briefly described Kaithlin's West Coast life, then wondered aloud who might have killed her.

"Someone like her"—she shrugged scornfully—"it could be virtually anyone. She used sex, seduced my son, and ruined all our lives."

"She was very young," I said, startled, "and your son was a grown—"

"She was a little nobody from nowhere," Eunice snapped. "I knew from the start she was a schemer, a social climber, a conniving gold digger."

"The business stories indicated that she was dedicated, talented, and successful and that she made a lot of money for your stores. I thought you were fond of her."

"Conrad liked her," she said dismissively, "but he never was a good judge of women." She paused to give me a meaningful once-over. "You are very much like your mother."

Not what I needed to hear.

Eunice scrutinized her flawless manicure, then summoned the woman to begin her pedicure, making it clear our interview was over. "Kaithlin's talent," she said in closing, "was for getting what she wanted. She nearly killed us all."

I passed sparkling fountains, sculptured hedges, and riotous flower beds in rainbow colors as I left, thinking, *No wonder you ran, Kaithlin. Good for you. Your only mistake was coming back.*

The killer tornado that savaged Stanley, Oklahoma, ten years earlier was all too real, the story true. Onnie and I tracked it down. Twenty-seven victims, including an entire family, the Sullivans, had perished. National news stories recounted the horror of one member killed by winds that tore her infant son from her arms. But the obits, published in the victims' hometown newspaper, listed no surviving sister Shannon.

"How convenient," Onnie said. "She just plucked a tragedy from the headlines and claimed it for herself. Wonder what she would have used had there been no twister?"

"She would have found something," I said. "There's always a fresh disaster somewhere." Was she drawn to it? I wondered. Did she relate to the symbolism inherent in an infant son torn from his mother's arms and in images of lives spinning out of control?

Onnie said she'd track down last summer's wire-service piece on death-row inmates and check to see where it had been published. I called the Florida Bureau of Corrections with a question. Their spokeswoman said she'd get back to me with an answer as soon as possible.

As I scrolled through my story exposing Kaithlin Jordan's second identity for a final read, a towering presence peered over my shoulder.

"What do you think? Does the lead work?" I glanced up, expecting Fred or Onnie.

"Works for me," Fitzgerald said.

"How did you get up to the newsroom?" I asked. "Security is supposed to announce visitors."

"I told your buddy you were expecting me."

"Swell," I said, as Rooney waved happily from the hall.

I hit the SEND button and smiled up at Fitzgerald. He smiled back.

Onnie interrupted with a printout of the wire story. The *News* hadn't used it, but it had been published by a number of subscribing papers nationwide, including the *Seattle Times* on June fourth. A paragraph devoted to R. J. identified him as a "wealthy Miami department-store heir facing death for the murder of his young wife nearly a decade ago." His mug shot ran as well. I imagined Shannon Broussard, prominent Seattle socialite, devoted wife and mother, opening her newspaper. What happened when she saw the photo and read that he was about to die for her murder? Was that why she returned?

Gretchen eyed us suspiciously from the city desk as Fitzgerald and I headed to the cafeteria for coffee.

"Let's take the stairs," I said, as he punched the elevator button. "That thing's too slow."

"Saw that coming up," he said. "Thought I'd need a shave by the time I reached your natural habitat. So this is where you disappear to." His deep-set eyes scanned the newsroom. "It's like a roach motel; once you come in here, you never come out."

"Oh, I manage to skitter out and about," I said, "here and there. Did you talk to R. J.?"

"No, that SOB isn't talking to anybody."

"Oh?" I feigned smug surprise. "I just left him over at Williams Island. We spent a little time together. He's working on his tan, looks good, sends regards."

"No shit," Fitzgerald said. "What did he say?"

"The usual, that Kaithlin's death was his big break. Claims he has no idea who did it or why. He's still pissed off at your office. He was curious about Preston Broussard—jealous, actually. Have you met Broussard yet?"

Fitzgerald said he'd been present when Rychek interviewed him at the station after he'd identified the body. Broussard, still shaken, told them that Shannon had withdrawn large amounts of cash over the past seven or eight months, money still unaccounted for. He had been unaware of the transactions until after she disappeared.

I thought I knew where the money went, but I asked Fitzgerald anyway.

He shrugged. "Could be a lot of things. Blackmail, hidden vices, a boy toy on the side. Maybe she was gearing up to cut and run again."

"And leave her kids? I doubt it. I think she saw this wire story in her local paper and decided to save R. J."

"After all the pains she took to frame him?" Fitzgerald asked.

"It would explain the calls she made to Kagan," I said. "Maybe she never expected R. J., with his rich parents and high-priced lawyers, to be sentenced to death. Maybe it was okay with her if he did time, but she couldn't let him be executed."

"A real sweetheart." Fitzgerald frowned skeptically. "But why would she risk it all to save that son-of-a-bitch?"

"Maybe she found religion, or a conscience. Maybe she still cared. R. J. was her first love."

"Not the sort of first love people write poetry and songs about," Fitzgerald said patiently. "The way I see it going down is Kaithlin's afraid he'll kill her, so she strikes first and makes a run for it."

"Right," I said. "She sees no other escape. She's a casualty of the ever-escalating war between her husband and her mother. Even if she survives a divorce, she loses the only thing she has left—her career. The mystery of the missing money is not going to enhance her résumé. With nothing left here, she fakes her death, frames him, and puts as many miles as she can between her and Miami.

"While she's doing that, alone and vulnerable, she meets a man who will protect and care for her. She uses a handy disaster in the Midwest to create a tragic past and, fearful of losing him, never reveals her true identity to the new husband."

"Okay," Fitzgerald said agreeably. "We're on the same page. So far, so good."

"Right," I said. "She's at peace, Miami only a memory. Unlike Lot's wife, she never looks back—until last summer. She sees the story; R. J. doomed to die. Maybe motherhood raised her consciousness."

"You're saying she identified with R. J.'s mother," he asked, "another woman about to lose a child?"

I paused to think of Eunice. "Nah, scratch that one," I said.

"I don't buy it either," Fitzgerald agreed. "People capable of what Kaithlin Jordan did aren't altruistic. They never have high-minded motives or morals. There isn't a noble deed in them. The basics are what drive them: money, sex, jealousy."

"You're a cop, you're cynical," I protested.

"Hey, no offense." He patted my hand. "I'm glad that after all you see on the job, you're still naive enough to think that way. It's nice."

Nice. He thought I was nice. I wished I could confide all I knew, without betraying Frances—and Kaithlin.

I kissed him hard just outside the building's back door, trying to ignore Rooney, who lurked nearby, apparently looking out for my well-being. And I promised to join Fitzgerald for a drink when I got off, no matter how late.

I called Kagan's office from the newsroom.

He wasn't in, Frances said.

"Good," I said. "I need to know the approximate dates that those checks arrived—"

"What did you do?" she whispered urgently. "He's been trying and trying to reach you! I've never seen him like this! He and Rothman quarreled. He's out of his mind. He punched right through the drywall—"

"Okay. I need to know—"

"I can't talk to you on this line! Call me later, at home." She hung up.

I redialed. "Would you tell Mr. Kagan that I returned his call?" I said sweetly, as though we hadn't just spoken.

"I'll see that he gets the message," she said crisply.

He called thirty minutes later.

"So what happened? Your story this morning didn't mention me or Rothman."

I imagined him and the detective dashing out of their respective residences in their jammies at dawn to comb the pages of the morning paper for their names. "Right," I said. "We held those details back due to new developments. In the morning we're running the story on her other identity and what brought her back to Miami. It's turned into much bigger news."

"Whattaya mean?"

"You know. The money. What she hired you to do. The Seattle husband has bank records showing all her withdrawals. A paper trail proves it was sent here, to Miami. . . . I'm doing an investigative piece. You should try to tell your side before the story hits the street."

"Look," he said, "I don't know what other people are telling you, but I have an obligation to protect the lawyer–client privilege."

"The client's dead. Murdered," I said.

"I can't discuss this over the phone," he said.

"In your office?"

"When?"

"Now?"

He took a deep breath. "Thirty minutes."

"Make it an hour," I said. I needed Frances to get home first.

I called Broussard at his hotel.

"I've been on the phone for the last hour. Making

arrangements." His voice quavered. "I'm taking Shannon home. The children don't know yet. I want to tell them in person. I have to be there."

"That's good," I said. "They'll need their dad. I'm still trying to piece together why she came here and what happened after she arrived." I asked about the cash withdrawals.

He had the dates. There were five, beginning with $50,000 on June 12. The others ranged from $35,000 to $70,000 for a total of $250,000.

No wonder Kagan was living large.

"Would you do something for me?" Broussard's voice dropped to a weary whisper. "Tomorrow, before I leave, I want to go back to that place you showed me, where she was found. Just to—to see how it was, to say a silent prayer or something. Would you be there, to sort of walk me through it?"

"Sure. I'll call you in the morning. Try to get some sleep. Also," I said, loathing myself, "my editors would like a picture of Shannon, maybe a family portrait with you two and the kids, or a wedding photo. Something representative of her life out there, with you."

"I'll see what I can do," he said hesitantly. "Someone at the house could overnight it."

Frances answered her home phone. She sounded frightened. "What are you doing? You're going to get me in trouble!"

"Look," I said, "we need to find out the truth. If your boss killed Kaithlin he's dangerous and we have to get you out of that office. If we prove he didn't, it'll give you some peace of mind. I need to know about the money. Does two hundred and fifty thousand sound right? She withdrew that much since June in increments from thirty-five to seventy thousand."

"Probably," she said slowly. "I knew the first was about fifty. I didn't realize the total came to quite that much, but the ballpark sounds right."

"Do you recall any of the dates that money arrived?"

"I looked them up after you called. Let me get my notebook."

She rattled them off. Each envelope had arrived in Miami within twenty-four hours of the Seattle withdrawal.

"Frances, please, would you talk to a detective? For your own safety."

"No!" She sounded shocked. "He would know it came from me. You promised!"

"All right," I said. "I promised not to drag you into it and I won't. I was only asking. Did Kagan deposit the money into his own bank accounts?"

"Some," she said guardedly, "in different banks. But never enough to tip off the IRS. He spent a lot and paid cash. Remember"—she began to sound agitated—"you can't tell anyone we talked. I spoke to you in good faith."

I reassured her, said goodbye, and told the desk I was going to interview Kagan. "At the very least, Kaithlin Jordan hired him for something," I told Tubbs, who was in the slot. "At the very worst, he killed her."

"Do the cops know about this?" he asked, his round face puckered into a frown.

"They asked, he lied."

"Need somebody to go with you? A photographer,

another reporter?"

"No," I said. "It would only spook him more."

"Well, be careful," he said doubtfully.

Traffic was a nightmare, bumper-to-bumper on the Dolphin Expressway where a jackknifed tractor-trailer had dumped a load of produce across two lanes. I arrived exactly ten minutes late.

Kagan's office looked dark in the growing dusk but was unlocked. His secretary's desk looked tidy, no lights lit on the telephone system. The door to his inner office stood ajar.

"Hello?" I called.

"In here." He stepped out from behind his big desk, pointedly checking his gold Rolex. "I thought reporters were always on time."

"I am," I said innocently. "Your watch must be fast."

He frowned at the timepiece, probably worth more than my car.

He wore another expensive Italian suit; his shoes were polished to a high gleam, but unlike at our last meeting, shadows ringed his eyes, a bottle of Chivas Regal stood on his desk, and there was a fist-sized hole in the drywall between his office and a file room.

He motioned me to a leather chair, while he sat on the edge of his massive desk, looking down at me from a position of power.

"What happened to the wall?" I asked, wide-eyed.

"Cleaning service accidentally pushed a piece of furniture into it."

"What a shame," I said. "You should make them fix it."

"Look," he said. "I'm gonna be straight with you."

"That would be nice."

"Me to you," he said. "Marty to Britt, one on one."

I opened my notebook.

He held up a cautionary hand. "No notes. Hear me out first." He licked pale lips as if they were dry, then offered a drink. "It's after hours," he coaxed.

I declined. His hand shook slightly as he poured his own. He drank it neat, the first swallow followed by a long shuddering breath.

"Okay," he said, fortified. He paused. "You're not using a tape recorder or anything, right?"

To reassure him, I upended my purse on his desk. We stared in dismay at the contents. I'd forgotten the remaining half of that greasy day-old grilled-cheese sandwich. Another surprise tumbled out with my comb, a lipstick, and small change, a *resguardo,* a tiny cloth pouch filled with herbs and other items, a talisman for my protection. My Aunt Odalys must have slipped it in there during our last visit. Would the Santería saints be offended by the melted cheese stuck to it?

"You don't practice that crap, do you?" Kagan asked.

"I have this relative." I sighed. "My father's younger sister."

"Tell me about it," he said. "You remember my father, don't you? Everybody does."

"Sure," I said. "He specialized in death-penalty appeals."

"Yeah, till he stroked out six–seven years ago. Anyhow, here I am, beating the bushes to make a living, and one day last year I get an out-of-town call from some broad. She's looking for my old man and finds me, the only Martin Kagan, attorney-at-law, currently in the book. Won't give her name or number, but she wants help on a death-penalty case.

"I tell her she's got the wrong guy, the old man is gone, but somehow she gets the impression I'm a knight on a white horse, young blood still fighting my father's crusade."

I wondered how she happened to get that erroneous impression but curbed my smart mouth.

"She wants me to stop an execution, get the sentence commuted. She's not local, she says, and wants to stay anonymous. Wants me to claim I'm taking up the cause pro bono, like my dad used to do, but behind the scenes she'll foot the bill.

"I snatch a figure outa the stratosphere and say here's what it'll cost you. I'm expecting an argument. Instead, in a heartbeat, she says she'll send the money. Sure, I say, you got a deal, never expecting to hear from her again. But what do you know, next day an envelope arrives. Swear to God! I never dreamed she'd really send it."

"What did you do?"

He stretched out his hands, palms up, in a gesture of helplessness, his expression ironic. "The sentence she wants commuted is R. J. Jordan's. When my old man did his volunteering he worked to save poor bastards who were indigent, without a dime. The Jordans have more money than God. Heavy-duty legal power's been hammering at that case for years, doing everything any legal genius could possibly conjure up. Those pros already filed every appeal in the book and then some. And despite it all, the case still looks like a lost cause.

"What am I supposed to do, show up, announce my

arrival? Tell all that high-powered talent, 'Here I am, guys, joining your team, uninvited? I never had one-a these cases but don't let it worry ya, it's not gonna cost ya a dime.' They'da laughed their asses off. They'da told me if I wanted to volunteer, I should join the army."

"And, of course, you couldn't give the money back," I said, "because you didn't know where to send it, right?"

"Right." He jabbed a finger in my direction, nodding emphatically, apparently pleased that I perceived his predicament. "I didn't know who the hell the broad was."

"So what did you do?"

"Had a clerk monitor the case for me, all the motions, pleadings, and appeals, so whenever she called," he said, "I could provide her with an update, let her know what progress was being made."

"Of course she probably misunderstood and believed you were generating some or all of that paperwork."

His Adam's apple lurched. "Could be that she did." He reached for his glass.

"So she sent more money, because she thought you were really working to save R. J."

His head shot up, eyes darting.

"Hey, who wouldn't have done the same thing? Everything on earth was being done for the guy, and then some. I didn't go looking for her. She fell off a Christmas tree. She found *me*."

"But you led her to believe there was progress, that there was hope."

"Well, you know, there's always hope."

"You did do something," I said. "You hired Rothman."

"That bigmouthed son-of-a-bitch shouldn't have talked

to you," he said testily. "I don't know what he said. But you can't trust him."

His righteous indignation was impressive.

"I wanted him to find out the broad's story, where she was coming from. I mean, I hadda protect myself. Maybe I was being set up. Why would some outa-town philanthropist suddenly become a rich guy's benefactor? She hadda have an angle. So Rothman, he's good; he tracks her down, even makes a trip out there at my expense. Shoots surveillance pictures and, lo and behold, we put two and two together and realize the broad with the bucks is the victim in the homicide Jordan's about to fry for!

"All of a sudden, everything makes sense. I don't even hafta feel guilty. Taking her money is absolutely justifiable. Broad's just buying off her own guilty conscience. I'm helping her sleep nights. What is she gonna do, file a complaint against me with the bar association? She's not even divorced. She's sure as hell not gonna blow the deal she's got out there, the big house, the new husband, the kids.

"So I go on keeping her apprised as usual. Everything's going along fine until last month. All of a sudden, the supremes shoot down Jordan's last appeal and some goddamn tabloid TV show profiles 'R. J. Jordan, millionaire heir, about to die for murdering his beautiful young wife.'

"My luck, the bitch sees it. Shows up in Miami a couple days later, mad as a wet hen."

"She was shocked by the story," I said, "because she thought your legal work was successful and he would escape execution?"

"She mighta had that impression," Kagan confessed. "So she shows up here and has the chutzpah to accuse *me* when *she's* the one hung the poor bastard out to fry. She's belly-aching that I took money under false pretenses. Me! That's when I drop the bomb, let her know I know she's living her whole goddamn life under false pretenses. I tell her if she don't shut her yap I might just call in the cops and a camera crew."

"What did she say?"

"Ah, the usual female rants, raves, and threats, but eventually we cleared the air, worked out an amiable compromise."

"Oh?"

"Yeah. I was gonna sorta keep working for her, on a regular retainer. Even had a meeting with Rothman. Had it all worked out."

"When did you see her last?"

He shrugged, eyes darting. "Doesn't matter."

"Somebody killed her," I said.

"Think it was me? Think I'm crazy? You don't butcher the cash cow." He leaned close, his voice a raspy whisper. "What you do is you keep on milking it. Kapeesh?"

I stared back, at a loss for words.

"Look," he said, "the way I see it, she was a legacy. A gift left to me from my old man. Like all families, we had our ups and downs, but we happened to be on a downer when he had his stroke. Left me in a awkward position. He sure as hell didn't leave me much of anything else. This is no story. There's no witnesses. I'll deny it. What I told you here is deep background, just to clarify the situation, so you don't get the wrong idea and write something that makes me look like the villain here. The real story is who killed her, and I had nothing to do with that. I'm an innocent bystander."

"An innocent bystander?" I said. "You were an officer of the court, willing to let an innocent man die so you could keep taking money from his alleged victim."

"Naw, naw. I never woulda let that happen. If it came right down to the wire, I'da done something." His eyes were furtive.

"Too bad," I said. "You blew your chance to do the right thing, to be a hero, a crusader like your dad."

"The old man ain't here," he mumbled. "You don't know what he was like. Even if he was alive, he'da never believed I did anything right." He stared, eyes moist.

"Did Kaithlin ever tell you why she wanted to save R. J.?"

Kagan averted his eyes to pour himself another drink. "Who knows what goes on in a woman's head?"

"But you must have picked up a sense of why. Was she still in love with him?"

"She didn't want a new trial, didn't want 'im to walk or ever draw a free breath. All she wanted was to keep his ass outa the hot seat, keep him alive and in a cage. If that's love"—he shrugged and lifted his glass—"ain't it grand?"

16

I'd missed something, I thought, as I drove back to the office. Something obvious that nagged, just off center in the shadowy reaches of my mind.

I called Stockton, R. J.'s lawyer, at home. He wasn't there yet so I called the Elbow Room, the downtown bar where lawyers from his building congregate. The bartender said he'd just left, so in five minutes I called his car phone.

He recalled the tabloid show well, he said, words slightly slurred. He had appeared briefly on camera himself, but refused to allow a death-house interview with his client. R. J. was the problem. Defendants who confess, find religion, and heartily repent their crimes are those whose sentences are most likely to be commuted. But, ever the bad boy, R. J. refused to repent. He kept insisting he didn't do it.

I could stop by his office and watch the tape anytime during working hours, he offered.

"The TV people love this case," he said dreamily. "It has it all; greed, sex, and violence among the beautiful people." He was more than a little annoyed that, after all he had done for the man, R. J. was behaving churlishly, refusing to cooperate with the big network shows now eager for interviews.

I told him I'd come to see the tape in the morning, then checked my messages as I navigated through traffic on the Dolphin Expressway. The Department of Corrections spokeswoman had left an answer to my query. Bingo, I thought, and beeped Rothman. I was almost back at the *News* when he called.

"Where you been?" he said. "I tried to get ahold of you."

"Working on the story," I said. "I was hoping to talk to you before it goes to press."

"Where are you at?"

"The *News*," I said. "Just pulling in."

"Okay, I'm close by, checking something for a client. How's about we meet over by the Casablanca on the MacArthur Causeway? Ten minutes."

"The fish market? They open this late?"

"No." He sounded disgusted. "That's the idea. It's private."

The world's freshest fish is sold at the Casablanca outdoor fish market on Watson Island, along the causeway that links Miami and Miami Beach. The small island is also home port for commercial fishing boats, a shark fishing fleet, a sightseeing helicopter service, and Chalk's seaplanes, with regular routes to the Bahamas and Key West.

"Okay," I said, "I'll see you there. What are you driving?"

"A rental. Dark-colored Blazer."

"I'll be in—"

"A white T-Bird. I know," he said, and hung up.

Magenta lighting illuminates the swooping new design of the recently elevated west bridge. A $1.4 million necklace of high-intensity bulbs stretches for 2,500 feet. Its eerie purple glow reflects off the water and the sheer concrete bridge supports, disturbing the dreams and nightmares of the homeless and hopelessly deranged who dwell there. Their nights now a purple haze, they have become edgier, more prone to psychotic episodes and violent outbursts.

I hit the brakes near the fish market as a stick-thin figure in tattered clothes stumbled across my path. How many like him, I wondered, could be fed and sheltered with the $20,000 a year spent on electricity for the purple lights?

The wind had picked up out of the east, the temperature was in the 60s, and the blue lights of the port span, the purple of the bridge, the cruise ships, Bayside, and the city skyline were as breathtaking as a bejeweled kingdom in some ancient fable. The huge moon, in all its splendor, paled by comparison.

I parked at the windswept fish market, a narrow one-story building, dark and boarded up for the night. No one else seemed to be there as I marveled at the view, inhaling the scents of water, fish, and the city night. Then the Blazer rolled up out of the dark.

I knew that Rothman, like most private eyes, was an ex-cop. But his strong telephone presence had led me to expect a bigger, more imposing man. He wore a short-sleeved guayabera. Beefy and middle-aged, his hairline was receding, and his eyes were hostile and alert.

"Beautiful, isn't it?" I said.

He looked startled, then eyed the view suspiciously, his glance hard and sweeping.

"Yeah," he said. "It was right over here, 'bout this time last year, they found that hooker floating facedown. Name was Norma. They think she bought it over there at Bayside and rode the tide over here."

"That's right." I recalled the case. Was that a veiled threat, I wondered, or was this the man's version of small talk? "Did they ever solve that one?" I asked.

"Not that I heard. You know how some cases tend to fall through the cracks."

He must wish the Jordan case would do that, I thought.

"So you're still sniffing around, huh?"

"Right," I said, remembering how R. J. had reacted to the man's name. "The story's finally coming together. I just found out about the business you did with R. J."

Rothman shook his head slowly, eyes incredulous in the shifting light off the water. "You must be one hell of a poker player. You should come work for me if you ever need a job."

"I never got into card games," I said mildly. "Saw R. J. this afternoon, over at Williams Island."

"He mention my name?" he said skeptically.

"It came up in conversation."

He shook his head, smiling.

"And, of course," I added, "there is also the fact that you were placed on R. J.'s visitor's list and made a trip up to see him, two days before Kaithlin Jordan was murdered."

Rothman's smile faded. "Not unusual for private investigators to visit inmates. It's not like they can visit us."

"But you were never part of his defense team. You had to fake it for permission to see him."

"Look," he said. "I just do my job. Sometimes you stumble onto a piece of information that's valuable to various parties in a situation. That's what keeps this business interesting."

"So." My voice sounded thin in the rising wind. "Kagan hired you to find out who she was. How did you do that, by the way?"

"You expect me to share trade secrets?" He sniffed the air and shifted his weight, eyes on the move. "Let's just say nothing's impossible when you got a direct link."

"Was it the money deliveries or her phone calls?" I asked.

"I've said all I'm gonna say about that."

"I was just curious," I said. "You're good. Once you made Shannon Broussard, the leap to Kaithlin Jordan wasn't all that tough. You were out at the cemetery too, right?"

He smirked but didn't answer.

"When you did put it all together, you not only collected from Kagan, you sold the information to R. J. You told him where she was, right?"

"In good conscience, I couldn't let the guy die."

"You could have told the police or his defense team."

"Yeah, but why not accomplish the same thing and make a buck? Kagan's one stingy bastard, and I'm not in business for my health. You ever freelance? You ever write stories for somebody besides the *News*?"

"Sure," I said.

"I'm betting you don't do it for nothing, am I right? Same premise. We all gotta make a living in this world. Never give away what you can sell. And the end result was justice. The guy was exonerated."

"But not until later, after her body was found and identified. Why the delay?"

He shrugged. "Don't know, ask him. Day after I went up there, Jordan's mother paid my bill and I provided the info on where her late daughter-in-law was staying."

"So Eunice also knew Kaithlin was alive?"

He nodded, then sighed. "I did nothing illegal."

"When I freelance nobody dies."

"You're saying Jordan might be responsible?"

"Right."

"The man was behind bars."

"What better place to hire a killer?" I said.

"I hafta admit the thought might have occurred to me. But if he's guilty, he's got the best damn alibi I ever heard—at the time of the crime, he's on death row for her murder. But if it's him, the M.O. makes no sense. Her body coulda washed out to sea easy. She coulda wound up shark food or been lost in the Gulf Stream. He hadda make sure she was found and identified."

"But why didn't R. J. blow the whistle right away once he knew she was alive? Her body wasn't identified for another two weeks."

"Maybe the guy gets off on near-death experiences." Rothman gazed pensively out across the water.

I wondered what he was really thinking. "Maybe," I said, "there was a misunderstanding. Maybe he or Eunice hired a hit man who didn't get the concept."

"Or maybe she just didn't want junior back on her hands. From what I hear, he was always a pain in the ass."

"So Eunice hired somebody to send Kaithlin out to sea? Hard to believe that of a mother," I said, "even that one."

"You'd be surprised what some mothers will do to their kids," he said.

"That was you, wasn't it?" I said. "At the cemetery?"

He cocked his head to stare at me for a long moment.

"What were you doing out there?" he countered.

"Trying to piece things together, figure out who was who and what was going on."

"See, I told you," he said. "We think alike. You oughta come work for me."

"You met Kaithlin, right?"

He nodded.

"Why did she want to save R. J.? What brought her back?"

He gave me a toothy smile, as though happily surprised that there was something I didn't know. "Maybe he had something she needed, or thought she did," he said wryly.

"Like what?"

He shook his head. "Why don't I see you to your car. You don't want to hang around here alone in the dark."

"What was Kaithlin like when you met?" I asked, as we walked to the T-Bird. "Was she scared?"

He paused as I unlocked my car. "I'm the one shoulda been scared," he said. "She was one cold, scary bitch."

I sat in the car, scribbling in my notebook. I had more questions than before. What exactly did he mean by that last remark? Troubled, trembling suddenly in the chill, I stepped out to ask, but his Blazer was gone. He had pulled away, lights out, and vanished in the darkness.

The newsroom had emptied after deadline for the final. The office was quiet. I had a message from Myrna Lewis, but it didn't say urgent and it was too late to call her now. I'd try her in the morning. I typed up my notes from Kagan and Rothman, then tried to draw a timeline of Kaithlin's final days in Miami, but too many gaps existed and the list of suspects was growing.

R. J., Eunice, Kagan, and Rothman. Who else knew Kaithlin was alive and in Miami?

I scooped up my ringing phone, with a wave to Rooney as he passed by, whistling on his rounds.

"Britt, thank God you're there!"

"Mr. Broussard? What's wrong?"

"You haven't heard? It's terrible. What more can they do to me?" He sounded barely able to speak, choked by rage, pain, or grief. "How much more can I take?"

"What is it? What's happened?"

"I was taking Shannon home tomorrow. Arrangements

are made, a service at our church, where we were married, where our daughters were christened. But the funeral home handling things called me a couple of hours ago. The medical examiner's office refused to release the body to them."

"Don't worry," I said, relieved. "It must be a mistake, some clerical error—"

"No. You don't understand. It's Jordan. He's claiming her body. They said that legally he's her next of kin."

"R. J.? But from what I understood, he refused to—"

"He's changed his mind. She's my wife, Britt. Our children—"

"That bastard. Why would he—?"

"Is there any way to reach him? Can you help me appeal to his better side?"

If R. J. had one, I'd never seen it.

"I called my Seattle attorneys," Broussard said. "They recommended some lawyers here. I wanted to run their names past you. We need to seek an emergency injunction, go before a judge. I just want to take her home on schedule tomorrow and see my girls, tell them about their mom." His voice broke. "Why is he doing this?"

"I'm not sure," I said. "Maybe it's a mistake. Let me make a few calls and get back to you."

Pearl, the overnight attendant on duty at the M.E. office, answered. A determinedly cheerful and savvy black woman, she backs up ten years' experience at the office with a keen intelligence and innate common sense. Few mistakes occur on her watch.

"Oh, that one," she said indignantly. "Nobody wanted that woman for weeks. We were stuck with the body, thought the county was gonna have to bury it—now everybody wants it. They're fighting over her."

"Everybody?" I asked.

"Yep. Two husbands and a friend. She mighta had a short life, but she musta lived it to the hilt. Looks like she never got divorced. Now the lawyers are getting into the act."

"Friend? What friend?"

"Lemme see. Got the file right here." I waited while she shuffled papers. "One Myrna Lewis," she said. "Claims the funeral for this one was prearranged, that the deceased's late mother left specific instructions years ago."

"I'd forgotten about that, but it's true," I said. "But I thought other arrangements had been made, to ship the body to Seattle."

"That's right. She was going outa here to Lithgow's this evening, to be prepped for shipping. Then this afternoon, the Lewis woman shows up with a copy of the mother's will. Wants the deceased picked up by Van Orsdale. An hour later, a hearse from Riverside shows up at the loading dock with a release signed by one Robert J. Jordan, husband. This gal's got too many dates for the prom."

"Did they take her?"

"No. The chief said to wait, hold onto the body, and straighten things out in the morning. All three parties say they're hiring lawyers. At one point I had the Lewis woman on hold, husband number two crying on one line, and husband number one cussing me out on the other. But I can tell you one thing right now: Florida State Statute eight-seventy-two, the one that deals with the custody of dead bodies, puts the legal spouse at the head of the list. Then comes a parent. If none of the above claims a deceased, the body goes to anybody willing to pay for the burial."

251

"But she and Broussard, the second husband, lived together as man and wife for the last nine years in Seattle. They have two little daughters."

"Then tell me what the hell she's doing dead in Miami."

"That's what we're trying to figure out."

"I tell you," Pearl said, "my heart goes out to the man with the little girls, but from a strictly legal standpoint he's last in line. That marriage was bigamous. The first husband is her legal next of kin, followed by the mother's representative."

"The one with the children is talking about an injunction," I said.

"So is the little lady, a senior citizen, who claims to represent the deceased's mother. Should have seen the snit she was in about the first husband getting into the act. I tell you, Britt, a judge is gonna have to rule on this one. And who knows how long that'll take? Meanwhile, she's getting raunchier in the fridge. You should see how that body is deteriorating," she said, annoyed. "Eyes drying out and sinking, fingers getting all shriveled and mummified."

"Oh, for Pete's sake," I said, my head beginning to ache. "I really didn't need to know that."

"Well, you called me, I didn't call you. And that's the straight scoop," Pearl grumbled. "We're probably gonna have to embalm that woman ourselves before her body gets any more—"

"Okay, okay," I said, wincing. "I'll call tomorrow. There won't be any new developments before then, will there?"

"No way. She's not going anyplace tonight."

What time was it anyway? I wondered, exhausted. Something throbbed behind my eyes. Did I really want to meet Fitzgerald for that drink? I should have called Myrna

Lewis. I called R. J. instead. He answered on the first ring.

"Oh, hey," he said, his voice thick as though he'd been drinking. "I was expecting someone else."

"Sorry to disappoint you," I said. "I understand you're claiming Kaithlin's body."

"News travels fast."

"Why are you doing it?"

"I'm her legal next of kin."

"I guess you knew that her—the father of her children planned on taking her home tomorrow."

"Miami is her home," he said. "That's where she was born, raised, and married to me." Ice tinkled in a glass close to the phone.

"Why not give the guy a break?"

"That son-of-a-bitch was screwing my wife while I was sitting on death row!"

"But he was unaware. He's an innocent victim."

"*I'm* the victim!" His voice rose. "How do I know he didn't influence Kaithlin to do what she did? They might have planned it together."

"That's ridiculous," I said. "They met out west after she left you in Daytona."

"Nobody has ever even apologized to me!" he shouted.

There was no reasoning with him.

"Why didn't you immediately inform your lawyers when Rothman told you Kaithlin was alive and in Miami?"

He hesitated. "How did I know he was telling the truth? Nobody ever believed me. We had to find her and produce her first. She wasn't at the hotel where the detective said she was. My mother was still looking into it when the body was identified."

"Why not just hire Rothman?"

"My mother didn't trust him."

I sighed. "So many people are hurting," I said. "Why not let him take Kaithlin back to their little girls?"

"Hell, no," he said emotionally. "In fact, my lawyers say that as surviving spouse I can file claims against any property she holds jointly with Broussard out there."

"How could you?" I said. "You don't need the money."

"Listen," he said, his tone changing. "I want your honest opinion. Why do you think she came back? Do you think it was that news story, that she realized for the first time that I was close to execution and wanted to prevent it?"

"I think that's exactly why she came back," I said. "She spent a great deal of money, risked everything, and lost her life. Why do you think she did it?"

"Because she loved me still." He spoke the words like a prayer, the arrogance in his voice overtaken by something tender and vulnerable. "She always loved me."

"Will you let him take her home?"

"I'll never let her go again."

Heart-heavy, I reached for the phone to call Broussard with the bad news, but it rang first.

"Britt, thank God you're there!"

"Angel?"

"It's time." She sounded breathless. "I have to go to the hospital. The baby's coming and I can't find Rooney. His beeper isn't working."

"He walked by here just a couple of minutes ago," I said, looking wildly around. "He's here somewhere."

"Would you please find him, Britt? I know he wants to

be there, to do this together. We went through all those Lamaze classes."

By this time, I thought, Angel was qualified to teach them.

"Don't worry. I'll go find him right now. Hang in there."

I stepped into the long, dimly lit corridor. No sign of him.

"Rooney! Are you there?" Nothing but my own voice bouncing off the walls. I hurried back to my desk, fumbled for the Acme Thunderer police whistle on the key ring in my purse, then ran to the fifth-floor lobby.

"Rooney Thomas!" I shouted. I took a deep breath, then blasted my brains out on the whistle. I listened but heard only the ringing in my ears.

"For Pete's sake!" I was furious. Normally, the man is lurking around every corner.

"Rooney!" I shouted down the stairwell, then blasted the whistle so hard that spots appeared before my eyes.

Blinking them away, I dashed down two flights and sprinted down the hall to the cafeteria. It was empty, lights turned low.

"Rooney!" I took another deep breath. As I placed the whistle to my lips, a figure loomed at the coffee machine in the back. "Rooney!"

He glanced up, startled. "Britt?" He squinted across the room. "Something wrong?"

"Your beeper isn't working!" I dashed toward him, babbling. "Angel's trying to reach you. She has to go to the hospital! You're about to become a father!"

His reaction made me smile in spite of myself.

"Oh, my God! It's time! I don't know if I'm ready for this!"

"Too late now, it's happening!"

"The baby!" He directed a wild near-miss kiss to my cheek, fumbled for his keys, and dashed for the door. "Thanks, Britt!"

"Be careful," I shouted after him, heart pounding, still out of breath.

I punched the elevator button but gave up and took the stairs, grinning. Rooney and Angel were lucky I happened to work late, I thought, as I trotted up to the fifth floor. And if Rooney is forced to deliver that baby himself because he didn't check his beeper, it's his own fault. About time those two grew up, I thought righteously.

I caught my breath back at my desk, then called Broussard, who answered immediately. Nobody was sleeping tonight, it seemed.

"It's no mistake," I said miserably. "In fact, a third party's involved now. A representative of Kaith—Shannon's dead mother."

"I heard." He sounded calmer. "I spoke to an attorney here, who was good enough to call me back at this hour. He's going to file something first thing in the morning. He sounds resourceful. His name is Pollack, specializes in probate law."

"I don't know him," I said. "Does he think you can win?"

"He said the only way is to present an overwhelming body of evidence showing that Jordan has no legitimate interest. He said we have three things working for us. Jordan has already refused to claim the body. Second, revenge is his only motivation, and, third, we can question his claim of being still legally married to a woman declared dead ten years ago."

Clever. I thought. Leave it to the lawyers. Win or lose, those arguments would certainly prolong the process and excite the press.

"What do you think?" Broussard asked hopefully. "He said not to worry. Sounded sure of himself."

"It might get expensive," I warned.

"Money doesn't matter," he said. "How can I leave her? She was running for her life when we met, running from him. I have to take her home."

What a story, I thought, regretting that it broke too late for the morning paper. As I cleared my desk, the elevator clanked and the door slowly moaned open. I glanced up, expecting the overnight cleaning crew.

"Angel! What are you doing here!" She hobbled off the elevator, holding her lower back as if in pain. "Why didn't Rooney take you to the hospital?"

She stopped to lean heavily on Ryan's desk.

"He's not here?" she gasped. Her breath came in little puffs and pants.

"No! He left like a bat out of hell, to take you to the hospital!"

She looked confused. "But I thought he'd wait here for me. When he wasn't downstairs, I had to come up."

"This is the craziest thing I ever heard of," I muttered angrily. "Angel, if you plan to marry this man, the father of your child, you will have to learn to communicate with him. What's your phone number?" I demanded. She told me and I dialed. A busy signal.

I sighed.

"The kids must be on the phone," she gasped.

"Sit down," I said.

"No," she said, puffing. "It's better if I stand."

"Should I call nine-one-one?" I reached apprehensively for the phone.

"No," she panted. "I think I can make it."

Her use of the word *think* troubled me. I was about to retry her number when my phone rang.

"It's Rooney! He's at your place." I handed Angel the phone. Would this night ever end? I wondered.

"Honey, the baby is coming. I have to go . . ." She winced and doubled over.

I snatched the phone back.

"Stay right there!" he was shouting. "I'm on the way!"

Oh, right, I thought. I'd seen his car, a bucket of bolts held together by rust.

"Oh, no, you don't," I said. "She can't wait. Meet us at the hospital. We're on the way. I'm taking her to the ER right now! If you get there first, start the paperwork."

He tried to argue, but I hung up.

I turned to Angel. "What's that?" A puddle had formed on the scruffy newsroom carpet.

"My water broke," she whimpered.

I flashed back to all the women and their war stories on birthing during my last date with McDonald.

"Come on, Angel, let's go. Let's go." I picked up her little overnight bag, grabbed my purse, and took her arm.

"Aren't we waiting for Rooney?" she panted.

"No! He'll meet us there." I paused. "He knows the right hospital, doesn't he?"

"Of course," she said indignantly. "Our Lamaze class is there."

"Thank God for small favors. Come on!" I charged

ahead, punched the DOWN button, then returned to lead her to the elevator. She winced, whined, and doubled over.

I looked around for help. The newsroom was deserted. Where are people when you need them? I thought, irritated. They're always in front of you in traffic, at the post office, on line at the supermarket; where were they now? "Come on, come on," I said. "Get on the elevator."

"Britt, I'm scared." Her face was drawn and pale. The contraction must have passed.

"It'll be all right," I said soothingly. "It's not like you haven't done this before."

"I'm scared," she said, puffing. "I think this baby is coming faster than the others."

"It's okay," I reassured her, and smoothed her hair. "My car is right downstairs. There's no traffic at this hour. We'll be there in ten minutes. Come on," I implored impatiently. "Get on the elevator!" Shoulders hunched, she took little baby steps as I steered her inside. I sighed with relief and pressed the lobby button.

She leaned heavily against the back wall, eyes shut tight. "We're on the way," I said cheerfully.

The elevator groaned, began its descent, then lurched to a sudden stop as the lights went out.

17

O h, my God!" I groped for the control panel, stabbing buttons frantically. One had to be the alarm bell. Nothing.

"Oh, no, no," Angel groaned in the dark.

"Don't worry." I tried to sound calm. "This elevator is always sluggish but it never gets stuck. It'll restart in a second."

"Push the buttons," she gasped.

"I am," I said. "I am." My fingers played them like a piano virtuoso.

Angel hiccuped in pain. "Oh, Britt. I'm having this baby!"

"No, no, Angel." I fumbled for the cell phone in my purse, reassured by the key pad's familiar green glow. "I'm calling for help. They'll get us right out of here."

I hit 911. Nothing. I hit it again and heard a distant ringing.

"Nine-one-one, what is your emergency?" asked a faint, faraway voice.

"Hello," I said breathlessly, "you've got to help us. We're trapped in an elevator at the *Miami News* building. My friend here is in labor, we were on the way to the hospital. You've got to send—"

"Nine-one-one, what is your emergency?"

"Hello, hello? Can't you hear me?"

The line crackled, alive with static, then went dead.

"What's wrong?" Angel shrieked. "Are they coming?"

"The signal's fading in and out, probably because we're between floors inside the building."

"Britt, I'm having this baby, now!"

"No, Angel," I said firmly. "Don't. It's not feasible. You can't do that here. This is not a good time. Just hang on and I'll keep trying. When we don't show up, Rooney will send someone or be here himself in a few—"

She gave a fierce growl of pain. "Son-of-a-bitch!" she

screamed. "Get us out of here!"

I joined her hysteria, kicked viciously at the elevator door, then reached for Angel, to hug and reassure her that everything would be all right. My arms flailed in empty space.

"Angel? Where are you?"

"Down here," she groaned. "On the floor."

"Oh, no."

I knelt and found her. Her skin was clammy.

"Good idea." I tried to sound cheerful as she writhed in pain. "Try not to move until they come." Fear in my heart, I redialed 911.

"Don't hang up," I shouted. "It's an emergency!"

"Are you on a cellular?" a far-off voice asked.

"Yes," I bellowed.

"Can you move to a better location?"

"No! I can't! We're trapped!" I gave our location time after time until he finally repeated it correctly.

"Who is that screaming?"

"The mother, for God's sake! She's having the baby!"

"Calm down," the operator said.

"Would you please just send somebody to get us out of here!"

"I have your location. We're sending the paramedics. How do they gain entry to the building?"

"It's locked at this hour, you have to get the security guard to open . . ."

Oh, no, I thought. Rooney. He's at the hospital.

"Tell them to get in here any way they can! Now! I don't care if they use dynamite!"

"Is this her first pregnancy?"

"No!" I said. "She's had eight prior children. Hurry!"

"We're dispatching a crew. What is the time between contractions?"

"Angel," I asked her, "how long between contractions?"

"Less," she panted, "less than two minutes apart."

I told him.

"Okay," he said calmly. "You need sterile sheets and towels. Do you have rubber gloves?"

"No, no," I said. "Don't you understand? We have nothing!"

"Can you wash your hands?"

"We're in an elevator, for God's sake."

"Okay." His voice faded, then returned. ". . . you to stay calm. I'm with you. I want you to examine the mother for crowning, in other words, can you see the baby's head?"

"I can't see anything!" I screamed. "I told you, we're in a goddamn elevator in the dark! Wait, wait a minute." I fumbled in my purse for my penlight. The weak, pale yellow beam wavered, the batteries nearly dead.

"Use pillows to elevate the mother's head," he said.

"Here, Angel," I said. I emptied her little overnight bag and propped it beneath her head.

"I have to go to the bathroom!" she wailed.

"How long before they get here?" I asked frantically.

"They're already there," he said, "trying to gain access to the building."

Thank God, I thought. "Hear that, Angel? They're outside."

"How's she doing?"

"She has to go to the bathroom."

"That pressure probably means the baby has moved into

the birth canal and is about to arrive."

"Oh, no, no, not yet," I told Angel. "They'll be here in a minute."

"You have any newspapers, plastic sheets?"

"No!"

"If you have a mask or gown, put them on. Make sure the mother's head is turned to one side in case she vomits."

"Wait!" I used the penlight. Things were happening fast. Too fast.

I spread a bathrobe, a small towel, and a dress from her bag out on the floor. At least they were clean.

"It's okay, it's okay," I told her, snatching up the phone again. "Take deep breaths. We can do this together." Can this be happening? Is this really happening? I thought desperately.

"I want you to place one hand under the baby's head as it emerges," the operator was saying, his voice nearly lost in the crackle of static. "Do not pull on the baby. Did you get that?"

"No pulling. I can hardly hear you," I gasped; my eyes teared. What if something goes wrong, if something happens to the baby or to Angel? How will I know what to do? I quit saving the battery, slid the penlight under my watch band, and prayed. I thought I heard shouts in the building, but too much was happening and I was too busy to respond.

All of a sudden I was cradling the baby's head, horrified, yet thrilled beyond belief as an upper shoulder began to emerge and I somehow guided a tiny new life into this big and scary world.

"A boy! A boy!" I sang out to Angel. "Whoops, he's a

slippery little devil." I fumbled frantically to hang on to him.

I cleared the baby's nose and mouth with my handkerchief, then groped for the phone. Everything was warm, wet, and sticky, the air thick with the strong smell of iron.

"Is he breathing?" Angel cried.

"Is the baby breathing?" the operator echoed.

"I'm not sure," I said, panic rising.

"Keep the baby on its side," he said coolly. "Make sure the mouth is clear. Then lightly snap your index finger against the soles of the baby's feet."

My frantic fingers found his feet. My God, they were so tiny.

"Lightly," he repeated. "Snap your index finger against the soles."

That did it. We cried, all three of us: me, Angel and her baby.

Her shoelaces were all we had to tie off the umbilical cord. While the fire department plotted our rescue, I cut the cord in the middle, using the miniature Swiss Army knife on my key chain. The elevator, like the entire damn *News* building, was as dark and cold as an editor's heart. I gingerly wrapped the baby in my cotton blouse, then my sweater. When none of the firemen's elevator access keys worked and they were unable to access the hatch at the top, the medics decided not to wait for the elevator company's emergency crew. They cut the power, brought in bright lights and a portable generator, and used the jaws of life to peel away the doors between the third and fourth floors.

The noise was earsplitting, bright lights blinding. The first paramedic dropped down four and a half feet to join us. I was happy to see him but reluctant to give up the baby. The husky firefighter had to nearly pry him out of my arms. "Be careful," I warned tearfully. "Watch his head. He's little, and he's been through a lot."

I rode in the ambulance, a blanket around my shoulders, determined not to allow mother and child out of my sight.

"Look at him," I told Angel. "He's beautiful. The most beautiful baby I've ever seen."

She, and everyone else, agreed.

Rooney dashed to meet us as the ambulance arrived at the ER. The baby kicked and gurgled as I watched the little family, eyes brimming.

"Congratulations," the husky medic said. "Good job."

"Right." His partner shook my hand. "Welcome to the Stork Club." The members, he said, are cops and fire-fighters who have delivered babies in the field.

He fastened a tiny stork-shaped pin to the paper hospital gown a nurse had given me.

I wore it over my stained slacks two hours later when a still-giddy Rooney drove me back to the *News*, where my car was parked.

"Your life is changed forever now," I preached, all hyped and on a roll. "He's a huge responsibility."

"I know," he said solemnly. "Angel and I won't let him or the other kids down. But we need all the help we can get. That's why Angel and I want you to be little Rooney's god-mother. We'd been talking about it even before tonight."

I accepted, of course.

Fitzgerald was seated on my doorstep. "Hey." He sounded

grumpy, got slowly to his feet, then did a double take. "Holy shit! Britt. Are you all right? Whose blood is that? What the hell happened?"

"The most wonderful thing!" I said, euphoric as a rosy dawn erupted around us. Fluffy white clouds drifted across the horizon, dewdrops sparkled on brilliant pink hibiscus, and songbirds greeted the sun in this beautiful world, the first dawn in the life of little Rooney Thomas Jr.

18

I was babbling nonstop about the baby, so Fitzgerald eventually fled, giving me the chance to shower, wash my hair, and call everybody I knew with the news.

Babies, I thought. They do change people forever. How could anyone give hers up?

Still on an adrenaline high, there was no point trying to sleep. I walked Bitsy as threatening rain squalls blossomed like bruised flowers on the eastern horizon. I threw a raincoat in the car, relished a hot breakfast at the Villa Deli, then drove through increasingly windy streets as storm clouds crowded a darkening sky.

I called my mother, who didn't answer, then Frances Haehle, who annoyingly pretended we were strangers. Mr. Kagan was in court, she said stiffly, but would soon return. Preston Broussard was also unavailable, still conferring with his attorney, which left me time to raid the baby department at Burdines Department Store.

I had no idea so many tiny garments were designed with little feet in them, even a miniature Florida Marlins uniform. Rooney Jr. also needed a rattle, a Pooh Bear shirt, and a hat with wee sunglasses to shield him from the South Florida rays.

Angel was in surprisingly good spirits when I swung by the hospital, bright and perky, despite all she'd been through. The woman was definitely a natural mother, and her rosy, dimpled baby even more beautiful than I remembered. Rooney snapped Polaroids and gave me a few to take with me.

Stockton's secretary located the tape and used her key card to settle me into a cubicle adjacent to the conference room. I watched the tape alone, in a comfortable chair, my pen, notebook, and a steaming cup of coffee in front of me.

The show's host referred to R. J. as "the millionaire department-store heir now facing execution after losing his final death row appeal."

There were pictures, R. J. young and husky in a football uniform; a full-length shot of Kaithlin, with two other swimsuited teenage girls at the beach, mugging and laughing for the camera. Kaithlin gazed directly into the lens, her smile fresh and certain, as Amy Hastings hugged her neck. Any Seattle viewer who noted a resemblance between the long-dead murder victim and local socialite Shannon Broussard must have deemed it coincidental. After all, the dead woman's name was different and her photos, shot long ago, aired only briefly.

The segment's most riveting moments came during a video of the once-happy newlyweds: a beautiful couple, lighthearted in the joy of the moment, blissfully unaware of their future. Kaithlin fit perfectly into the arms of a much younger R. J., laughing as he whirled her around the dance floor at their wedding reception.

Several small children darted across the dance floor and Kaithlin greeted them tenderly, a graceful arm entwined around a little fellow's waist, hands fussing with a tiny girl's hair.

Her full-skirted designer gown pooled around her in creamy satin waves as she knelt among the exuberant children. Her features were obscured, but the children's were alight in response to her.

I replayed that moment again and again. How stupid I've been, I thought. I should have known.

The sky, so crystal clear and full of promise at dawn, was now gray and grimy and leaked a chill drizzle. The desolate weather fit the mood. Preston Broussard clutched a half-dozen white roses. Her favorite, he said. I already knew that. Introspective and brooding, he listened intently to my running commentary.

"Here's where I came onto the beach. The weather was perfect, the way it was first thing this morning. Two uniformed police officers were right down there." I pointed as we slogged through damp sand.

"She surfaced only slightly south of where it happened." I pointed again. "The man up in that window, the one who witnessed it, called the police when he spotted her. So did a woman, a tourist from New York, who was sunbathing with her little boy, Raymond. Detective Rychek arrived, and the officers brought her up onto the sand. She wore an earring. That was all. They covered her with a yellow blanket. Her swimsuit top, a rose-red color, was retrieved by another swimmer farther south." My eyes strayed to Marsh's window, and I gave a little halfhearted obligatory wave. "He spotted it too, called it in while we were standing here.

"He said later that he'd seen her arrive. He knew where she'd been staying because of the hotel logo on her beach towel. Did you know," I said, turning to him, "that she registered under the name Morrigan?"

He smiled wistfully. "The detective mentioned it. She read stories about Celtic goddesses to the girls. The Morrigan, an Irish goddess of war, had the power to decide who died in battle. She could take the form of a bird, and when she hovered above them, warriors saw it as an omen of death." He shrugged. "I assume that's where she picked up the name."

I continued my narrative. "The man up there said she sat on the sand watching an intriguing cloud formation. As it began to break apart, she walked down to the water and dove in. She was swimming, when suddenly the killer was there. It was over very quickly." I touched his arm.

Tears coursed down his cheeks. "That man up there, his name is Marsh?"

I nodded.

"How on earth could he simply watch and do nothing?"

"There's not much he could have done. He's disabled, in a wheelchair." I didn't mention that, even if able-bodied, Marsh's instinctive reaction probably would have been to reload his camera. "He watches the sea and the people near it, shooting pictures and videos. It's his hobby," I said.

"Why didn't he shoot pictures of the killer?"

"He'd been photographing the clouds, the same unusual

formation she was watching, and ran out of film. He said he couldn't reload fast enough."

"Could he recognize the man?"

"Not from up there. A senior citizen who exercises here every day saw another swimmer near her. He assumed they were together."

Broussard hunkered down at the surf's lacy edge, gently dropping the roses onto the outgoing tide, one at a time. The scene would have made a poignant picture, but I hadn't told the photo desk. The man deserved his moment of privacy.

We returned to his hotel and a corner booth in the bustling coffee shop. His attorney, he said, was seeking an emergency injunction to prohibit release of the body until a hearing, hopefully within twenty-four hours. The lawyer had already spoken with Myrna Lewis's attorney. The woman was passionate about keeping R. J. away from Kaithlin's corpse. The lawyer felt, however, that if R. J.'s claim was denied, she might be persuaded to drop hers.

"I'm stuck here for at least another twenty-four hours," Broussard said grimly. "The girls can't understand why they're being kept home, but I can't risk their hearing the news from someone at school before I can break it to them myself. Reporters are calling the house. My family is under siege," he said bitterly. "I hate Jordan for this. I could kill the man myself."

"He's not getting any joy from it," I said. "He's miserable, his own worst enemy."

Broussard turned to me, eyes watery. "Do you think he had anything to do with her death?"

"I don't know."

"Will we ever know, for sure? Will the police ever solve it?"

"That's hard to say," I said truthfully. "The longer it takes, the less likely that will be. What often tips the scales is working to keep the case alive. Call, write, push for answers. Otherwise, it's too easy for the cops to shelve it and forget it. Most victims naively think it's wise to be patient, to let the professionals do their jobs. That's a huge mistake. Detectives become distracted, involved in other matters, refocused on new and easier cases. Especially here, where tourist officials prefer to see high-profile investigations like this one die quickly and quietly."

"Thanks, Britt." He sighed. "You don't know what a help it is to be able to talk to you. By the way." He reached inside his jacket for an envelope. "Here's that photo you asked for. I hope it's what you want. My mother sent it Federal Express last night." Eyes haunted, he stared longingly at it before handing it across the table.

He and Kaithlin had posed on a sofa, near a huge Christmas tree, the two little girls on their laps. A dog, a yellow Lab, sat at their feet, wearing silly reindeer antlers. A fire roared in the background.

"I wanted it to be our Christmas card this year, but Shannon didn't. She was very private. . . . You can print it now if you want to." He shrugged hopelessly. "It doesn't matter anymore. I want people who knew her here to see she was happy, that we were a family. Family meant everything to her. My parents are devastated. She got along better with them than I ever did."

"She was a good mother, wasn't she?" I said, studying the faces in the photo.

"The best." Warm memories filled his empty eyes. "Her children were her life."

"I thought so," I said.

The storm had passed but the sky remained gloomy as I drove again to the Southwind Apartments. Myrna Lewis didn't answer. I left a note in her mailbox, but as I left the building she was getting off a bus a block away. I wasn't sure it was her at first. She was dressed up, in an outdated navy-blue suit over a starched white blouse with a little cameo pinned at the throat. Her iron-gray hair had frizzed in the dampness, and her limp was more pronounced.

Out of breath, she clung to the banister as we climbed the stairs to her apartment. She limped into her bedroom to change her shoes and hang up her jacket before rejoining me at her kitchen table.

"I went to see the lawyer," she said, still breathing hard. "I'll do whatever I have to. Would you like something to drink?"

"Stay, sit," I said, taking over. "I'll do it."

"I don't have a lot of money," she told me, as I put the kettle on and lit the burner, "but Reva left enough for Kaithlin's burial. Legal fees are expensive, but I won't give up," she said grimly. "Reva was my friend. I saw what she went through. The worst grief on earth is to lose a child. It's even worse when it's sudden and violent and could have been prevented. Worse yet when you have no body to bury. Every time an unidentified skeleton was found in the swamp or out the woods somewhere, she swore it was her Kaithlin. That's why I have to do this. She would never rest in peace if R. J. was allowed to steal Kaithlin again."

"Kaithlin's second husband wants her too," I said flatly. "I saw him today."

"From what I hear," she said wistfully, "he sounds like a decent man, like a real husband. I'd love to see a picture of Kaithlin's little girls, Reva's granddaughters."

"Here! He gave me this today." I removed the envelope from my bag and took out the photo. "Aren't they beautiful? Like Kaithlin at that age." I gave it to her, then fetched her spectacles from the sideboard.

She stared at the happy faces for a long time. The kettle whistled and I went to find the cups, teabags, and spoons. When I returned, she had both hands to her face, weeping.

I set the steaming cups on the table, then stood patting her shoulder helplessly, looking down at the pink scalp through her thinning hair, tears in my own eyes.

"I'll have a copy made for you," I promised.

"What are their names again?" she said, making little snuffling sounds.

"Caitlin and Devon," I said, and handed her a tissue from my bag. As we talked and sipped tea, her eyes kept returning to the photo.

"They even had a dog," she whispered.

"What I need to know," I said, getting down to business, "is the date Kaithlin's son, her first child, was born."

She lifted her eyes and blinked. "Why?"

"It's very important," I said urgently. "When exactly was he born?"

Her brow creased. "I don't remember now. It was in the spring, I think, or maybe the fall. It was so many years ago. I remember, she was showing at Easter time," she said vaguely, "or was it the feast of St. Stephen?"

"I need the precise date," I coaxed. "Can you remember anyone else who might recall it, who was there at the time?"

She shook her head. "Reva didn't want anyone to know," she said. "There was a friend of Reva's, a woman. She had tried to help with Kaithlin. But I don't recall her last name."

She pursed her lips, frowning over her teacup.

"Her first name was Catherine. She worked at Jordan's. She was very kind, tried to help, but there was nothing—"

"Catherine?" I stared at her. "Kaithlin's supervisor at the store?"

She nodded. "Reva knew her. She came to the hospital to comfort Kaithlin when the baby was born." She frowned. "But I wouldn't know where to find her now."

My hands shook as I put down my cup. "I do," I said.

I called her office from my car. The sun had reemerged and the air was clear and bright again.

She wasn't in, the receptionist said.

"Are you sure?" I asked, impatient. Was she ducking me even at work? "When do you expect her?"

"Who's calling, please?"

Swell, I thought, if I blow my cover she'll never come to the phone. "Her daughter, Britt."

"Her daughter?" The woman sounded puzzled. "Hi, Britt. Are you in town?"

"Yes, is there a problem?"

"Ms. Montero has been out sick all week. I don't know when she'll be in."

"Sick?"

"I assumed you'd know."

I mumbled something and hung up, the distant, neglectful, uncaring daughter. Was she really ill?

I remembered the name of the insurance agency Nelson operated and called him. "Have you spoken to my mom today?" I asked. "She's not in her office."

"I know." He cleared his throat. "I'm concerned about her."

"What's wrong?"

"She's been down in the dumps lately. Depressed."

"What's the problem?" I asked.

"Well," he said, "you should know."

Her convertible sat in its reserved slot outside her building. I parked next to it and waved to the doorman, who buzzed me in. When she didn't answer her bell, I rapped loudly with the metal knocker. No answer. Nothing. I dialed her number on my cell phone and heard it ring inside. Still no answer. Dread gnawed at my stomach. I fumbled for the key she gave me in case of emergency.

Before I found it, I heard a sound on the other side, a movement at the peephole.

"Mom? It's me, Britt."

"Can you come back later?" she said. She sounded groggy, as though she'd been sleeping.

"No," I said. "Open the door."

"I'm not dressed."

"I don't care. Open it."

I thanked God she was all right as I heard the chain lock clatter.

Pale without makeup, her hair tousled, she was barefoot

and wearing a rumpled full-length cotton nightgown in midafternoon. The nightgown looked like she'd slept in it, normal for the rest of us, unusual for my fastidious mother. Her pastel apartment, always so full of light, looked gloomy, drapes drawn. The odor of stale cigarette smoke hung on the air.

"Do you have a fever?" Instinctively, I reached for her forehead. "Are you sick? Why didn't you call me?" Her skin felt cool.

"I just don't feel well," she said weakly. "I need some rest and time alone."

"When did you eat last? Why is it so dark in here?" I opened the drapes. Slumped on the couch, she looked more fragile than I had ever seen her, one hand shielding her puffy, red-rimmed eyes as though the light hurt them.

"Is it the flu?" I asked.

"No," she said softly.

"When did you eat last?"

She shook her head.

I checked her kitchen, opened the refrigerator. The only even remotely edible item was a long-wilted corsage in the vegetable bin. A bottle of vodka sat on the counter, half empty.

"What is going on here?"

"The third degree *again?*" Her back straightened as she reached for her cigarettes.

"Is all *this* about *that?*" I asked in disbelief.

She looked up, and I saw it was true.

I sat in an easy chair across from her, still shocked by her appearance.

She stared back. "You don't look so spiffy yourself," she

said. "Where'd you get those circles under your eyes? When did you sleep last? And that lipstick." She grimaced. "It's all wrong. Glossy is out."

"You're never depressed," I said. "At least you haven't been for years."

"So maybe it's time. One occasionally has to take stock of one's actions." She reached for an ornate lighter and, after several frustrating tries, managed to light her cigarette.

"They're not good for you," I said disapprovingly. "I'll fix you something to eat, or order out if I have to. But I need to ask you something first."

She rolled her eyes and exhaled.

"Do you know any way I can find out the exact date that Kaithlin's baby was born?"

"April seventeenth, nineteen eighty-two." She flicked her eyes at me. "At four forty-five A.M."

I dropped my notebook. My jaw nearly went with it. "How did you do that?" I said, stunned. "You're sure?"

She gazed at me through the smoke.

"Some things," she said, "you don't forget."

"So you were closer to Kaithlin than you ever said."

She nodded sadly. "From the moment I met that girl it was obvious she would go far." She give a brittle little laugh at her own joke. "Little did I know how far. But she always had something special."

"I know," I said. "You wished I was more like her."

She looked startled. "Surely you're joking, Britt."

"No."

She laughed in utter astonishment. "You think that for a moment I'd prefer a daughter like Kaithlin? Someone who got pregnant as a teenager? Who made her mother's life hell? Who wasted her own life? Her talent? And broke the hearts of everyone who loved her?" She stubbed out her cigarette fiercely in a shell-shaped ashtray, then leaned forward, expression intent. "You're serious," she said, in disbelief. "How could you ever entertain such a thought? Perhaps I wasn't as affectionate as I should have been, but I was always trying so hard to be a mother, a father, and a provider that I . . .

"Britt, do you have any idea how incredibly proud you make me? Even when you involve yourself in events that stand my hair on end, I am so thrilled that you are my daughter! I admit I nag sometimes, but that's only because I want so much for you. And I do worry, but that's because you're so brave, like your father. It makes me afraid of losing *you* as well. I couldn't love you more."

"I always think I'm a disappointment to you," I said, scarcely believing her words.

She shook her head. "You're a better person than I am. I've let so many people down." Tears filled her eyes.

"You've never let me down," I said, and opened my arms for a long warm hug. Our tears weren't only because we were both overtired.

It appeared to be my day for kitchen duty. I rechecked my mother's pantry, then called a nearby Chinese restaurant. I used her antique-style white phone, like one I saw Lana Turner use in an old black-and-white film on late-night TV, and then I sat next to her on the couch and we talked.

She was depressed, she said, because of the guilt she'd carried all these years.

"Poor Reva," she said. "God rest her soul."

"I can't picture you two as friends," I said. "You were

so unalike."

"She was older, of course, but we shared more in common than you might think," my mother said. "We'd both been abandoned, or at least at that time I still thought I'd been, by men who left us with little girls to raise alone. We were both working mothers struggling to survive.

"She showed up unannounced one day after Kaithlin first came to work at Jordan's and asked me to watch out for her daughter. She was a cautious and protective mother, and it was Kaithlin's first job. I could relate to that. I promised her there'd be no problem; that, in fact, I'd take a special interest in Kaithlin and mentor her. And I did.

"It was obvious to everyone when she caught R. J.'s eye. He was never subtle. Right then, while it was still a brush fire, I could have, should have, done something to extinguish it. But R. J. . . ." She closed her eyes tight, hugging her arms as though cold. "He was my boss's son, the heir apparent, the man I fully expected to be working for someday. I swear, Britt," she said, opening her eyes wide, locking them on mine, "it wasn't ambition on my part, trying to further a career. Hell, in those days I just needed a job. We needed the security. I told myself that R. J. flirted with everyone, that this little episode would be short-lived, like all the others—and I looked the other way.

"I hoped it would burn itself out. I was wrong, of course. Reva trusted me, and I never even warned her. By the time she found out, it was an out-of-control three-alarm fire. I was ashamed to admit to her that I knew all along. Kaithlin had become defiant, refusing to quit her job. Reva was frantic. She begged me to do something."

"What did you do?" I said.

"Very little." Her voice was empty. She reached for her cigarettes, jiggled the box, and slid one out. "As Kaithlin's supervisor I revamped her hours, juggling them about so she'd be less likely to see R. J. or be able to meet him afterward, but it was like trying to stop a force of nature. I told myself it was the best I could do. Reva pleaded with me to fire her, but I had no legitimate reason. Kaithlin was professional on the job, and the man Reva wanted kept away from her was my employer's son."

"What more could you have done?"

"Lots." She shrugged hopelessly, struggling with the lighter. "I could have talked to R. J. I could have gone to his father. The girl was underage. He wouldn't have wanted a scandal. I could have warned Kaithlin about R. J. She wouldn't listen to her mother, but she might have listened to me."

"Chances are none of that would have worked," I said.

"Well, now," she said, finally coaxing a flame from the lighter, "we'll never know, will we? Because I never tried. When Kaithlin was pregnant, Reva went to R. J. herself. He was horrid; he behaved terribly. She was crushed. But Con, he would have listened. We were close. He wasn't that happy at home. He relied on me—for many things."

"Mom!" I said, dismayed.

"We were friends," she said firmly, exhaling bluish smoke in the slanted light, "kindred spirits. He needed a woman to talk to, to confide in, to brainstorm with. His life wasn't easy. But he was good, a man of character. He would have tried to do something.

"But," she said, eyes stricken, "I was a total coward. I did nothing."

"You can't blame yourself."

"Oh, but I do," she said earnestly. "How can anyone not blame me, after the way it ended, with all of them dead: Kaithlin, her mother, Con? He was a broken man after R. J.'s conviction. And here I sit, the one person who might have prevented it all, and I never lifted a finger. My chief concern, instead, was my job and being the sole support of my daughter.

"Is it any wonder," she said ruefully, "that I was so hard on you when you began to date? That I've always been so crazed about your safety?"

"That does explain some things," I agreed. "But you're far too hard on yourself."

She shook her head. "When I saw that terrible photo you had and you began to ask questions . . . Then it was all over the news again, everyone talking about it. It brought back all the old memories, the guilt. I've been wondering why I'm alive when they're all dead. For the past few days I haven't even been able to get out of bed and function. I've been horrible, to you and to Nelson. I haven't been to the office all week. I'm a mess," she moaned.

"You had all you could handle back then," I protested. "Other people were responsible for their own bad choices. What if?" I said. "What if Kaithlin and R. J. had lived happily ever after? They might have, you know. You had no crystal ball. No one did."

She wiped her eyes. "Thanks, Britt. I'm so lucky to have you." She took my hand. "You know, I never saw Reva or even thought of her without thinking, There but for the grace of God. . . ."

The food arrived and we ate it off her good china, at her

dining room table. She'd put on lipstick and a flowered silk wrap and combed her hair.

"Why," she asked, as I served up the Kung Po chicken, "is the baby's birth date important?"

"I'm not certain," I said, "but I think he's the key somehow."

"I saw him once," she said, with the whisper of a smile, "the day he was born. I went over to Jackson Hospital to see Kaithlin, poor thing. The delivery was difficult; she was so young. I took Reva to the cafeteria for coffee and a bite to eat. Then we saw the baby, cute as a button. His new parents were coming for him later in the day."

"How did you still remember the actual date and his time of birth?"

"I had asked Reva to call when it happened, to let me know everything went well. She woke me at five A.M. to say the baby had been born about fifteen minutes earlier.

"The date wasn't difficult to remember. It was the twelfth anniversary, almost to the hour, of when I last saw your father, before he went off on his ill-fated mission to liberate Cuba. It's always a bad day for me. I try to stay busy. Now, whenever I think of Tony Montero on that date, I remember that poor little tyke having a birthday out there somewhere."

"You and all your secrets," I said. "You never mentioned that anniversary."

"Well, it isn't the sort of day one celebrates. Why burden you with it?"

"Hey, Ma," I mugged. "It's you and me. Your burden is my burden."

"You are the world's wackiest daughter," she said,

and giggled.

Back at the office I surfed the Net, seeking the right web site. I never knew so many were devoted to adoption. I finally tapped into the registry where children adopted from Florida and the parents who gave them up can each check to see if the other is searching for them.

I scrolled through all the hopeful people seeking others lost long ago. Those hoping to be found leave only a first name, the date and place of birth, and the location of the adoption, with a few exceptions.

Kaithlin's son was among them. April 17, 1982, time of birth: 4:46 A.M., Jackson Memorial Hospital, Miami–Dade County. Oh, my God, I thought, it has to be him.

A tag directed me to a site for a special message. His information request was not routine.

More than a message, brief and to the point, it was a plea.

"I am nineteen now," it said, "and have wonderful parents, but unless I locate my birth parents I will never be twenty."

He was a college sophomore, he said, with excellent grades—and leukemia. He had relapsed recently, he said, after a two-year remission. His only hope, all that could save him now, was a bone-marrow transplant from a parent or a sibling with the correct and rare AB blood type.

I gasped aloud. He might already be dead.

I reached for the trial transcript, thumbing frantically through the testimony on forensic evidence. Kaithlin's blood, identified on her torn clothing and in the motel room, was A-positive.

R. J. had to be the only one who could save him.

19

I e-mailed the site administrator.

The response: DO YOU THINK YOU MIGHT BE A RELATIVE? NO, I messaged back. I'M A JOURNALIST. IT'S A MATTER OF LIFE AND DEATH.

The response: WE AREA WARE OF THAT PARTICULAR CASE. WE CAN HOLD YOUR MESSAGE FOR HIM BUT IT'S NOT OUR POLICY TO PUT YOU IN DIRECT CONTACT.

IT'S A MATTER OF LIFE AND DEATH. I CAN HELP.

I'M ONLY A VOLUNTEER. THERE'S NO ONE ELSE HERE RIGHT NOW.

A MATTER OF LIFE AND DEATH.

HE HASN'T BEEN IN TOUCH RECENTLY. WE'VE BEEN CONCERNED.

My heart sank. The message continued.

BOCA RATON, FL. NAME: DANIEL SINCLAIR.

I tapped into recent obits for the Boca newspaper, in Palm Beach County. I didn't find his name. There might still be time.

The white pages on-line showed only one D. Sinclair, with an address. I called R. J., who wasn't in. I left him an urgent message.

I told the desk I'd be out of touch for a few hours on a personal errand and drove to Boca, fearing what I might find.

The drive, north on I-95, took forty-five minutes, then another fifteen to locate the address. The one-story stucco duplex with single-car garages on each side was modest for

Boca, or anywhere.

An aging Buick, the hood up, stood in one driveway. A long lean young man in a T-shirt and blue jeans appeared to be changing the battery. I parked on the street and approached, notebook in hand.

"Daniel Sinclair?" I knew the answer before I asked. Though slightly taller, he was the image of his father. Close up, I saw Kaithlin in his lighter hair and full mouth.

"That's me," he said cheerfully. He lifted out the old battery and placed it on the ground. He looked robust, his color good. Perhaps he was back in remission.

I introduced myself as he installed the new battery and reattached the cables. I offered my card.

He slammed the hood and wiped his hands on a clean rag before taking it. "You're a reporter?" he said.

"Right," I said, relieved. "And I'm so glad to see you looking well."

He slowly raised his eyes to mine, puzzled.

"I'm working on a story about adopted children who seek out their birth parents," I lied, "and saw your message on the website."

"Oh, jeez." He flushed, embarrassed.

"Have you had any luck?"

"Yeah." He shifted his weight as though uncomfortable. "My mother contacted me."

"You saw her?"

"Yeah, so to speak." His eyes flashed, bright with tears. He leaned back against his car, arms folded across his chest. "It was a disaster." He shook his head. "I screwed up. I screwed up bad."

"What went wrong?" I flipped my notebook open.

He glanced up and down the street, as though fearful that a camera crew might suddenly materialize. "Want to come in for a minute?"

"Sure. Where are your folks?" I asked, as he opened the screen door.

"My mom's dead. A drunk driver hit her car when I was nine. It was his fourth drunk-driving arrest. My dad's in a nursing home. He was older, in his fifties, when they adopted me. That's why they did the private adoption. The agencies wouldn't even put them on a waiting list because of his age. Want a Coke?" he said.

A small wooden crucifix hung on the wall near the front door. I followed him into the kitchen, where he peered into the refrigerator, dug out a couple of cans of cola, and handed me one. The curtains were sunshine yellow. An angel plaque mounted on the wall over the sink said GOD BLESS OUR HOME.

"Dad's had a couple of strokes," he said, as he popped the top on his drink. "Last one put him in the nursing home. He's gonna have to have a lot of therapy before he can come home."

"How terrible," I said, shocked by the sadness in his young life in this "good home."

"For him, yeah, but for me, naw. I'm okay." He showed me out onto a shady screened-in back porch, where we sat in wicker chairs. "I'm making it," he said, head tilted in a posture that reminded me somehow of R. J. "I'm going to school, work nights in a restaurant. Even sell a picture once in a while. You know"—he grinned—"amateur artist."

"But what about your health?"

His smile disappeared. "You can't write about this," he

pleaded. "I never should have done it. I'm fine. I've never been sick. Never had leukemia."

"You lied?"

He sighed, nodding. "Cindy, a girl I date, warned me. She kept saying, 'Danny, don't do it.' But I was stupid. See, I'd been trying to find my birth parents since I was sixteen. That's when I first registered. My dad didn't object; in fact, he gave permission. But I never got a response. After he had his bad stroke last year, I saw a story on TV about a woman who was adopted and needed a kidney. She had to find her natural parents; she did and there was a big happy reunion. She found out she had brothers and sisters, a whole family. That gave me the idea.

"Everybody's on-line now, and I figured if my birth mom saw it and believed it was a matter of life and death, she might respond.

"Worked like a charm. She never would've contacted me otherwise. She was real reticent, out of state, wouldn't give me her real name. Said she wasn't the right blood type, but she knew where my father was. I thought, Great, I get to meet both of them. Who knows? I thought. Maybe they'd even get together again. I know it all sounds stupid now."

"No," I said, mind still reeling. "Every kid wants a mom and a dad and wants them to be together."

"I guess I just really wanted something, somebody. Cindy's premed. She helped me learn all about the disease, so I could keep up the story. I figured—and I know it was stupid—but I figured once she saw me, everything would be all right. I mean"—he opened his arms, appealingly— "what's not to love?" His grin was self-deprecating. "What a mistake."

"Where did you see her?"

"She didn't want to meet in public, guess she didn't wanna be seen with me. I thought here would be good. Then she'd get to see my trophies, my artwork, you know, stuff she might like. I wanted to impress her.

"So the big reunion I'd waited for since I was a kid finally happens. She shows up in a cab, wearing a scarf and shades like she's incognito. It started out okay. Then I told her I had a surprise. 'Good news,' I say. 'I'm not dying.' "

He shook his head, expression pained. "I thought she'd be happy, relieved to find a healthy son—instead of some needy guy who wanted something from her. It was a disaster. She was furious."

"What did she say?"

" 'You don't know how much you've cost me,' or words to that effect."

"What do you think she meant?" I asked.

He shrugged. "Must have lost time from work, her family. Airfare's expensive; she's from out of state.

"I said, 'You're my mom. How can you say that?' But she just took off. Her parting shot was that I'm just like my father. The way she said it made it obvious that they aren't getting together.

"I botched it. Totally. She didn't want to see or hear anything once she knew I lied. Shot me down and took off, really pissed. Haven't heard her from her again. She's not even on-line anymore. Her e-mail address is shut down. I don't blame her. I never should have done it. Maybe she'll cool off someday and make contact again. If not, I sure learned a lesson. The reunion fantasy is always better than the real thing.

"You should put that in your story," he suggested thoughtfully, leaning back in his creaky chair, long legs stretched out. "When you're adopted you tend to day-dream, to fantasize that your birth parents are fabulous strangers out there somewhere. But if they were really fab-ulous . . . I mean, there's a reason people give a child away. It means you were a mistake.

"I've done a lot of thinking since then," he said, "and I'm grateful for what I do have. I've got my feet back on the ground. No matter what my problems are, I'm a damn sight better off than ninety-nine percent of the people on the planet—and if I want something of my own, if I want a family, I have to create it myself. And I can do that—in time. But"—he turned to me, eyes pleading—"I'd hate to be any more embarrassed about this than I am already, so please don't write about it. Or at least not until I get out of town."

"Where are you going?"

"Got a full scholarship to Boston College. Dad has a sister up there. Once he's well enough, I'm gonna move him north too. I just got back, spent a couple of weeks there getting to know her and her family, checking out the facil-ities. I'm really up for the change. Sometimes you just have to move forward and be your own person," he said. "Travel down your own road and make your own life."

"True," I said, closing my notebook. "Who cares about ancient history?"

"Right." He grinned. "Hey, look at the time. I've got to get ready for my shift tonight."

He spent a few more moments showing me his artwork, charcoal sketches and watercolors, sunlight and shadow on bridges, picturesque buildings, and old cars. They filled the wall space in his room and were stacked against the furniture, competing for space with his baseball and debate team trophies and his computer, its screen dark, on a small corner desk. A recent painting was still on the easel. A sandy-haired girl and a medium-size shaggy dog posed on what looked like the same back porch where we had just talked. "That's Cindy," he said, "and Boscoe."

"Lovely." I admired the softness of her face, the graceful flow of her scarf and the dog's whiskery grin.

Danny Sinclair walked me out to my car, smiling and clear-eyed. "Good luck with your story," he said, and waved as I drove away.

"Good luck to you too," I told him.

I played the radio, turned up the volume, and sang along loudly to keep awake during the long drive back. It's true, I thought, babies do change people. They change lives forever. I went directly to Kagan's office.

"Is he in?"

"Do you have an appointment, Miss . . . ?" Frances asked, eyes wary.

"No," I said, "but I hope he can spare a moment."

"I see," she said crisply. "Your name again?"

Too tired for her paranoia, even when no one was watching, I stared her straight in the eye. She gazed back like a total stranger.

"Montero," I said wearily, wondering what frightened her so. "Britt Montero from the *Miami News*. He'll remember."

She rapped on his office door, stepped inside, then

emerged after a brief exchange.

"He's with a client," she said. "He can see you in a few minutes."

She averted her eyes, tapping her computer keys primly, as I leafed through a dog-eared office copy of *The American Trial Lawyer* magazine.

As I skimmed a piece on libel law, an older black woman stepped out of Kagan's office, a sullen teenager in tow. I assumed she was grandma and he was trouble. He slouched out the door after her, at that awkward age, somewhere between juvenile hall and state prison.

"What did he do?" I asked Kagan, when Frances showed me inside. "Steal cars or snatch purses?"

"My clients are innocent until proven guilty," he said. In shirtsleeves, documents strewn across his desk, he looked almost like a real lawyer.

"Or until he pleads."

"What now?" His look said, Cut the small talk.

"You forgot to mention Kaithlin's son."

He rapped his expensive fountain pen on his desk blotter, his small smile ironic. "Rothman spilled his guts, right? That son-of-a-bitch."

"It wasn't R. J. she wanted to save," I said, "it was their son. Right?"

Kagan pushed a button, told Frances to hold his calls, then clasped his hands before him in a failed attempt to appear sincere. "She was a teenager when she had the kid. All these years later, she'd pulled it off, she's sitting pretty in Seattle. But, like most broads"—he leveled a meaningful gaze at me—"she can't let well enough alone. The Internet, God bless it. That started it. Playing around on her computer, she can't resist surfing the sites for adopted kids looking to find their natural parents." He spread his hands apart in a gesture of wonderment. "Lo and behold, her kid is registered."

"So?" I prodded.

He hesitated, then fished his keys out of his pocket and unlocked a desk drawer. Shuffling through a thick file, he withdrew a single sheet of paper and handed me a printout of Danny's message, his phony plea for help.

I merely glanced at it. "I've seen it," I said. "She thought R. J.'s execution would kill their son as well. The mother-child bond was the only tie strong enough to bring her back to Miami. I should have known. How did she plan to reunite father and son without exposing herself?"

"Who knows?" Kagan shrugged. "It never got that far." He licked his lips. "When she showed up here to blow her top, I whipped out my file on her. In fact, I gave her a copy. The photos, Rothman's reports, old news clippings he dug up on her and R. J. It was a real blow, a shock to her that we knew her story and who she was.

"Evidently she goes off next to meet the kid, check out his condition, see how much time she's got to work things out for him. Next day she calls and wants to meet with me and Rothman. Seems the reunion was another shock."

"She learned the kid wasn't sick, never was," I said.

"Right. She comes in; you shoulda seen her. First time she'd ever mentioned the kid to us. Apparently he's a dead ringer for his ol' man. She says he lied and tried to manip- ulate her just like R. J. did. Actually, the kid was pretty smart," Kagan said, admiring the boy's ingenuity.

"So she risked her family and her new life to save her

long-lost child, only to find out he didn't need saving. But now you and Rothman know her identity, she's been sold out, and somebody wants her dead." I imagined Kaithlin as she watched the life she had so carefully constructed start to collapse around her. She had to know the end was only a matter of time.

"Why didn't you mention the boy to me before?" I said.

"You never know," he said, eyes shrewd, "when this kind of information might come in handy, have some value in the future."

Still playing every angle, I thought, still hoping to make a buck off somebody else's misery.

"She was mad as hell that he sucked her in," Kagan was saying. "That she bought his story in the first place."

"When did you see her last?"

"She got real paranoid after the second meeting with me and Rothman. Said somebody had seen her and she couldn't leave her hotel room. So I went there that night, for dinner. I was trying to salvage the situation, so to speak. You know, talk her outa doing anything crazy."

"She was okay when you left?"

"Fit as a fiddle," he said.

"She was killed the next morning," I said.

He shrugged and looked innocent.

"Did she say who saw her?"

"No, but it freaked her out, big time."

"What craziness did you try to talk her out of? Going public? Exposing you?"

"Hey, a helluva lot more than that. She was furious, hysterical, first time I saw her. The second time, she was ice cold, which in her case was a helluva lot more scary. Tell you the truth, I liked her better hysterical."

"Scary in what way?"

He lowered his voice and leaned forward. "She figured that since we made her, the kid could do it. She was afraid he was gonna be trouble, like his old man. Woman actually asked whether we knew somebody who could get rid of the kid, for good, if he gave her any problems. She was afraid he'd show up on her doorstep in Seattle and give her a little 'splaining to do. Me and Rothman, we couldn't believe what we were hearing. We just looked at each other."

"What did you tell her?"

"Hell, even I've got scruples."

"Could have fooled me," I said bitterly, wondering whether to believe him.

"Hey!" His lips curled defensively. "Everybody hates criminal defense lawyers until they need one. This ain't the first time one of my own clients scared the shit outa me." He pushed up from his chair so hard it bounced off the wall. "That broad," he said, pointing his finger at me and pacing the room, "had a history, a track record of making bad things happen, and she had a helluva lot to lose." He paused, arms folded. "If she could consider putting out a hit on her own kid, who's to say what else she coulda done? Coulda decided to whack us too. She'd be home free."

I almost laughed. The man's cash cow had turned on him baring its teeth. Was he claiming self-defense? "How was she," I said pointedly, "when you left her that night?"

"Not bad." He sat on the edge of his desk. "Good, in fact. She'd quit talking about the kid being a threat, seemed better than I'd seen her. Relaxed. Maybe it was Prozac, or she got her PMS under control, or something. Seemed like she'd adjusted. She was feeling better, even smiling. So was I. She was upbeat when I left."

"You knew Rothman sold her out to R. J., told him where she was?"

"He did that?" Kagan's eyes narrowed in what appeared to be genuine surprise. "How much did the son-of-a-bitch get?"

"Ask him," I said, shrugging. His indignation was probably only because Rothman beat him to it.

"You try to be a nice guy," he said bitterly, "throw a little business somebody's way, and he gets greedy and blows things for you."

"Yeah, life's a bitch," I said, "and then you die. Who killed her, Kagan?"

He contemplated his expensive Italian leather shoes. "I'd say R. J. had a helluva motive; maybe Rothman wanted to shut her face. Who knows?"

How much of what he said was true? I wondered, as I drove back to the paper. Faced with the prospect of endless blackmail, Kaithlin may have threatened to expose him. The statute of limitations had lapsed long ago on any crime she might have committed. All she wanted was to protect her marriage, her family.

Repairmen in the lobby were working on the stalled elevator. The other worked fine, though my stomach flip-flopped as I stepped inside.

Fred waited in the newsroom. "Just what exactly happened in the elevator last night?" He studied me quizzically.

"You don't want all the details, trust me," I said.

"The fire department did thousands of dollars' worth of damage to the doors of the damn thing."

"Put it on my expense account," I said.

"Well, tell me one thing," he demanded. "What were you and this pregnant woman doing in the newsroom after midnight?"

I explained.

"Are the mother and child in good health?"

"Fine." I dug out my photos. "That damn elevator never should have been the only one in use overnight. Everybody's complained about it."

He nodded solemnly as I showed off my favorite: Rooney Jr., his face in a pout, tiny fists clenched.

"We should send flowers," he said, studying the photo.

"That would be nice," I said. "Diapers would be better."

Angel got flowers. I got a call from Zachary Marsh.

"Guess who I saw out there today?" he greeted me.

"Me?" I said, resigned.

"You've got it," he chortled. "Is that a new boyfriend, the dead woman's husband, or both?"

"Not funny, Zack. You saw the poor guy."

"I'm looking at him right now."

"What?"

"I developed the pictures. The sequence with the roses is very touching. You look a bit tired, though."

"I was, and I am. Had a rough night."

"Tell me about it." He sounded eager.

"I will," I promised, and relaxed for a moment. "You'd enjoy the story. It has a happy ending. But right now I have to work. I'll tell you all about it later."

I rang Eunice and lied to her housekeeper. She put me right through after I identified myself as the paper's fashion editor.

"I thought this was Helen," Eunice sputtered, annoyed that it was me.

"I'm sorry," I lied again. "The person who answered must have misunderstood. I have a question about Kaithlin."

"I—am—so—tired—of—her," Eunice enunciated succinctly. "Even dead, she never goes away."

"I can understand your feelings after all you've been through."

"She's still all R. J. talks about. Now this dreadful scandal, him wanting to claim that woman's body." Her voice became self-pitying. "It's going to be in the newspaper, isn't it?"

"I'm afraid so," I said. "It's a matter of public record. I can imagine how embarrassed you are. You did everything a mother could do. You even tried to find her, to save your son, after Mr. Rothman, that detective, gave you the information that Kaithlin was alive in Miami."

"That awful little man," she hissed. "I never had to deal with people like him in my entire life."

"He is sleazy," I agreed. "What did you do after he told you where she was?"

"Well." She hesitated. "Before making a fuss and looking the fool, I had to see for myself whether it was really Kaithlin. I didn't know if it was true or some scheme that horrible little man had cooked up with R. J. I thought she'd been dead all these years. So I went to the hotel where he claimed she was staying."

"The day after you got the information?" I said.

"Correct. I sat in that lobby, all day long, just watching, to see if she was really there. I never even had lunch. Hardly went to the powder room. Just waited and watched."

"Did you see her?"

She paused. "I caught a glimpse of someone I thought might be her, but only for a split second. Then she was gone. I couldn't be sure."

"Did that person see you?"

"She might have. I'm not sure."

She was the reason Kaithlin holed up in her room, I thought. The reason she had met with Kagan there that night.

"I returned in a day or two," Eunice said, "with an old photo of Kaithlin that I'd managed to find. A hotel employee said she looked familiar but must have checked out."

She had. By then, Kaithlin lay unclaimed at the morgue.

Eunice's halfhearted detective work suggested that she might have feared the information was accurate. Maybe she really didn't relish the prospect of R. J. coming home. Maybe she wouldn't mind sending him back.

"I know he's your son, and you love him," I said gently. "But do you think he might have hired someone to kill her? Did he ask you to do something like that?"

"Of course not," she snapped. "The stupid fool is still obsessed by her. And he knows better than to ask me to become involved in anything so unsavory."

A hearing into the legal tug-of-war over Kaithlin's corpse

had been set for later in the week. I had nearly finished the story when Fitzgerald called.

"I've got somebody here who wants to talk to you," he said, over the sound of music. The background noises were too loud and happy to be anywhere but a bar.

"Who?"

"Hey, kid."

"Emery, what's up?"

"You ain't gonna believe this, kid. We're celebrating," he said jubilantly. "The Jordan case. *Finito.* It's all wrapped up. You can't write nothing yet, you have to wait till we talk to the M.E. tomorrow. But the case? It's solved."

20

"What do you mean, suicide? That's impossible."

"Nope," he said. "The FBI came through, God bless 'em. Their lab and ESDA, short for Electrostatic Detection Apparatus. Size of a fax machine. Amazing. They re-created what she wrote on that legal pad in the hotel room. Definitely a suicide note."

"To whom?"

"The husband, Broussard. Who else?"

"But he never—"

"Evidently he ain't picking up his mail these days. Here, listen to this, kid. Hey, Dennis, hand me the file. Okay," he said. "Get this."

I took notes as he read.

"Darling Pres,

"When you read this I will be dead. My morning swim, my love, is to where the horizon meets the sky. I won't be back. I don't know whether I'll be found or not but, rest assured, I am gone and at peace. I love you and the girls too much to burden you with ancient history. I tried to protect our life together, yet follow my conscience to atone in some way for past mistakes. Instead I made a far bigger mistake, one that has trapped me between my ugly past and uglier people. My life has come apart with no way out.

"I could never look in your face again, once you knew my story. I know the value you place on truth, and I couldn't bear to see you turn away. Here is one absolute truth: You were my final reprieve in a life gone wrong. Unfortunately, the past hounds us to our graves and beyond. Believe that I never intended to hurt anyone, especially you and the girls, the lights of my life. That's why this is going to your office, so it won't fall into the wrong little hands at home.

"We were so lucky! How many people ever share such a wondrous ten years? What a blessing that I found you when I did. You saved me. It was you and no other. Please don't hate me.

"Love forever,

"Shannon.

"Now," Emery said. "Does that, or does it not, sound like a suicide note?"

"But what about the medical examiner? The injuries he saw? He ruled it a homicide."

"Some of them mighta been what I thought in the first place," he said, "inflicted by sea life, from being dragged along the bottom by the tide; maybe some were even self-inflicted or she got banged up in a little scuffle she mighta had with somebody. They were all minor."

"She did quarrel with Kagan and maybe even Rothman," I said doubtfully. "You know, that private detective?"

"See?" he crowed. "The chief M.E. is good, but the guys in that office, they've been wrong before. Ain't the first time, won't be the last. That's what I got to meet with him about. I'm gonna ask him, in light of this, to take another look at her and reclassify it as a suicide. This also explains why she cut the labels out of her clothes and stripped the tags off her luggage. Out-of-town suicides do that all the time to conceal their identities."

"You're sure she wrote it?" I said doubtfully.

"Gonna have a handwriting expert take a look," he said, "but the signature looks identical on the copies of her checks and whatnot that we got from Preston Broussard. And there's that line from her wedding ring. You know, that 'you and no other' crap. That's her talking. She wrote it. I caught a break for a change. Maybe my luck is changing. God love the FBI. The only person happier than I am to get this monkey off my back is the chief. This brings down our murder rate and closes the case without a three-ring circus in court. Perfect."

"It is pretty damn neat," I agreed. It explained why Kaithlin didn't run after seeing Eunice lurking in the lobby. She'd given up. She didn't intend to run anymore. "You're sure?"

"Think I'd close it if I wasn't?"

"But Kagan was with her that last night," I protested. "He's the one who had dinner with her in her room. He just admitted it. Said she was in good spirits, better than

301

she had been."

"See, whad I tell ya? Makes sense," he said. "Would-be suicides always feel better after making their final decision. Once they know what they're gonna do, they feel good about having some control over their lives again. That's why next of kin always has trouble accepting it. They're always saying, 'But he was in such good spirits, finally got a grip,' then *boom!* Happens all the time."

"Yeah," I said uncertainly. "But what about Zachary Marsh? The witness? My God, Emery, he saw her struggling with somebody in the water."

"That," he said, "is a problem. But between you and me, we both know Mr. Zachary Marsh ain't no bird-watcher. He's a publicity hound. He lives for attention. If you remember, he never breathed a word about homicide till after the fact. He reads in the newspaper she got whacked; then, all of a sudden, he remembers: Oh, yeah, by the way, I seen somebody kill her. Saw the whole thing go down. Yeah. Sure.

"Interesting he didn't happen to mention none-a that when he called to report the body. He's like the freaks who crave attention so much they start confessing to every unsolved murder in town. You gotta take Mr. Marsh and his little personal crime watch with a grain-a salt."

"What does Broussard say?"

"Didn't talk to him yet. Stopped by his hotel, but he was out. Just do me a favor and hold off; don't write nothing until after I get squared away with the M.E. tomorrow. Meanwhile, me and Fitz are here at the Eighteen Hundred Club, celebrating. Care to join us?"

"Maybe later," I said.

I went back to my story on the legal battle over the body and changed "unsolved murder" to "drowning." Instead of homicide, I wrote that the death was "still under investigation by homicide detectives."

Then I called. "Hey, Zack," I said. "I need to talk to you about the Jordan case."

He sounded pleased. "Didn't expect to hear from you again so soon. What happened last night?"

"The police say they've solved it."

"They arrested the killer?"

"There's been no arrest," I said. "Can I drop by? I'm about to leave. I can be there in thirty minutes."

"Fine," he said. "I can fix you a drink. You can tell me all about your rough night and I can show you the shots I took today. You and the husband."

"Right."

"I'll be ready," he said. "Looking forward to it."

It took me longer than I thought to clear the newsroom. Tubbs questioned my sudden qualifiers in the story. Then I had trouble moving my car out from under the building. Cuban exiles were protesting out front again, blocking traffic and waving signs. Apparently the latest *News* editorials weren't anti-Castro enough to suit them.

I am half Cuban myself. Castro killed my father. But at moments like this I wonder why these people are not in Havana to protest, block traffic, and wave their anti-Castro signs. How does blocking Miami traffic help the cause? My father didn't thumb his nose from a safe distance. He fought on Cuban soil to free his country.

The streetlights blurred, as I blinked and rubbed my eyes in the misty winter evening. It had been a long day. I could do this tomorrow, I thought. But some inner compulsion drove me to follow through, to find the answer tonight. I was lucky to find a metered space on a side street. I hate valet parking, giving up my car to strange men eager to put their heavy feet on my gas pedal.

The mirrored elevator zipped me straight to the sixteenth floor. I stepped off, grinning again about little Rooney's arrival—about how two of us boarded an elevator and three got off.

I rang, then rang again. Marsh knew I was coming, I thought, annoyed. Impatient and weary, I rang a third time. A well-dressed middle-aged couple emerged from an apartment down the hall. They stared, without speaking, all the way to the elevator. They probably know Marsh, I thought, and are wondering why anybody in her right mind would visit the man. I pressed the doorbell again.

Why didn't I play Twenty Questions when he was on the phone? I'd be home by now. But if he lied to me, I wanted to look him in the eye. Maybe that's why he didn't answer. I rang again and was startled by a sudden buzz as the door clicked open.

My steps echoed on the tile floor.

"Hello?" I called.

"In here," the metallic voice said, as before, "to your right." The lock on the second door disengaged with a click as I approached.

I entered his aerie, distracted again by my life-size image in living color on the big screen. My hair was a mess, my blouse wrinkled. I needed a good night's sleep. The wide windows exposed the dark sky and sea beyond. Inside were all the toys, electronic equipment, the slight smell of antiseptic on the air, and something else, an unpleasant yet familiar odor that I couldn't quite place.

His wheelchair faced the windows and the horizon as usual.

"Sorry I'm late," I explained. "Cuban protestors are tying up traffic around the paper again."

He kept his back to me. Pouting, I presumed, because I'd kept him waiting.

"I need to talk to you about the day Kaithlin Jordan died."

He mumbled something. It sounded odd. I didn't understand his words.

"What?" I stepped toward him as his wheelchair spun around with a sudden whine of the motor.

I gasped. Was I hallucinating?

"Surprised?" he said softly.

The man in the wheelchair was Preston Broussard.

21

I laughed in amazement. "What on earth are you doing here?"

"I came to speak to Mr. Marsh about what he saw," Broussard said quietly.

"Where *is* Zack?" My eyes roved the dimly lit room. Everything appeared in place except for an eight-by-ten photo face down on the glass-topped table, but no sign of Marsh.

"I hear the case is solved," Broussard said, ignoring my question.

"How did you know?"

"Mr. Marsh happened to mention it, and a desk clerk at the hotel informed me that a detective was looking for me."

The apartment was silent.

"Zack?" I stepped toward another door, presumably the master bedroom and bath. "Where is he?" I persisted. "He's expecting me."

"Indisposed." Broussard explored the controls, touched a button, and the chair swung abruptly to the left. "What did the police say?"

"Does Zack know you're playing with his chair? The man is very finicky about his stuff," I warned, irritated as he swung back to the right.

"What did the police say?" he repeated, his voice expressionless.

I sighed, then perched on the arm of a sculpted chair. "There are some things you should know first."

"Quite so." He stopped toying with the controls to stare at me, eyes expectant.

If Marsh was in the bathroom, no water was running, no toilet flushing, nothing.

"Were you aware," I began, "that Kaithlin had R. J.'s child several years before they married, while she was still an underage schoolgirl?"

He looked startled. "No."

"It was a boy," I said. "Kaithlin's mother arranged a private adoption."

"Wait." He waved a finger at me, as though I'd been naughty. "The name is Shannon. My wife's name was Shannon."

"Right," I said, too exhausted to debate the point. "Later,

after they were married, R. J. wanted to seek custody. But her mother refused to cooperate. He never succeeded in finding the child and was furious. The issue created major problems in their marriage."

Broussard's fingers tap-danced impatiently on the chair's metal arm-rest.

"Remember, when you said Shannon began to spend a great deal of time on the Internet?"

Curiosity flared in his eyes.

"Her son was the reason." I leaned forward and explained in detail how she found her lost son, his lie, and her reaction. How she had sought out Kagan because of his father's reputation, her fatal mistake in hiring him.

"That's where the money went, to Kagan. She returned to Miami to save her son."

Broussard looked bewildered.

"To do that, she thought she had to save R. J. But Kagan defrauded and then threatened to expose her. Then Rothman, the private detective who found out who she was, *did* expose her. He sold her out to R. J. She felt desperate, betrayed, and saw no way out of her situation."

His expression remained one of disbelief.

He said nothing, so I went on. "Kagan had dinner with her the night before she died, in her hotel suite. His plan was to go on taking money from her. She had threatened to go public but was afraid of losing you. Kagan said she appeared to be in better spirits that night, but—"

"That was him?" Broussard whispered in astonishment. "The man in her room was the lawyer?"

"Yes. She couldn't go out by then. R. J.'s mother had been snooping around the hotel looking for her. I'm sure

Kaith—Shannon saw her. She knew it was all over. She had nowhere to run."

"That was the goddamn lawyer at her hotel?" he repeated, voice rising.

"That's right."

"My God. Oh, my God!" He clutched at his forehead as though too shocked to comprehend my words. "Shannon came here to save a dying son?"

I nodded. "That's right. She thought he had leukemia."

He gulped deep breaths as though in pain.

"She didn't want you to know; she was afraid it would destroy your relationship. She really—"

He shot out of the wheelchair, gripped my arms, and jerked me to my feet so abruptly that my pen and notebook fell to the floor.

"Do you have any idea what you're saying?" he shouted. "Oh, my God!"

"Stop it!" I firmly shook away his hands. "I know this is painful but control yourself!"

Where the hell was Zachary Marsh? For once I would have been delighted to see him.

Broussard stood panting, eyes wild.

"I gave her everything." His voice quavered. "Anything she wanted. All I asked was honesty. She knew I didn't tolerate liars. Three years ago," he said, "at a cocktail party, I overheard a conversation. Someone asked where she grew up. She said Omaha. That startled me. There's a big difference between Omaha and Oklahoma. But the hour was late, and she'd had a cocktail. I attributed it to a slip of the tongue but never forgot it. Last year at a business conference in Seattle, I met a man from Stanley, Oklahoma. 'You must know my wife,' I said innocently. 'She lost her family in the twister.' He knew the Sullivan family. He grew up with the young mother killed with her infant. He said I was mistaken, there was no sister Shannon. She had no sister at all.

"I checked it myself. He was right. That's when I knew I couldn't trust her. Her brooding about the past wasn't grief, it was some secret part of her that I knew nothing about. I began watching her."

He paused, face wet with tears; his mouth worked silently until he could continue.

"I saw my worst fears come true. The time she spent on-line, her cash withdrawals, her secretive behavior—"

"You knew before she disappeared that she'd been withdrawing cash?"

"When loved ones lie, you make it your business to know theirs."

"But that's not what you told the police, or me."

"I could see she was planning to leave me, to leave us. I knew her sudden trip alone wasn't to New York. I heard her inquire about flights to Miami and hotel accommodations. I wasn't stupid. I knew she and her on-line lover planned to meet."

"You were spying on her."

"What other recourse does a man have when he's deceived?" His voice trembled. "I followed her, booked myself into the hotel next to hers. When I saw a man leave her room that night, I knew it was true."

"You thought—"

"You don't know my pain and suffering that night." He shook his head grimly. "I knew she would swim in the morning. She was a creature of habit in so many ways." His voice dropped to a whisper. "I dressed like a tourist, shirt and shorts over a bathing suit. Once she left for the beach, I went to her room. Told a housekeeper I'd forgotten my key. She let me in. I wanted her lover's name, I wanted to know who the son-of-a-bitch was. What I found was far worse than I imagined."

He slumped down in the wheelchair, head in his hands.

"I found a file in the wastebasket, thrown away. Copies of old news stories, photos of her with a different name, another husband. Stories about her 'murder,' missing money, his trial. The whole tawdry scenario. She had abandoned and framed her first husband and apparently planned something similar for me.

"How do you think I felt?" He raised his head, eyes flooded, lips tight. "I wanted to destroy her, to tear her apart. I was temporarily insane," he pleaded, "about to explode."

He stared past me, voice low. "I surprised her, out beyond the breakers. I wanted to hurt her for all her secrecy, her duplicity, her lies, her adultery." He gasped, as though in pain. "But I can't forget her face. It haunts me still, the way she looked when she saw me. Astonished, yet her eyes lit up with something tender, as though she actually did care. She opened her mouth, but I couldn't stand any more lies. I didn't give her a chance."

In that brief moment before the terror, I thought, suddenly sick to my stomach, she must have believed he was there to save her again.

"Where is Zachary?" I demanded, fearfully. "Is he all right?"

Broussard shrugged, a small, noncommittal gesture. "I thought he might have taped or photographed me that morning. You see on TV all the time how police can enhance video, even blurry photos of bank robbers, until the faces are identifiable. I called to sound him out and he admitted he'd seen me down on the beach, even said he had photos that might interest me."

Oh, Zachary, I thought, what did you do?

"I knew," Broussard was saying, "he'd blackmail me for the rest of my life, torture me until he finally turned them over to the police."

"No," I said quickly. "He's harmless, a sick, lonely man who wants attention. He's handicapped. Where is he?" I pleaded.

He shrugged sadly. "I can't leave my children orphans. You can understand that. I came here to destroy the photos and the negatives to save myself. Marsh said you had just called, that the police had solved the case. He wouldn't give up the pictures, denied having them. He kept lying. I didn't believe anything he said. But later, when I used his phone to check my messages at the hotel, they said the police had been there."

"You hurt him, didn't you?" Don't let him be dead, I prayed.

Eyes cold, he nodded.

"Is he still alive?" I said quickly. "We can call nine-one-one."

He smiled, eyes shiny, like a mourner at a funeral.

"You didn't have to do it," I croaked, my mouth dry, vocal cords suddenly gritty. "He only took photos after they pulled her from the water."

"Don't you lie to me too," he warned, voice menacing. "I do not tolerate liars. What about this?" He went to the table, snatched up the photo, and thrust it at me. It was him, hunkered down at the water's edge, casting the last white rose into the foaming surf. I saw myself, in the frame's lower left-hand corner, watching.

"You see?" He snatched it back. "He's hidden the others, but I know they're here somewhere." He regarded me soulfully for a moment. "I wish you hadn't come here tonight. I liked you."

"I like you too." I tried to sound calm. "You've been through a great deal. Anyone would understand—"

"Too late." He shook his head, conviction in his posture. "The police want me. I'm still looking for the pictures, but I'll find them."

"The police are only looking for you to say that she committed suicide. That she left you a note."

"What note?"

"A suicide note. They're closing the case," I said desperately. "The FBI lab enhanced the handwriting indentations left on a legal pad in her room."

"I saw it," he said, disdainfully, "beside the bed. It was blank."

"She mailed the letter to your office," I explained. "It must be waiting there now. The cops didn't believe Zachary. They were happy to write her off as a suicide. She never intended to come back from that swim."

"You're lying."

"I can prove it right now! I can read you exactly what she wrote. I took it down as the detective read it to me. It's there," I said, catching my breath, "in my notebook."

"Get it," he demanded.

I scrambled to retrieve it, then riffled frantically through the pages.

"Darling Pres," I began, voice cracking.

He sat stiffly in the chair, wary eyes riveted on me. He groaned as I went on, a sound that sent icy ripples across my skin.

"How could she think I'd turn away?" he cried as I finished. "If I had known, if I only knew she really . . ." His voice wavered, hopeless.

"That morning . . . it was like a dream. I couldn't believe I'd done it. My whole body shook. I didn't know if I would still be able to walk when I left the water. But instinct took over; it does, you know, in emergencies. The need for self-preservation. For my daughters. They need me. I wouldn't let my parents raise them." He rambled on, bitterly. "They're incapable. When I was a child they left me with paid strangers, some abusive and disgusting, while they traveled, enjoying themselves, doing as they pleased. We were estranged for years, until Shannon brought us together. I have to protect the girls. Everybody knows a victim's spouse is always the number-one suspect. It was dangerous, but I had to take the risk. I went back to her room. I had picked her key up off the dresser the first time. I thought she'd forgotten it. . . ." His voice trailed off.

"She didn't forget it," I said. "She knew she wasn't coming back. She didn't need it."

"I went to cover my tracks, to erase every link to Seattle. I took the files as well. I knew she was registered under a phony name. If she was never identified as Shannon Broussard, she couldn't be connected to me. But it was the oddest thing," he said, looking up at me. "The labels had already been cut from her clothes, the initials removed from her luggage."

"She did it for the same reason," I said. "She didn't want to be identified."

"I could have saved her," he said numbly.

"Yes," I said. "You could have."

Eyes calculating, he savagely chewed his lower lip. "Would you take money?" he said. "You're what, a four-hundred-dollar-a-week reporter?"

"I'm underpaid," I said, "but not that underpaid."

"What about your future?" he demanded. "You expect to chase fire engines until you're sixty-five years old?"

"I have to leave now," I said quietly.

He sighed despairingly. "Too late. There's Mr. Marsh to consider. No," he said sorrowfully, "you can't leave."

"Don't make it worse than it already is."

"Come on." He reached for me. "We're taking a walk."

"Where?" I stepped back, heart thudding.

"It can work," he said, as though thinking aloud. "No one saw me come up. Marsh found you attractive, he told me that. You and he had some sort of a relationship, then quarreled, struggled, and you both fell."

"No." I tried not to panic or look at the windows, the dark sky and sea beyond. "I didn't even like the man. He's a news source. Everybody knew that."

"More reason for him to lose control when you resisted."

"He was in a wheelchair, for God's sake," I said, my voice thin with fear. "This is insane. You'll never pull it off."

"Why not? The man was an MS victim. He had good

days and bad ones. He was stronger than I expected."

I sprang toward the cordless phone on the glass table. Even quicker, he caught my wrist. The phone clattered to the floor, spiraling across the shiny tile, out of reach.

We grappled, as he forced me toward the bedroom. I kicked, screamed, and shoved him back into the three-legged telescope. He was caught off balance as it toppled and crashed to the floor. Wrenching away, I dashed through the still-open door to the outer room. I expected him right behind me, but glanced back and saw him at the wheelchair instead. He removed something from the pocket. The remote.

Skidding on the polished tile, I nearly crashed into the front door. Locked. Twisting the knob, I wrenched it both ways in a frantic search for a button, a lever, some sort of release. It wouldn't open. "Fire! Fire!" I screamed, pounding on the heavy wooden panels, praying for someone in the corridor. "Fire! Fire!"

Tall and moving lightly on the balls of his feet, Broussard came toward me, the remote in his hand. "Shut up!" he said. "Don't make this more difficult."

"Stay away from me!" Huddled against the door, I watched our macabre dance reflected in the mirrored wall.

He pointed the remote at me like a gunfighter leveling a weapon. He flicked a finger and the door behind me snapped briskly, the lock disengaged. As I reached for the knob he tapped the button again and it locked. He hit another button and the sound of music, sweepingly sentimental strings and piano, instantly filled the room.

I screamed as loud as I could, did an end run around him, and fled back toward the room we had left. The door stood open. I could reach the phone, dial for help; then he wouldn't dare . . . I was only inches away when the door slammed and locked.

He smiled grimly.

"Let me out of here!" I demanded furiously, shouting over Dean Martin crooning, *When the moon hits your eye like a big pizza pie . . .* "Or you'll wind up on death row yourself!"

His jawline tightened.

There was so little furniture. I looked wildly about for something I could use to break windows.

He attempted to cut me off, sidestepping and parrying, as I darted to a door at the far left, hoping it wasn't a closet. The knob turned and it opened. A short hall led to the kitchen. Low counters and sinks. A wall phone, mounted waist high, to accommodate Marsh in his wheelchair. I whipped a knife out of a wooden cutlery block on the nearest counter and wheeled to face him. Broussard, right behind me, cursed and slipped on the floor.

He caught his balance as I backed toward the phone, brandishing the knife. Its long blade glinted in the dim light. "I'll kill you!" I warned. "Come near me and I swear—"

In a single swift motion he snatched a heavy copper-bottomed pot off the stove by its handle and swung it at my head like a baseball bat. It connected with the sound of a church bell pealing.

When I opened my eyes, he was straddling me on the cold floor. My ears rang, my head throbbed, and my elbows hurt, as though they had hit the tile floor before I did. The taste of blood in my mouth, I groped feebly for the knife and saw it in his hand.

"Let's go," he said.

Nauseated and dizzy, as though seeing strangers, I watched in the huge mirror as he half dragged me back through the apartment. The door to Marsh's study sprang open and we faced ourselves on the big screen, life-size and in living color. The fear in my eyes terrified me more than the blood on my face or the blade at my throat. He saw the image too, tightened his grip, and waggled the knife under my chin. I dragged my heels, resisting every step, as he wrestled me into the bedroom. Sliding glass doors stood open to the wraparound terrace. Sheer white drapes swayed and billowed like angels' wings in the wind off the sea.

He forced me through them, hand clamped over my mouth, then cursed as we stumbled over something. It was Zachary, curled in a fetal position, arms across his narrow chest, as though trying to protect himself. His face was blue.

I ripped Broussard's hand from my mouth, gagging. "Think of your daughters," I gasped. "If they could see—"

"I *am* thinking of my daughters." One hand under my armpit, he reached down with the other, gripped me between the legs, then lifted me off my feet and over his head. In that dizzying instant, my cries lost in the wind, I glimpsed the fenced-in pool sixteen floors below and remembered the jumpers I had seen, skulls shattered like eggs, the contents spilled around them. My free hand clawed furiously for his face, to mark him, so that Rychek or somebody would know how I died.

The night air whooshed around me as he hurled me, still

struggling, over the railing. My fingers scrabbled frantically against an unyielding surface, then caught the narrow ledge on the sky side of the stone balusters. I clung there for a heart-stopping moment, legs flailing in empty space. He tried to kick my fingers away, wedging his foot between the balusters, but they were too closely spaced. He cursed, threw one leg over the railing, and leaned down to push me away.

My legs swung forward, as my fingers slowly lost their grip and I fell. Cut off in mid-scream, I slammed with a painful crash onto the identical terrace of the apartment one floor below. Stunned, I rolled to my hands and knees, crawled painfully to a small patio table and two chairs, dragged myself to my feet, and beat on the sliding glass door.

"Help me! Open the door! Please!" I pleaded. No answer. The interior remained dark.

Overhead, Broussard's legs swung over the balcony as he came after me. I staggered to yet another sliding door around the corner. I fumbled desperately with the latch but it, too, was locked. Sobbing and shaking, I shouted, pounded, and kicked at the door, then peered inside. I saw ghostly shrouds, sheet-covered furniture, and the silhouettes of a ladder and paint cans. My face left bloody smudges on the tinted glass—only a hint of what was to come. I moaned at a sound behind me. Broussard had lowered himself and was clinging to the ledge, ready to swing onto the terrace after me.

"Get away!" I screamed.

With no place to hide, I snatched up a patio chair, brandishing it as one might to fend off a wild beast.

His long legs swung toward me, knees flexed, feet together. Taller by six or seven inches, he had to lift them to clear the railing. Screaming, I charged as though wielding a battering ram. The legs of the chair caught him just below the belt.

His expression, mouth open wide, was one of total surprise. He clawed at thin air for a moment, then fell away. The chair clattered after him, bouncing off the building.

His scream faded, but I did not hear the dreaded impact. Lost on the wind, I thought, as I crumpled to the floor, limp and weeping. I sat for a time, trying not to think, focused only on breathing. Finally I dragged myself to my feet, fighting back nausea as I gripped the railing with both hands and forced myself to look down. No crowd gathering below as I had expected. No cops. Preston Broussard had not slammed into the paved pool deck. Instead, he stared up at me, suspended face-up in space, six feet off the ground, impaled on the spear-sharp supports of the wrought-iron security gate that separates the pool area from the street.

22

Numb and shivering, I sat with my spine pressed to the cold outside wall of the empty apartment and waited for sirens. But all I heard was the wind.

My mind wandered. Would I see my mother again or be doomed to this high tomb forever? The dead moaned around me, or was that the wind? In my mind's eye, or was it ancient memory, I saw a distant time in a far place when

I stood alone on a towering cliff high above the raging sea, the wind wild in my hair. Stars shone above, doom waited below.

Eventually, I was roused by bright flashes of color bouncing in eerie patterns off the south side of the building: the spiraling lights of emergency vehicles. I stood up slowly and waved stiffly, trying to shout from my open air prison 'n the sky.

It seemed to take hours before the flashlight beams of two uniformed cops pierced the dark interior of the apartment behind me.

They found the light switch and unlocked the sliding glass door, and I stumbled toward them. "You know anything about that guy down there?" one asked, steadying my arm.

"Everything. There's another one upstairs," I mumbled, and burst into tears. "Call Rychek," I said, as my knees gave way.

"How did you get out there?" The cop frowned as he bent over me.

"Fell," I rasped, my throat raw from screaming. "He threw me off," I said, "from up there." I tried to point, but a dark-eyed medic in a blue jumpsuit refused to free my arm. He was taking my pulse.

I hadn't seen the medics arrive. They asked how I felt. Tearfully I displayed my bloodied and broken fingernails.

They exchanged glances, fastened a brace around my neck, and lifted me onto a backboard. "I'm not a victim," I insisted. "I'm okay." They wanted to wheel me out. I said I wanted to walk—in a minute or two. Until then it felt good to lie down. The blanket was soft and warm and I closed my eyes for a moment. I opened them after my teeth stopped chattering and saw an IV in my arm.

I had to wait for Rychek, to explain everything, I said. The medics insisted I go to the hospital instead. They won.

The stiff collar around my neck made it difficult to talk or turn my head. I told the medic with the brown eyes I didn't need it and that Billy Boots had worn one like it after his surgery.

"What did he have done?" he asked, humoring me as I was wheeled onto the elevator.

"Neutered," I said vaguely. "Maybe that's why he eats toothbrushes."

"Makes sense to me." He raised an eyebrow at his partner.

I frowned, trying to focus. "Listen. It's important," I pleaded, then forgot what I wanted to say. "I'm a member of the Stork Club," I mumbled instead.

In the emergency room, they discussed shock, a hematoma, and possible cervical injuries. I tried to see who they were talking about. All I needed was to go home for a good night's sleep, I insisted. They wanted CAT scans. I lost.

Rychek and Fitzgerald appeared somewhere between X-ray and the MRI.

"Broussard is dead. Marsh, too," I greeted them, thinking more clearly now despite a throbbing headache.

They knew. They had been to the Casa Milagro. Rychek took notes as I told them almost everything. Fitzgerald held my hand and stroked my hair.

No one else saw Broussard fall, Rychek said. He was discovered when a honeymoon couple returning from a romantic stroll on the beach followed a rapidly running river of blood to the iron gate and looked up.

"The fire department and a crew from the M.E. office are having a hell of a time getting 'im down from there," Rychek said. "They're using an acetylene torch on the gate. Too bad he's dead, we coulda charged him with breaking the law of gravity."

"No way," Fitzgerald argued. "He proved the law of gravity."

I was lucky. No broken bones, no permanent physical damage. My cuts and bruises would heal. Treated for shock and a concussion, I went home after twenty-four hours. They wanted me to stay for forty-eight, but I insisted. My mother, Lottie, Onnie, Mrs. Goldstein, and Dennis Fitzgerald all took good care of me. Even Kendall McDonald called. I was fine, I said, in good hands.

Janowitz wrote the deadline story on the deaths. My in-depth piece followed two days later.

I left someone out, the same person I left out of my statement to police. Danny Sinclair.

I left him out one more time.

"I know why you called," R. J. said, referring to the urgent message I left him so long ago, before driving to Boca to find Danny. "You found out I was right. Kaithlin couldn't forget me. She still cared. That's why she came back."

"Right," I lied. "She cared."

"I'm glad that son-of-a-bitch is dead," he said. "He murdered my wife."

R. J. allowed Myrna Lewis to bury Kaithlin at Woodlawn. He even offered to pay the bill. When the woman, who barely survives in her shabby apartment, refused his money, he was surprised. I wasn't.

The two of us paid her a visit. My mother drove because my head still ached. We drank tea in her kitchen and talked about Danny.

"Do you think he should be told?" I asked.

"Would you want to know," my mother asked, "if they were your parents?"

"He sounds like a wonderful boy," Myrna said wistfully.

"They weren't rich or well-known and they had their share of bad luck, but Reva did a good job choosing his parents," I said. "She'd be happy at how her grandson is turning out."

I smiled at them both. Some truths are better left untold.

Relieved that her boss hadn't killed anybody, at least not anybody we knew about, Frances Haehle finally confided why she'd been so afraid of going to jail if he was arrested. Her sister had died three years earlier. While she was still grief-stricken and vulnerable, Kagan had asked her for the dead woman's date of birth and social security number. When she gave it to him, he had put her dead sister on his payroll, a phantom employee to beef up his business expenses and cheat on his taxes.

Kagan saw me right away when I dropped by his law office.

"Didn't I tell ya?" he crowed, jubilant at being cleared in Kaithlin's murder. "And you were looking at me like I was responsible."

"Indirectly, you were," I said. "You were no innocent

bystander."

"You look all banged up." His expression was arrogant.

"Yeah. I look like I ran into one of your swell clients in the alley. Look," I said. "I want you and Rothman to forget about Kaithlin's son."

His ferret eyes glittered. "Sure, sure," he agreed. "No problem."

"Good," I said. "Now shred her file, the one you took out of that drawer last time I was here. Do it now."

He licked his lips and smirked. "Now, why would I do that?"

"Because," I said, "the cops know exactly how much money Kaithlin sent you. They won't go to the trouble of reporting it to the IRS, but I will. I'll go right to their office from here. I know a few agents who'd be delighted to have the information. Who knows what they'll find when they start examining your returns for the past seven years." I smiled.

"I'll deep-six the file," Kagan said. "Take my word for it."

"No," I said. "I can't. Take it out now, call in your secretary, and we'll watch her shred it."

He took out the file, then slammed the drawer hard.

"Get in here!" he bellowed.

Frances stepped into the office, avoiding my eyes. I checked through the file, then watched at her elbow as the machine reduced it to confetti.

The last item fed into the blades was a Rothman surveillance photo. Kaithlin, coffee mug in one hand, a leash in the other, laughing at the big dog as he romped around the two little girls in riding gear as they left their Seattle home.

The haunting irony is that she successfully escaped the violent husband she feared, only to be murdered by the mild-mannered second husband she loved.

Love is so fragile and so often fatal. I am amazed when people are brave enough to risk it.

The wedding was beautiful, sweet and simple, like fortunate lives. Fitzgerald drove down from Daytona to be my date. The big event took place in the little church on Lincoln Road. The radiant bride wore spring flowers in her hair and a long off-white dress.

The ring bearer, Harry, age five, took his mission so seriously that he briefly refused to relinquish the matching wedding bands when the moment came.

Misty, eleven, looked lovely, her blond hair long with silky bangs that brushed her eyebrows. Lottie wore her red hair piled elegantly atop her head. I liked the swishing sound of our salmon-pink gowns as we slow-stepped down the red-carpeted aisle to the march from Wagner's *Lohengrin*. Perhaps I just loved life and all it brings on that day so bright with promise.

The twins dropped rose petals, and little Beppo escaped his seat with the others next to Angel's mother, who held the baby, and scampered up to join the bridal party at the altar. No one objected when Rooney swept him up and held him in his arms while he and Angel exchanged vows.

"I think I'm going to faint," the bride whispered as the soloist sang.

"No, you're not," the minister firmly corrected.

He was right.

So was Lottie, I thought, as the newlyweds swept out of

the sanctuary to the joyous strains of Mendelssohn. The world has so few happy endings.

Love and decency still survive, though my belief was briefly shot down by a subpoena server who recently nailed Lottie and me in the News lobby. He grinned and skittered off like a cockroach.

We had been summoned as witnesses for depositions in a civil lawsuit filed by "Janet and Stanley Buckholz as the natural parents and guardians on behalf of the plaintiff, Raymond Buckholz, a minor child." A Miami Beach hotel, a travel agency, and the city's chamber of commerce were named as defendants.

"Hell-all-Friday." Lottie furrowed her freckled brow. "Who the heck—"

"Raymond!" I said. "The little boy who spotted the body at the beach that day!"

The New York couple alleges that, as a result, Raymond suffers from "post-traumatic stress disorder, mental anguish, psychiatric trauma, and emotional distress." They are seeking damages based on "false and deceptive advertising" that lured them to Miami Beach for a family vacation.

Otherwise, Kaithlin's story is old news. She haunts me still. I believed that, with persistence, I would learn who and what she really was. But the more I reported, the more I learned, the less I knew to be true. Was she victim, villain, or simply human, caught up in passions and events that spun out of control? I realize now I'll never know. All those who are still alive have different, conflicting stories, and the dead don't talk. The past is an unsolved mystery and the truth a moving target.

I jog the boardwalk at dawn, swim, and then sunbathe on golden sand along my favorite stretch of beach. I daydream and contemplate the comfort of a limitless horizon despite the long shadow cast by another landmark. Each time I am there, I can't help but turn away from the bright sailboats that dart beyond the breakers, their colors etched against flawless blue sky, and look up to a high window over-looking the sea. I always wave.

Acknowledgments

I am grateful to the usual suspects, generous as always with their expertise, friendship, and support, especially Dr. Joseph H. Davis, real live hero and the world's best pathologist; real friend and true seeker, Renee Turolla; my own dream team of super lawyers Joel Hirschhorn, Arthur Tifford, and Ira Dubitsky, along with the Honorable Judge Arthur Rothenberg; and high-flying jet pilot Captain Tom Osbourne. Thanks, too, to ace photographer Jared Lazarus; my longtime accomplice Arnie Markowitz; Jerry Dobby; Bill Dobson and his beautiful Amalia; Douglas A. Deam, D.M.D.; Dr. Howard Gordon; Patty Gruman, who manages to always be in the right place at the right time; Brooke and Dr. Howard Engle; my agent, Michael Congdon; my patient editor, Carrie Feron; and those stalwart men of the FBI, Terry Nelson and David Attenberger. Janet Baker keeps me honest, and I am blessed to have the ebullient Cynnie Cagney and Dr. Garth Thompson in my corner, along with my true sisters Molly Lonstein, Karen

McFadyen, Ann Hughes, and Charlotte Caffrey, who share their friendship, insight, and efforts to keep me out of trouble. It's my good fortune to have co-conspirators like Pam Stone Blackwell, the best emergency room nurse in the world; and William Venturi, ace private detective, and, as always, I am ever indebted to the cool and resourceful Marilyn Lane, my getaway driver.

My life does have a sterling cast of characters.

Center Point Publishing
600 Brooks Road • PO Box 1
Thorndike ME 04986-0001 USA

(207) 568-3717

US & Canada:
1 800 929-9108